175

PATRICE PERIOT

By the same Author

SALAVIN (*novel cycle*)
translated by Gladys Billings

THE PASQUIER CHRONICLES (*novel cycle*)
translated by Béatrice de Holthoir

LIGHT ON MY DAYS (*autobiography*)
translated by Basil Collier

PATRICE PERIOT

Georges Duhamel

TRANSLATED FROM THE FRENCH BY E. F. BOZMAN

LONDON: J. M. DENT & SONS LTD

VICTORIA COLLEGE
LIBRARY
VICTORIA, B. C.

All rights reserved
Made in Great Britain
at The Temple Press · Letchworth
for
J. M. Dent & Sons Ltd.
Aldine House · Bedford St. · London
LE VOYAGE DE PATRICE PÉRIOT
First published by Mercure de France, 1950
English translation, 1952

843.7
D86vo
E1

CHAPTER I

THE Montmartre cemetery is no haven of eternal silence. Over this place of perpetual repose reigns the tumult of a mountain storm, the roar of a torrent in flood, the clamour of a marching host, the din of battle, and the Parisian dead must be heavy sleepers indeed to enjoy any sense of peace in their beleaguered sanctuary. All round it life is firmly entrenched and jealously clinging to its territory. The houses beyond the walls stare acquisitively at the little pentagon of earth where the tombs are huddled together like packing-cases in a warehouse. To the north stands a hospital, separated from the cemetery by a miraculously quiet street which threads its way symbolically between hope and finality. The adjoining back streets, lined with sleepy hotels and whelk-stalls, bear the stamp of obscure artists and bankrupt bankers, and a Joseph de Maistre has to rub shoulders with a Hegesippe Moreau. The hawkers from what used to be called the outer boulevards have parked their barrows on the pavement right up against the very walls of the burial-ground, still displaying on their superstructure pictures of the Snake Lady and the Strong Man. Every now and then a motor-bus glides

5

down the slope, scattering the street pigeons, which leave it to the very last moment to fly away, gauging to a nicety the speed of their mechanized adversary.

To the south, where the cemetery seems to climb the hill one step at a time, the battle of life is even more strident and merciless. The rue Caulaincourt leaps in one bound over the graves, the deserted walks, the bizarre monuments, and the decaying flowers. Hooters, klaxons, and motor-engines create an unbelievable din. Two streams of pedestrians hug the pavements nervously. Here the cemetery debouches on the nothingness of life, here is its solitary gate for the use of hearses and visitors alike. The blind alley that comes to an end at this disconcerting spot is one of the strangest corners in all Paris; there are plants and flowers for sale, meals, funerary monuments, and dubious attractions. The cabarets, with their shaded lights and their smell of spirits, come to life late at night in the very estuary of death. By day the roadway is black with parked cars, for space is scarce in this crowded quarter. On the asphalt of the pavements artists exhibit pictures which may or may not be their own . . . overblown flowers, erotic landscapes, and female nudes in a sickly pink reminiscent of strawberry ices. Finally the road disgorges itself open-mouthed into the drunken din and sombre fury of the boulevard, where the great city seems to be trying to affirm, to proclaim to high heaven its all too ephemeral power.

So thought the man who, black felt hat in hand, his unkempt grey hair ruffled by the breeze, paused before a tombstone on which the moss was just beginning to grow. It was one of those spacious family vaults where the vacant places are promptly claimed and

6

occupied by each successive generation. About eight names were carved on the slab. The latest, and most legible, dated back several years, and announced that Clotilde Périot, *née* Demoncelle in 1882, had been buried there in 1943.

For some ten minutes Patrice Périot paced to and fro beside the stone. He had thrown away a bunch of heather which had withered in its pot, and with his bare hands had brushed away the dead leaves blown by the wind. With thumb and forefinger he re-arranged some tulips, still fresh from his last visit, then drew himself up in front of the stone. 'Now for my short meditation,' he thought to himself, almost speaking the words aloud. In the course of a long life devoted exclusively to the pursuit of knowledge and the things of the mind, to research and discovery, he had formed the habit of dealing with everything methodically, even sorrow and joy. He was temperamentally too cautious ever to speak of very intimate matters, but he had what he called a set of personal rules, which in his self-imposed discipline he was careful not to disclose to any one; there were different rules for meditation, work, and sleep, and ingenuously enough he applied similar rules to the other functions of life, with the result that he was firmly convinced, whenever he had a stomach-ache at the end of the day, that he must have absent-mindedly broken one of his rules of eating and drinking.

He drew several deep breaths, for it was his belief that this process induced muscular relaxation and prepared the mind for thought. Actually, after some false starts and hesitations his thoughts did begin to sort themselves out. 'The believers are the lucky ones,' he mused; 'they have the best of all possible disciplines. They say a prayer they have said a thousand times, and while their muscles and the superficial functions of their intelligence are thus engaged, behold, they may succeed in liberating the soul itself, by which I mean that faculty which is not a faculty, that indefinable reality which forms the immaterial core of personality, the hub of being. . . . My poor Clotilde! What an anxious person she was! How she worried! How distraught she would be, if she were alive to-day, at the incomprehensible behaviour of her children! She would never have consented to call her little Christine "Vera." I am as tolerant as most men, but that Vera business is the height of absurdity. And I hardly dare think about Hervé! Hervé worries me even more than Edwige, which is saying a lot. Thierry is a saint, at least that's what Cazenave says in his admirable, and in my opinion very misguided, article, but he is by no means easy to live with. The saints are all of that ilk. . . . Ilk, ilk. . . . I must ask my friend Cauchois the derivation of the word some time. The three grandchildren are delightful in spite of being badly brought up. If only I could get Christine married. . . . Christine, I can never bring myself to call her Vera. . . . Poor Clotilde! She used to tell me always to think of her when anything went wrong. And I do think of her. I come twice a month to make a visit like this. I think of her every day and still I don't see a solution, or anything resembling one. Gérin-Labrit is a remarkable man, and yet he bores me. He—he—how shall I put it?—he makes me clench my teeth the instant I set eyes on him. All the same I must work, and what is more they must let me get on with my work. As between Gérin-Labrit and Schlemer I prefer Schlemer. He is more my type—mentally and spiritually—it's impossible to find the right expression. Poor Clotilde! The cardiologists called it "myocardial infarct." In my young days it would have been either endarteritis or coronary disease. I don't even know which now. All these things change so quickly. In medicine only death remains the same. Better not let the imagination run riot, better not think of my poor Clotilde's body, or of what may have become of it, lying there, only a few yards away from me. No! I'd rather think about my confirmed little saint, Thierry. But enough! The great thing is that I must be able to work. If I go on like this I shall turn into a man who although inundated with work not only does nothing but is incapable of doing anything. Yes, and I must read my mail this evening—I must dispose of it at all costs—and then write my speech for next Wednesday's function. Peace? Peace? Can there be anybody so insane as not to be in favour of peace? What's the time? Five? Or is my watch wrong? Farewell, dear Clotilde, and forgive me all these distractions. They are inevitable even when I keep to my rules!'

Patrice Périot stepped back two paces, and with a friendly nod turned away, still carrying in one hand the little round black felt hat like those affected by the professors of his younger days, while the fingers of the other fumbled with his overcoat buttons.

To reach the bridge Patrice Périot left the cemetery by the spiral staircase on the right. Children were sliding down the central bannister without doing themselves any harm, in spite of the fact that a gap had been purposely left in it. He gained the pavement but dared not cross the road, slippery after the morning rain, and so reascended the curious inclined bridge to the cross-roads, where as usual he was seized with doubt. To get to the rue Lamarck, in which his house stood, should he take the rue Caulaincourt or the rue Damrémont? Suddenly he plumped for the rue Damrémont, muttering to himself: 'There are moments when determinism has all the appearances of free will.' Reaching the raised part of the highway he foolishly decided to try to locate in the cemetery, far down below the parapet, the approximate position of the family tomb. This bright idea nearly cost him his life. A taxi missed him by a hair's breadth, and he had time only to hear the driver shouting in a stentorian voice: 'Look where you're going, you imbecile.' 'A Member of the Institute!' he thought. 'Fancy him speaking to a Member of the Institute like that!' No sooner had the thought occurred to him than he began to laugh at his own foolishness, but even as he laughed he nearly disappeared under an enormous lorry which rushed down the slope with all the brutal disregard of a huge animal protected by its bulk. Périot felt the hairs on the back of his ungloved hand stand on end as he leapt for the safety of the pavement. He walked slowly along the rue Damrémont keeping to the right, and began to debate with himself, as was his habit, on what he called 'self-evident propositions,' the chief merit of which was to make life more tolerable without exacting any creative effort. He would say, for example: 'To dream is becoming impossible for the civilized Parisian. But what's the use of a civilization which makes dreaming impossible?'

A little later, realizing that he was nearly home and back to his daily cares, he thought: 'Actually I would rather be dead. My children would be a bit upset, poor dears—but then it's their turn to be upset,' and after a few more steps: 'All the same they still need me. The little saint more than his brother—more than the three others put together.' At the corner of the rue Lamarck he squared his shoulders, and said aloud, to cheer himself up: 'I am always like this when I come out of that cemetery. I shall feel better soon. I can't help it.'

Patrice Périot had lived for more than twenty years in a large flat on the fourth floor of an imposing-looking house, built on the south side of the street so that from midday onwards the sun shone into most of the rooms. While his children were still young Périot had managed to rent two adjacent flats and to fix up a door leading from one to the other. Subsequently he had been urged, again and again, to move to the left bank, where he would be in the atmosphere of the Sorbonne and near his laboratory. But he had refused for various reasons that did not convince even himself. 'No!' he used to say, 'Montmartre is healthy, and as a physiologist I have a reputable patron there in Lamarck—a bit out of date, perhaps, but definitely respectable.' On other occasions he would say, without as much as a smile: 'The time I take to cross Paris is well spent; it is time given to reflection, time lost; or, in other words, time gained.' Among his old friends, the kind to whom he could pour out all his thoughts and a bit more into the bargain, he would add: 'As soon as I leave home I am plunged into streets crowded with the "common people." I walk, and as I walk I listen. I am genuinely sorry for those who never listen to the voice of the common people in the working-class districts.' And after a silence he would say, almost under his breath: 'I have been happy in my home there. Admittedly the happiness has not lasted; but then, it never does! Besides, I feel that to move at my time of life would be a betrayal of my joy and my sorrow. In any case I shall soon have to retire, absurd as it may seem, I who am full of energy, and have never worked better in my life; nevertheless, I shall have to retire.'

Patrice Périot walked on a few steps, raised his eyes, and smiled. In the sky above the street, outlined against the dark background of cloud, he saw, indistinctly in the twilight, a slowly moving object, not exactly like a bird, but rather resembling a miniature aerial car suspended above a valley. Screwing up his eyes he saw a double cable spanning the street. Patrice Périot shrugged his shoulders and continued to smile, no easy matter because he was nearing his front door and was busy composing his features, as he always did on these occasions.

'Excuse me, sir,' said the concierge, emerging suddenly from her lair, 'he called again this morning, the young man about the cable, you know, that copper, that police constable, I mean. Such a nice young man, but he wasn't in the know. I told him that M. Bouriette had put in a word for you with the commissioner and that the chief constable had agreed to shut his eyes until your daughter over the way had got her telephone in. He was impressed, I don't mind telling you, and he went off without a word. But he'll be back again—they come round every week—

he'll be back, only it won't be the same young man, of course.'

Patrice Périot said a word of thanks to this zealous person, made as if to raise his hat or give her his blessing—his gesture might have meant either—and began to climb the staircase.

At first he thought that all was silent in the flat, but while he was putting his hat and coat on the peg he heard a reedy yet musical sound coming from one or the rooms on the north side of the house, the one that overlooked the industrial suburbs of Clichy, Saint-Ouen, and Saint-Denis. This room belonged to Thierry, the youngest of the boys, the one Périot called his little saint. The light airy sound was not a song, but was more like the tinkling of a hand-bell in a vaulted church. And yet it had that quality one finds in the voices of children which rightly belongs to the angels.

'What is he up to now?' thought Patrice, opening the door as quietly as possible.

The middle of the room was empty except for a shabby carpet. A little girl with golden curls was kneeling there, and beside her was Thierry, also on his knees. A smile of radiant happiness gave his face an expression of ecstasy. His lips were moving as if he hoped by that means to help her pray. She was saying in a childish treble:

Where is dear Jesus?
He is in my heart.
Who lets Him in?
Grace.
Who drives him out?
Sin.
Naughty sin to drive away dear Jesus from my heart!

Come back!   Come back, my dear Jesus,
Into my heart.
My heart will not sin again.
In the name of the Father and of the Son . . .

The prayer ended and the sign of the cross made
with deliberate care, Thierry leapt to his feet, and
ran towards his father with arms outstretched in
welcome.

'It's wonderful, really wonderful, dad. . . .'

'Yes, indeed,' said Patrice nervously.

'Don't you think it's wonderful?'

'I should rather call it—charming.   And couldn't
you help her, while you are at it, with her pronunciation?   She says "grease" instead of "grace."   Being
careful to pronounce the words properly will not interfere with the ideas they express.'

Thierry raised his hands to heaven.

'Her ideas!   But, dad, I'm not thinking of her ideas!
I'm thinking of that beautiful little soul in all its
fervour and purity.   Her pronunciation, as you call it,
can come later.'

'Are you sure that our little Jeanne understands any
of the things you are making her say and do?'

'There's nothing she need understand just now, dad,'
said Thierry, more in sorrow than in anger.   And
anyway I didn't teach her that prayer, I regret to say.
She must have learnt it from the gardener's wife at
Jouy-le-Comte, or one of the others there, but that's
nothing against it.   This afternoon I heard a lecture
by Vigroux on the atom.   Yes, on the atom, and I
am willing to bet, although I know I'm attending his
course, that Vigroux doesn't understand the first thing
about the atom, and that everything he says will be

completely meaningless in twenty years' time. Understand! Dad, your attitude beats me.'

'Have it your own way,' said Patrice Périot, laughing, 'and there's no need for you to get annoyed with me. . . .'

'I never get annoyed with you, dad, for I know you mean well.'

'Thank you for the compliment, my son. I'm not used to such generous expressions. Have you discussed this orgy of religious instruction with your sister Edwige?'

'Edwige and I understand one another,' said Thierry, frowning. 'She gives me a free hand.' Then in a lower voice: 'She is at the mercy of the kids and her husband's tantrums. Do you realize that Maurice is actually getting jealous of a wife who gives him a baby every fifteen months. God forgive all such unhappy souls! I see they're drawing the curtain opposite,' he added, looking through the window, 'which means that Edwige will be over to fetch her little treasure any moment. By the way, did you know that M. Romanil is in your study? He has been waiting more than half an hour.'

'You should have told me before, Thierry. Clement Romanil is an important man, and his time is valuable. I'll go at once, but really you might have told me, instead of—— Oh, never mind, forget it.'

Patrice's study was in what was formerly the right-hand flat, the whole of which he had reserved for himself and divided up into a bedroom, a room known as the library crammed with mountains of books and magazines, and a study submerged inexorably by a rising tide of paper, despite the furious complaints of

Mme Hortense, who had ruled the Périot household for twenty years with a watchful, critical, and gloomy eye.

Seated in an arm-chair, his glasses perched precariously on his snub nose, Clement Romanil was smoking his briar pipe and ferreting among the periodicals scattered around him on and under the tables while waiting for Patrice. He greeted his host without rising from his seat, and held out a smooth fat hand.

'Forgive me, old man,' said Patrice, taking a seat in the one-armed chair that had become exclusively " the master's"; 'what's up?'

'Up? Nothing's up.' Romanil smiled broadly. 'Absolutely nothing, old chap. Simply a wish to see something of you. We never meet at the lab, and in any case every one talks and shouts so much there that talk is impossible. There's no chance even to enjoy small talk.'

He had bristling grey hair, a heavy stomach, and a thick red neck, but the intelligent and serene light in his eyes made one oblivious of the grossness of his body. He had the sing-song intonation rather than the accent of his native province. He suffered from emphysema and breathed unashamedly through his open mouth, disclosing two rows of stumps.

'The fact,' thought Patrice Périot, 'that he has nothing to say to me means that he *has* something to say to me—in other words some complaint to make. That's always the way with old friends.' With an air of studied indifference he began to glance through his appointment book.

'Are you expecting someone?' asked Romanil.

'What a question! Like you I'm always expecting someone.'

'Me?'

'Yes, we are all in the same boat. That is what makes life such a misery for us.'

'Not at all! *Your* life is a misery because you don't know how to say "No." You haven't learned the art of self-defence.'

'Let me turn on the light. I don't know how you can see to read. It's getting dark already, or else my eyesight is failing. I expect you are going to tell me, and not for the first time, that I allow myself to be exploited.'

'Nothing of the kind,' the fat man answered. 'I have said that so often, and with so little success, that in future I shall keep my mouth shut.'

'Listen! A ring at the bell!' said Patrice anxiously. 'My hearing is excellent—it's only my eyes that are beginning to let me down. It was a ring—I'm sure of it.'

'Don't worry, old man, I shall be going in a minute.'

'No, on no account. You stay. And I promise you, Clement, that I'll say just the same in your presence as I would if you weren't here. Who is it, Madame Hortense?'

A tall bony woman, severe of countenance, in widow's weeds, came into the room and looked about her with an air of commiseration.

'They've come, sir.'

'Who?'

'The usual crowd, more or less.'

'All right, show them in.'

Mme Hortense went out, leaving the door open

behind her, and a few seconds later three men came in. One was wearing a felt hat and a smart overcoat; the other two were in their shirt-sleeves, despite the end-of-winter nip in the air, one bare-headed and the other carrying an old-fashioned sports cap in his hand. A young woman slid into the room unobtrusively and made herself at home by perching on the corner of an old sea-chest that had been used by Patrice Périot since the early days of his marriage to contain the family papers.

'Allow me to introduce my old friend Clement Romanil, of the College of Science,' said Périot, ignoring the girl.

The old man made an abortive effort to rise from his seat and shook hands distantly with the three visitors. They sat in a row on the divan where Patrice frequently took his afternoon nap and which, by some miracle, at this moment was clear of the usual avalanche of paper.

'My comrades and I have taken the liberty,' said the first of the men, 'of bringing along the text of this petition for your signature, although Mlle Vera had offered to present it for us.'

Patrice took his reading glasses out of their case, put them on his nose, and accepted the paper he was offered. He spent two or three minutes reading and considering it, then without comment dipped his pen in a cheap bottle of ink and signed at the foot of the document.

'We know, sir,' said the leader of the delegation, 'that we can always count on you when liberty, justice, and peace are at stake. . . .'

Patrice Périot stood up, and his visitors followed

suit. The leader seemed to be all set to make a speech, but at the last moment he hesitated, and taking the paper from Patrice's hands, said simply, with a respectful smile: 'As soon as all the intellectuals behave like you our battles will be won. We thank you, sir.'

The girl, quiet as a mouse, showed the visitors out, closing the door carefully behind her.

Clement Romanil was still sprawled in his chair. 'Extraordinary,' he said, 'that I have known Christine since she was a baby, and she doesn't even say hallo to me nowadays. She behaves as if I were a total stranger.'

'All children are like that,' said Patrice reflectively. 'Maybe she knows you too well. I tell you, my grandchildren never think of giving me a kiss—apparently they don't find our generation very attractive—not even my darling little Jeanne. She's in the house now —did you see her? She takes as much notice of me as if I were a blank wall.'

'I congratulate you on one thing,' said Romanil; 'you read the document those lads gave you from end to end.'

'What a thing to say!' Patrice looked thoroughly shocked.

'Can you honestly tell me you always read the papers they bring you to sign?'

'They? Who do you mean by "they"?'

Romanil shrugged his shoulders and lapsed into silence. Then he went on, speaking thoughtfully and deliberately: 'When I was twenty I used to say, like the rest of my crowd, "none more left than I." But to-day I don't even know which is left and which is right, or what is free thought and what is not. . . .

Only three months ago you signed a petition for the release from prison of those two worthies in Venezuela. A little later it was proved that neither of these martyrs so much as existed. You were trapped. Trapped through your own kind-heartedness—I grant you that much.'

Patrice paced the room, steering his way among the piles of books. 'Clement, old man, I understand you well enough, believe me I do. As soon as you told me that you had come to see me for no particular reason I knew that you were going to preach at me. Do not deny it. I mean what I say—preach. That's what made me sign a petition on behalf of Seretti and Montecolla just now. *They* exist anyway—I am sure of that, and I am sure that they will die if we don't get them off. My attitude is simple enough; even at the risk of making a mistake I sign, and I will go on signing. Better make mistakes than be filled afterwards with self-reproach; better sign for ten ghosts than send one innocent man to his death. There's no need for us to argue about the rights and wrongs of each case, because you know perfectly well what I'm getting at. It was only out of respect for your freedom of action that I refrained from handing you that paper just now—and a pen to sign it with. I know you through and through. You are still liable yourself to fall into the traps laid for people you call soft-hearted—and think soft-headed.'

Clement raised his hands and coughed till he was red in the face. 'I say no more, old man. But tell me, was that really Christine they were calling Vera just now? What's the idea?'

'That's a long story.' Patrice looked uncomfortable. 'Vera's a sort of *nom de guerre*. . . . What do you want, Edwige?'

A young woman had just dashed into the study without even knocking, as if she were being hotly pursued. She was well set up, a trifle plump, with full bosom and smooth neck. She seemed to be choking with barely controlled sobs. To Patrice Périot's question she made no reply of any sort, and withdrew into the darkest corner of the room.

Patrice addressed himself to his friend once again. 'My plan, you see, is to give my children as much freedom as is humanly possible while reserving the right to issue occasional words of warning and advice. Actually I know, Clement, that my advice is entirely useless. A man's experience is of no use to any one, least of all to himself. Otherwise the world would be saved, and we haven't arrived at that point yet. Did you ever know Ernest Bovet? No? A pity. He used to say: "I want my children to belong to the left when they're twenty. Otherwise where will they be when they're fifty?" As for Christine . . . but here she is. You will observe, Clement, that my study is by no means a hermit's cell.'

Christine took not the slightest notice of this remark and went over to her sister, who was standing in front of the bookshelves rolling her handkerchief into a wet ball like a modern actress in her big scene.

Romanil heaved himself out of his chair. 'Good-bye,' he said to the girls. 'I would very much have liked to have a chat with you, but it is getting late and I have more than half an hour's journey by metro ahead of me. The stairs will kill me in the end. *Au revoir*, Périot, old man. Shall I see you at the College

21

of Science on Monday? Not that we can talk in that babel, but at least I will be able to throw you a friendly glance from a distance. Good-bye, Edwige! Good-bye, Christine!... your father told me you had a *nom de guerre* now.'

Christine shook her head. 'Not a *nom de guerre*. A *nom de paix*.'

'Have it your own way. Good-bye, all!'

The old man took his leave; even from a distance they could hear his wheezy breathing like the sound of a crane raising and lowering its bales.

'Now let me get on with my work.' Patrice's expression was pleading.

'Nonsense, daddy,' said Christine sharply, 'we're going to have dinner. The soup's nearly cold, and we should have been eating by now but for that dried-up old windbag.

'Christine!'

'Father,' sighed Edwige, 'I wish you'd call her Vera, just to please her.'

'All right, Vera if you like,' said the professor wearily; 'it's all the same to me. Edwige, I suppose you have come to fetch your daughter. She was with Thierry a little while ago.'

'Edwige has come in to give M. Ribeyrol a chance to recover his good humour,' said Christine accusingly. 'The Ribeyrols are at home this evening. They are not going over to the Puechs'. Incidentally M. Ribeyrol is jealous of M. Puech, among others.'

'Vera!' said Edwige appealingly. Then opening her mouth she proceeded to apply her lipstick, facilitating the operation with the oddest facial contortions.

'It's incredible,' thought Patrice, 'that Edwige, the

22

prettier of the two, a very good-looking girl in fact despite her air of misery, should so disfigure herself.' He ended this short meditation with a sigh, and said in a resigned voice: 'Come on then, let us have dinner, and quickly because I have my work to do. I haven't even glanced through my mail yet, and there's that speech to write. . . .'

Edwige, taking her little chatterbox Jeanne by the hand, left the family party, and Patrice put his hand on Christine's shoulder, allowing himself to be led, like Oedipus by Antigone. They found Mme Hortense and Thierry waiting for them in the dining-room, standing behind their chairs.

Places were laid for four. 'Needless to say,' said Patrice, 'Hervé is out.'

Silence fell. Then Mme Hortense said in her gloomy voice: 'I prefer to say nothing.'

'There is nothing to be said,' sighed Patrice. 'I am not surprised. In fact, I should be surprised if he were here. All the same I am surprised that you two, Christine and Thierry, are punctual for once. It is almost a miracle. My congratulations.'

'Father,' said Thierry angrily, 'you know that my one aim is never to offend you. Don't you, father!' He turned his chair round and went over to his father, face burning, lip trembling.

'I suppose you're going down on your knees now,' shot Christine, in her bitterest tones.

'And why on earth shouldn't I go on my knees?' said the boy.

There he stood in front of Patrice, his eyes shining, his breathing agitated. He was barely turned twenty and his complexion still held that fleeting freshness of

23

adolescence that is given only to a favoured few. While he stood, tense and emotional, Christine piped up again in dulcet tones:

'Take a seat, little curé.'

The young man turned towards his sister and replied: 'Don't mock me for being a Christian. I don't blame you for being a Communist. If your Communism were Christ-like, as it could be, I might be a Communist myself.'

Christine shrugged her shoulders in exasperation, and Mme Hortense rapped on the table for silence like a schoolmistress and said: 'Eat your dinner, both of you. You're getting on the professor's nerves.'

Thierry made the sign of the cross and began to swallow his soup. Patrice Périot seemed to be listless and care-worn, and Christine-Vera watched him intently, like a cat watching not a mouse but some much larger animal, a horse perhaps, whose every movement needs to be kept under observation. The girl was about twenty-five or twenty-six years of age. Her thin face and dull complexion were framed in blonde hair, entirely natural, and contrasting oddly with her dark, almost black, eyes. Her whole expression was one of hardness and abnormal seriousness rather than of charm or originality. Often Patrice, watching her without appearing to do so, used to think to himself: 'What is the explanation of those dark eyes? All the rest of us have green eyes. Clotilde used to talk about one of her uncles on her mother's side. It could be. Such characters can reappear after five or six generations. Nothing is lost. Everything comes to light again. But what beats me is that although she knows we are agreed on most points, she

24

persists in looking on me as an enemy or at best as an accomplice.'

The meal was finished quickly and in silence, and Patrice withdrew to his own quarters. On his way through the drawing-room his eyes fell on a beautiful cut-glass vase standing in a fine china dish, which he had been given at Prague at the congress of biologists. He paused for a few moments to contemplate this precious object, which was not as a rule used to hold flowers but which to-day contained a bunch of violets. 'Oh dear,' he said aloud, 'someone has broken my beautiful vase. Would you believe it? We have had it for fifteen years, and now its end has come as it comes to all of us in time. How on earth can any one have been so clumsy?' Patrice picked up the vase to examine the extent of the damage. Water had leaked out of the crack and the vase was sticking to the china dish, which came up with it and then fell, to be shattered into fragments on the stone floor. 'I'm just as bad as the others,' thought Périot, 'and the only reason I rarely break anything is that I rarely do anything.'

He went down on his knees and began to pick up the pieces. Where to put them? In the waste-paper basket? No. Hortense will find them there—and if she fails to see them she may cut her fingers. He heaved a sigh, and slipped the debris into his coat pocket. Disconsolately he thought: 'Everything we see, everything we love, will be destroyed, and everything we have created will turn to dust one day. Such is the order of things. . . . I am beginning to get too attached to my various possessions, my favourite cup or plate or candlestick—a bad sign, my lad, a very bad sign.'

He sat down at his desk, turned on the reading-lamp which was always either too dim or too strong, according to the state of his eyes, and picked up a bunch of unopened letters. He spread them out with a look of exasperation, then put them into a bunch again and pushed them on one side at the foot of a heap of papers. 'No letters to-night. They'll do to-morrow if I come home early. All the same I must work. That wretched speech! I'll have to make it up on the spot, and I mistrust all impromptu speeches —you never say exactly what you mean. Besides, there is bound to be a shorthand writer about some-where, and that means more trouble afterwards, for correcting a typescript takes longer than writing the stuff out correctly at first. So much for my speech! But I must work. I must be allowed to work. Every minute of the day someone insists on my lending a hand with something, presiding over something—and most of them seem to think I enjoy it! Actually, of course, I do it because my deep sense of public duty will not allow me to evade it. My life is becoming impossible, and if things go on as they are at present I will soon have to give up my beloved work of research and invention. The truth is that my friends are be-ginning to exploit me. They are turning me into a sort of symbolic figure. Symbolic of what? I ask you!'

In the pool of light shed by the lamp he had spread out a large note-book, bound in a strong spring folder. He turned through the pages covered with small, neat handwriting until he came to the point where the text suddenly came to an end in the middle of a white page, poised, as it were, over an abyss. Painfully recalling an elusive train of thought he re-read the last few lines of his manuscript. 'It remains to be demonstrated that placental immunity is strictly limited to those diseases which have definitely been contracted by the mother, and which can either be remembered by the household or are referred to in family letters and papers or revealed by laboratory tests. If so-called placental immunity were proved to extend to illnesses the mother has not had, then it would be necessary to seek a satisfactory explanation outside the field of determinism. . . .'

At that point the manuscript ended. Patrice Périot formed the last two words with his lips: 'Of determinism . . . of determinism. . . .' Then he took his pen and wrote in another word: '. . . of classical determinism.'

He worked on for some three hours, heard midnight strike, rose from his chair and stretched himself, then went off to his room and to bed. After an hour of futile and methodical attempts to go to sleep he thought to himself: 'I am a sleep-stutterer,' then he fell asleep. Soon afterwards he woke up, covered with sweat, to escape a nightmare that was almost instantly forgotten. 'There was a door that I couldn't open, except with a corkscrew . . . what could be the meaning of that? And what else? Oh yes, there were flames the other side of the door. And an animal was crouching on the bed. What a dream! How humiliating and what a warning to me! Imagine my having a dream like that. What a queer state I must be in! It just serves me right!'

CHAPTER II

SITTING in the car Gérin-Labrit crossed and uncrossed his long legs, put his hand to his mouth to stifle a yawn brought on by indigestion, and in his harsh voice reprimanded the driver sharply for putting on the brakes too suddenly. Then he turned to Patrice Périot and said: 'I suppose you are as over-worked as the rest of us, professor; but in this case you must accept . . .'

In the early stages of his association with Périot, which was hardly cordial enough to be called a friendship, he had waited a long time before deciding how to address him. Although he was at least fifteen years younger than the professor he was too proud to call him 'maître.' He argued that the word was bourgeois, and would add, screwing up his eyes, that in any case he himself was equally entitled to the honour. He refused to call him plain 'Mr.,' and 'comrade' seemed a bit out of date. Accordingly he had the idea of addressing him by his academic title of professor, and he used to say 'professor' or 'my dear professor' in a tone that was a mixture of respect and easy familiarity. The title was deferential without being too much so, he felt, and besides it was a simple statement of fact — Patrice Périot was a professor at the Sorbonne.

'I urge you to accept,' he went on, 'because there is no one more fitted than you to discharge such a high duty. I know what you will say—that you are over-whelmed with work. Nevertheless, you are now at a stage in your brilliant career when it is your duty to devote part of your energies to the advancement of pure knowledge and to the responsibilities of men of science. I mean just that—responsibilities.'

'I follow you,' said Périot uneasily, 'but as far as I am concerned——'

Gérin-Labrit forged ahead unperturbed. 'Our paper might be called *Pure Science*, or some such title. Have no qualms about the financial side. We have plenty of good friends and all the expenses will be guaranteed. We have only to invite public subscriptions and they will come pouring in. Each will give his mite. And as for the work itself, we can arrange for you to have half a dozen secretaries and an office. Ours will be a scientific organ, and you will not have to bother about political angles or legal complications.'

He spoke judicially, with an element of lofty detach-ment bordering on elegance. His excessively thin face was crowned by a mass of wavy hair, carefully trained to be disorderly and parted in the middle by a thick white line. His features were regular, almost handsome, but his impassive face was heavily lined and there were dark rings under his cold, grey, ex-pressionless eyes.

'You are a single man now,' he went on, 'and you ought not to shirk it. Who else could be entrusted

29

with such important work? Vuillaume lacks courage
and confidence. Laurent Pasquier lives in the moon,
and his reactions are completely unpredictable. Sterno-
vitch had a slight stroke a year or two ago, so that he
is out of the running. Besides, we must have a good
honest French name, like Dupont or Durand. Forgive my thinking aloud in your company—it is because
I can rely on you heart and soul. We thought
of Roch . . . but he is a bone-head, and he is afraid
of politics, Communism, truth, of everything in fact.
Here we are, at our destination already—perhaps we
can continue the conversation this evening or to-
morrow?—let me go ahead and make way for you.
All these good people admire you, and are anxious to
know what you look like.'

As soon as they were out of the car Gérin-Labrit
waved away the crowd gently but firmly. 'Make way
for our president,' he said. People stopped talking
and laughing for a second, and someone said : 'That's
Gérin. Did you see him? Yes, the tall one, the
writer. Who's the old man? Do you know?'
'Why, yes, he's a well-known scholar—his name's on
the bills.'

Gérin forged ahead, followed by Périot. 'Come
this way,' he said, smiling, 'otherwise we shall be
asked to pay an entrance fee, which would be too
much of a good thing. Do not get separated from
me, professor.'

Buffeted, pulled this way and that, at one moment
borne along by the crowd, at another engulfed in a
human wave, Patrice Périot at last reached the end of
the hall. Some young men were keeping order and
reserving places for the officials.

'We won't go on the platform yet, professor. I want to see if every one is here.'

Patrice was standing hat in hand and one of the stewards offered him a chair. This was by no means his first experience of a big public meeting. He had often been asked to appear in public, and sometimes to speak, especially since the famous occasion in October 1936, when a reporter had elicited the phrase from him: 'Having seen with my own eyes the sufferings of the people from whom I am sprung, I am resolved to spend my life among them, sharing their trials, their struggles, and their joys.' But the meetings were too frequent for a busy man and Patrice justifiably urged the pressing demands of his work. He rarely had his way. First Schlemer, then Gérin-Labrit, then Rebufat, famous mathematician and fellow member of the Institute, forced his hand by personal intervention, and he yielded grudgingly. Yet once he was facing the crowd, in spite of himself and his resolutions, he experienced a sort of warm and lucid intoxication, which, far from being disagreeable, had the effect of lulling his scruples.

Gérin-Labrit reappeared, accompanied by three men. Patrice recognized them at first glance. One was Joseph Mousselon, revolutionary veteran, grown white-haired in parliamentary service; the second was Joannic, a sculptor who had been tortured by the Germans and had eventually lost both his arms—he looked shockingly thin and worn nearly three years later; the third was our friend Schlemer, of whom Patrice was accustomed to think with a sort of tolerant indulgence.

'Let us take our seats, gentlemen,' said Gérin-Labrit,

leading Périot to the wooden steps. 'You will take the chair, professor, and we count on you for a few words.'

Patrice threw up his arms: 'I have made no notes at all—I simply haven't had the time.'

Gérin-Labrit laughed. 'So much the better! Your real feelings will come out when you speak impromptu. Now come on, we must waste no time. It's going to be a long evening.'

As the party moved they were greeted by a burst of hand-clapping and stamping of feet. The far end of the large rectangular hall was almost lost in the haze of cigarette smoke. Périot had to sit in the centre of the long platform and below him was the rostrum from which the speakers, standing in front of a reading-desk, would soon address the crowd.

Gérin-Labrit sat on Périot's right and passed him a slip of paper saying laconically: 'The minutes of the meeting—let's go. The microphone and the rostrum are yours!'

Périot rose to his feet, clapped his hands commandingly, and silence fell.

'My friends,' he said, 'we are met this evening to talk about peace——'

He got no further. The word peace was taken up in a thousand throats.

Périot signalled for silence and began again, trying to make full use of the loud-speaker system, though he distrusted it on the grounds that it distorted the voice and possibly the thoughts of the speaker; however, without it he could not have made himself heard by the thousands crammed between these four dingy walls.

32

'My friends,' he went on, 'you are about to listen to men you have learned to love and respect. I am only going to say a few words to introduce the speakers and to signify my deep interest. Peace! Who does not desire peace in his heart of hearts? Firstly peace in his own conscience. . . . I am speaking of course of honest men, not of madmen or criminals. Can any honest man, surrounded by those he loves and cherishes, accept even the mere thought of war? And if he thinks of the great working-class, who always bear the brunt of the casualties, then, truly . . .'

All the time he was speaking Patrice Périot was criticizing himself and biting lumps out of himself secretly. 'I might at least have thought out something beforehand. Listen to my platitudes. I am absolutely lost in public. And all because I hadn't a minute to myself, not even one minute, for creative thought. Never mind, it can't be helped. They asked for it. On with the nonsense. It may be nonsense but it's well meant, and after all, there is some truth in it.'

While these severe judgments were being formed in one region of Patrice's brain, another was selecting the necessary phrases and making the arrangements for speaking them correctly, and yet another was keeping an eye on the people round him and on the first few rows of the audience. 'Gérin-Labrit is making faces,' the third region registered. 'I must have touched on a point that he wants to make. Schlemer must weigh a good fifteen stone and he is emphysematous; but he has hours of talk in him.'

Patrice was standing against the long table, from which he borrowed support by leaning on his doubled forefingers which assumed a swollen and misshapen appearance under his weight. He had made up his mind to speak for only three minutes, but now he was all set for a quarter of an hour at least. One phrase after another tumbled out, before he knew where he was. Occasionally there was prolonged cheering. He should have taken advantage of one of these bouts to put an end to his speech, but he could not bring himself to do so, because he had not arrived at what he thought was a logical climax. Incidentally—in a thoroughly patriotic spirit, of course—he was quite enjoying the sensation of educating all these good people in the love of peace as a necessary condition of true civilization.

Eventually he spoke for twenty minutes, only too aware of the fact that he had given way to the temptation to be theatrical, notably in a flowery peroration comparing peace, in biological terms, to organic health. As he sat down at last amid thunderous applause, shaking hands with those around him, his face clouded. 'Christine! Christine is sitting in the front row! She didn't tell me she was coming. How annoying. Had I realized that Christine was here, I'd have spoken entirely differently . . . Christine is a thorn in my flesh.' Whereupon he rose to his feet again and said: 'I will now ask our friend Gérin-Labrit to address us. As you know, he is the well-known author of *Vagues profondes*.'

Gérin-Labrit took up his stand at the rostrum and placed his watch on the desk. 'Good heavens,' thought Périot, 'he has taken his watch out. That means we are in for an hour at least.' He had a well-developed technique for listening to harangues. 'There are two ways of putting up with speeches,' he thought; 'one is not to listen at all and to think about something else; the other is to listen and force oneself to be interested, cost what it may.' Feeling a bit tired he decided in this case to withdraw within himself and allow the storm to pass over him. It was then that he noticed the former minister, Bertrand Recordeau, sitting unobtrusively in the front row next to Christine. Recordeau was an extreme left-wing Socialist, who had been a member of several governments before and after the war. For over a year now he had been squeezed out of the various groups, and was unable to disguise his chagrin, making it perfectly obvious to every one around him that he was disgruntled at his enforced retirement, and that he would take no further interest in life until he was given another chance. 'There's no spectacle so depressing,' thought Patrice Périot, 'as that of a minister out of work. He's like a plaintiff who has lost his case, or a rejected applicant, or a deceived husband who lives apart from his unfaithful wife and has a bunch of flowers sent round to her every day. . . . But why is he sitting next to Christine? Is it by chance or design?'

A cloud passed over the surface of his mind, but he noticed that Christine was not talking to Recordeau, and began to feel more at ease when he saw that Christine, who was always so strangely cold, almost hard, in her manner, was furiously applauding the slightest points made by Gérin-Labrit. The latter had been speaking for nearly a quarter of an hour, eloquently but without fire. He punctuated each phrase by cutting the air vertically with one hand, and despite his rather shrivelled appearance the volume, control, and balance of his delivery were surprisingly good; he gave the impression of choosing his arguments from an armoury and using them with the devastating precision of the swordsman. Patrice Périot watched the animation growing on Christine's cheeks, and set his teeth as he always did when Gérin-Labrit was involved. 'Not that,' he said, 'anything but that. She's twenty-five, and I know I am her father, not her nurse—she's a sealed book to me. But not Gérin-Labrit! Not him, of all people!'

Just at that moment Gérin-Labrit turned round, as if to appeal to the officials. During this manœuvre Patrice noticed that Gérin-Labrit had a little brown froth at the line of junction of his lips, and that a drop of white secretion, like milk, had accumulated in the outer corner of each eye. 'There is the revenge of physiology.' he thought; 'this crazy intellectual has glands like the rest of us. All the same, he ought to wipe away all that secretion. It's rather disgusting.'

From then on Patrice made another attempt to forget the hall, which was rumbling and booming like a deep inlet of the sea on a stormy day. 'I must get on with my work; that is absolutely essential. If only people would allow me to stick to my job. Quite apart from anything else, it is in their own interest, because it is in the interest of science—at least so I manage to persuade myself. This attempt at introspection was interrupted by the increasing din of the meeting. Gérin-Labrit was obviously reaching his climax, and was saying: 'Let us unite in declaring war on war. We will impose our own peace, even if we have to resort to armed force in order to do so, even if we have to use the sword to incise the abscess

36

and heal the wound by evacuating the contents. And do not let us forget, in our struggle for peace, that those who are not with us are against us. Our prime duty, now and in the future, is to spew out the lukewarm.'

At this point the thunder of shouts and bravos was enough to lift the roof. It was the crowd's way of affirming their resolve to spew the lukewarm out of their mouths. Flushed with his success Gérin-Labrit walked slowly up to the platform and took his seat beside the chairman. Patrice was just wondering whether he would have to shake the speaker's hand when the painful decision was taken for him by Labrit, who grasped his hand, dragged him to his feet, and kissed him on both cheeks without further warning. The crowd roared their approval. Patrice was moved, but could not help thinking uncomfortably of the brown froth on Gérin-Labrit's lips. He sat down and took out his handkerchief, and while appearing to feel the heat mopped his cheeks surreptitiously. Then he announced Schlemer as the next speaker.

It was possible to avoid listening to Schlemer, continuously at any rate, but it was difficult not to admire him. He was enormously fat, but that did not prevent him from pacing up and down, waving his arms, and indulging in gymnastics that would have been exhausting for a trained athlete. He spoke freely, obviously enjoying the sound of his own voice, and he knew how to make his audience enjoy themselves, too. Périot made up his mind not to listen but to watch him for his entertainment value.

And as mental entertainment it was first class, giving Patrice fresh food for thought. He became prosecutor and defendant at the same time. 'I am addressing these meetings several times a month,' he thought, 'not to please Rebufat or Schlemer, but to deliver a message to all these good people from our secret world of science. The work I am doing is part of my duty towards myself. Towards myself—that is a point to remember.'

While Patrice was indulging in these reflections Schlemer had developed his usual technique of delivering carefully prepared allusions to the names of his opponents, and to their various theories. At each reference the huge man threw up his podgy arms to heaven, and was greeted by a volley of boos and whistles from the crowd.

It was past midnight before the meeting had carried unanimously several resolutions expressing its ardent desire for peace, and Patrice Périot left the hall, arm in arm with Gérin-Labrit. The author waved aside the crowd, with the words: 'Make way for our president, the great architect of peace.' Men and women gave way willingly enough, but there were remarks such as: 'Who is he? Who is that—do you know?' They had only seen Patrice from a distance, and failed to recognize him. Besides, he had been the first to speak, and since then a torrent of words had flowed over their unsuspecting and perplexed heads.

With difficulty they found the car, and Gérin-Labrit said: 'You must let me give you a lift home.'

Suddenly Patrice Périot felt very tired, like a man after a heavy and unaccustomed night out. Gérin-Labrit put on a cheerful air to cover his own fatigue, and made conversation with such abstract phrases as 'Communism will triumph because it brings a message of hope. Hope is an essential food for every one, and Communism alone supplies it.'

An awkward silence fell until Gérin-Labrit interjected: 'It is absolutely absurd, as I am sure you agree, professor, to expect a reconciliation between the classes. There will be no such thing.'

'So what?' said Patrice absent-mindedly.

Gérin-Labrit made no response except to raise his hand as if to make a clean sweep of something and consign it to perdition.

CHAPTER III

THE corridor in the centre of the house is a gloomy spot, where no direct light ever penetrates. Through it run the exposed central heating pipes, emanating a mild warmth, and various domestic smells carried by the draught linger and eventually die there. The walls are adorned with portraits which are so bad that no one dares look at them for fear of recognizing himself. A low-powered lamp has been condemned to hang in this unappetizing place. Every now and then the voices of children can be heard, singing or quarrelling in the adjoining rooms, or a water pipe gives vent to one of the rhythmic whistles and thumps that are the national anthems of this uncouth age. A door slams, shattering the silence, and the old corridor looks for a few moments like a sanctuary that has been profaned.

Hervé Périot knocked loudly and repeatedly at the bath-room door. Receiving no reply he called: 'Christine!'

From within could be heard the noise of clinking bottles, and he called again: 'Vera! Open the door!'

'You are the limit.' Christine's low voice was quite

unperturbed. 'You don't even bother to ask if I'm presentable.'

Hervé shrugged his shoulders. The voice went on from the other side of the closed door: 'What's the hurry?'

'I only want a word with you.'

'All right, you can wait.'

After a moment's hesitation Hervé Périot went into his sister's bedroom, took a seat on the arm of one of her chairs, and turned idly through a pile of newspapers. A few minutes later Christine appeared, tying the girdle of her dressing-gown.

'You really have got a nerve,' she said, without raising her voice, 'wandering into my room as if it were your own, and rummaging among my papers. . . .'

Hervé looked at his sister appraisingly out of the corners of his eyes. 'There's one thing about you, I must say. You never hide anything—your convictions, or your actions, or your dislikes. . . .'

'I do not even hide my suspicions.'

Hervé lit a cigarette. 'Exactly. People of your type have the unique merit of rendering indiscretion impossible. I came to your room to ask you a favour.'

'No,' said Christine firmly.

'No? What do you mean?'

'No, I will not lend you my car.'

Hervé Périot was rather undersized, but while this did not appear to bother him he was always seeking other reasons to explain away his habitual lack of ease. His sensitive face was distorted by uncontrollable tics, his hair was glossy and wavy, and he had what Christine used to call the oyster-coloured complexion of the Périots. He watched his sister attentively, like a cat its prey, and said: 'Not even for a couple of hours?'

'Not even for five minutes.'

'If you will trust me with it for two hours before lunch to-day, I promise to return it to you in perfect running order.'

'How kind of you. And give me a putty medal into the bargain, I suppose?'

'I'll tell you later what I'll do to show my gratitude.'

'Don't bother. I know that if I lend you my car for as much as five minutes it will never be the same again. Something will be broken, a bolt loosened, a control out of order, a mysterious rattle, something or other to mark the fact that you personally have been at the wheel. Other possessions may change hands, but a car never. Even if I had more confidence in you than I have, I should not lend you my car.'

Hervé looked innocently at the ceiling. 'Not even if it was a matter of life and death?'

Christine, filing her nails, said coolly: 'I warn you that your threat of tragedy is an unsatisfactory form of blackmail. It will not work because you have tried it too often, and you are still perfectly all right. The result is that you've lost face all round, except perhaps with daddy—I can't speak for him.'

Apparently Hervé did not even hear these strictures. He merely caught up the last few words and said: 'Daddy! Dad hasn't got a car. He either travels by metro—or goes on foot.'

'He argues that it's good for his health. And besides, he's too old to learn to drive now—he wouldn't dream of it.'

'You're the only one of the family with a car—

42

leaving out that supreme egoist Maurice. *We* have no car—but Vera Périot has.'

'It doesn't belong to me.'

'It is registered in your name. Lend it to me for a couple of hours this morning, not a minute more, and I'll let you have it back as I found it. Moreover, I'll undertake to say nothing to father about——'

'About what?'

'About the man you lend the car to every few days—your unique and invaluable car that doesn't even belong to you!'

By this time Christine was applying a flesh-coloured varnish to her nails with a fine brush. Without as much as looking up or raising her voice above its normal cadence she said clearly and deliberately: 'If you talk any of that rot to daddy, I warn you, Hervé, that I am in a position to get my own back.'

'Really? And how, I should like to know?'

'Firstly by spiking your guns; secondly by causing you, through enforced loneliness, to become a very different man from what you are.'

'Such as?'

'A rational, honourable man—a normal man, in fact.'

Hervé laughed nervously. 'A threat of vengeance is not a satisfactory form of blackmail, Vera. It won't work. I'm going to borrow your own line of talk. It won't work, because you've tried it too often and you've lost face all round, etc. Now come off it, Vera. I may be a bit off the rails, but you are downright wicked. You are horrible. And what is more, I tell you, when you are wicked you look ugly.'

His voice was getting louder and louder. Suddenly

he saw his brother Thierry in the doorway, pyjama-clad, hair tousled, arms raised.

'There you are,' said Christine, 'you're shouting so much, Hervé, that you have roused our saintly little Thierry from his prayers, or perhaps from his sleep. Now he's going to preach us a sermon, which is my cue to turn you both out and dress in peace.'

She began to shove Hervé, now silent and gloomy, out towards the passage, but Thierry said, almost tearfully: 'Christine, I wish to goodness you wouldn't keep on calling me a little saint. I am a sinner and a fool like the next man. But the thought that you two can't spend ten minutes together without having a violent quarrel upsets me so much that I feel it must all be my fault, and that I should somehow have managed to influence you.'

'You young ass,' said Christine, taking him by the shoulder, 'you must have the pride of the devil to think that you are to blame for all the sins and sorrows of other people. Run along, that's a good boy, and let me dress.'

In the doorway Hervé turned back, and whispered urgently in his sister's ear: 'Lend me a thousand francs, Vera. No, give me a thousand francs, because I know I shall never pay them back.'

Christine shrugged her shoulders, glanced round for her hand-bag, opened it quickly, and took out a note which she pushed into her brother's pocket. With clenched teeth she said: 'Clear out, now, for heaven's sake. Clear out, and don't say thank you, or I'll tear up the note. Don't tell me I'm not horrible. Don't tell me I'm not ugly. Don't have a moment of remorse, you ungrateful wretch!'

The two brothers met again in the musty corridor. Hervé was breathing fast and Thierry said: 'What's the trouble? I can hear your heart beating. You're ill.'

'I'm not ill. I'm fed up, that's all. Now I'm going to slip a coat on and try and have a word with dad. Have you had breakfast? No? Communion, eh? Good enough as long as you leave me to my own devices. I'll be in to lunch with the family.'

Patrice Périot was sitting at his desk in his dressing-gown. Seeing Hervé come in he said: 'I heard you all arguing—yes, even from here. I can't hope to stop you wrangling—I have too much else to do. Your mother died before her time and I shall never get over it. She might have been able to understand you and talk to you, but I can't. I certainly can't!'

'Father,' said Hervé, 'could you spare me ten minutes?'

'Not now, Hervé, not just now. I must read through my letters and think out the replies. Come and see me before lunch and don't be late. What were you saying to Christine?'

'A few sweet nothings,' sighed the young man, 'that she did not relish. She is as tough as a goat.'

'Off you go, now, there's a good lad. If you have a moment send a message to Edwige by the cable to tell them we shall be lunching at a quarter to one. That should mean that by half-past one—— Oh, for heaven's sake, let me get on with my work, Hervé!'

Patrice Périot sat lonely and care-worn at his desk, on which the mountain of letters, papers, reviews, and pamphlets rose in a maze of rock-ridges, valleys, cliffs, and precipices. The geological simile amused him for

45

a moment, but did not dispense him from the duty of getting to work.

After a long period of happy hard-working obscurity fame had come to him suddenly in 1935, when much to his surprise he won the coveted Gordon Pain prize, awarded for the second time to a French scholar by the University of Massachusetts. He had just published a work entitled *Biological Notes on the Natural Reservoirs*, which, although not entirely unintelligible to the ordinary reader, was addressed primarily to specialists. Périot's sudden fame resounded throughout France, and the popular writers put him over in the press as the discoverer of a new philosophy of animal life concerned particularly with the excretory organs. This gave the journalists a theme for plenty of wise-cracks, and they adopted Périot as if they knew all there was to be known about his theory of 'Natural Reservoirs.' Just about this time Patrice had been asked, among a number of other well-known people, to lend his name to the manifestoes issued by a certain political party. He used to read the documents submitted to him, and would sign them if he approved. Immediately the tone of the press altered, some papers referring to him with barely disguised bitterness, others lauding him to the skies. Poor old Périot was baffled by all this, and shook his head as he opened the papers. 'I am not the greatest scientist of the twentieth century. Far from it. I am simply one research worker among many. But they'll never understand that. The constant use of the superlative is a habit, and one for which the only substitutes are reliable information and a standard of comparison—a good general culture, in fact.'

It was in 1936, during an interview with a reporter, that he coined the phrase, seemingly sincere and innocent enough at the time, which had the most surprising repercussions. 'Having seen with my own eyes the sufferings of the people from whom I am sprung . . .' All perfectly true. He was of artisan stock, and his education had meant big sacrifices for the family. He had fought in the 1914–18 war as an infantry officer. He trod the streets of Paris every day, and he felt that he knew and loved the people. What could be truer? What could be more straightforward? But the phrase was quoted in type an inch thick by the left-wing press, which made it appear that Patrice Périot, recently elected Fellow of the Académie des Sciences and eminent scientist, no doubt, was a political party man. The bright young men of the right-wing papers published skits referring to Professor Périot as 'Bladder Périot' or sometimes 'Sphincter Périot,' and people in the train would ask : 'What's the idea of calling him Sphincter Périot—what's a sphincter, anyway?' to which the reply might be : 'I suppose it means sphinx—you know, those things in Egypt, something to do with the pyramids.'

During the years following his leap into the limelight Patrice had made some important researches on the organs controlled by the autonomic nervous system, which were the subject of keen discussion in scientific circles. But the public took not the slightest notice. The picture of Périot had already been painted and circulated—no alterations were required. It never pays to try the patience of the mob.

Périot was both amazed and upset by his sudden particoloured reputation. He soon began to look back with envy to the time when he worked on his own, untroubled by other people; and to a friend who congratulated him on the great success of his labours he replied: 'True enough, but I have paid dearly for it.'

Between 1936 and 1939 this unsolicited notoriety grew, and Patrice ended by taking a certain amount of illicit delight in it. Then came the years of disaster, and in 1940 Périot's home was unsuccessfully raided on several occasions by the Germans. In 1942 he was one of the group of Members of the Institute who were imprisoned for a few days and then thrown out on the station platform at Fresnes, even more bewildered than usual, wearing shoes from which the laces had been removed—a childish trick, typical of petty police regulations, aimed at humiliating the worthy old men.

Patrice stayed at his job as professor throughout the war, and when the liberation came, in an access of religious joy and exaltation, he began to appear in public again and to address great crowds, who made a legendary figure of him. But he had his difficulties, notably an endless, exhausting, personal stream of correspondence which took up most of his time despite the help of an efficient secretary who could write most of the answers with the help of an occasional word. And so he began to complain bitterly, to any one who would listen, of the burden which was weighing him down and distracting him from his true work in life. Occasionally the flood of letters would unaccountably dwindle, and then Patrice Périot would say that he was delighted by the falling off; but inwardly he thought 'people are beginning to forget me; I must be getting old,' and the temporary relief was poisoned by anxiety. Next day a mountain of paper would submerge his desk again, and the telephone would ring continuously. Personal visits were numerous, and Monday mornings which were reserved for them were not enough for his appointments. His train of thought was often interrupted by a delegation, respectful but ignorant of his real work, who would press him to open a suburban industrial exhibition or to make a public speech against the use of the atom bomb. He would plead, frowning, that he was far too busy, but his imagination would immediately begin to work on the subject suggested. He called to mind various calculations made by the physicists. 'The fusion of the earth under the action of the atomic bomb could hardly go deeper than five or six feet under present conditions. Therefore subterranean cities must be built, and people must learn to live like ants in the bowels of the earth. They must give up the light and joy of life—that was something a biologist could talk about. Before he knew where he was he was over-come by the virtuosity of his own imagination and had agreed to speak at the great atomic bomb protest rally. The mere thought of the sufferings of the rising generation, of his children and grandchildren, brought tears to his eyes. The delegation withdrew respect-fully. No sooner were they gone than the professor lashed out at himself for his weakness: 'A man of your type ought not to be addressing huge crowds, however worthy the cause, but should be getting on with the work he's most fitted for.'

This Sunday morning Patrice Périot had planned to put his letters in order and prepare the ground for his

D

secretary, after which he would lunch with his children and grandchildren, then pay a visit to his brother Gustave. He would give the end of this 'day off' to a little of his own work, hoping for the best.

With frequent head-shakings he opened the envelopes, read and annotated the letters. They fell into various categories, which he marked by special signs pencilled on the envelopes; invalids, criminals, fools, madmen. Every now and then he came across a purely disinterested letter, and savoured it in passing, but he knew well enough that one drop of bitterness was enough to spoil a whole cup of nectar. Then there were the anonymous letters, better left unread because of their disturbing or malicious nature. Finally there were generous letters from old friends to pour balm into his wounds; these were rare enough. Was not life becoming difficult for every one? Who had the time now to sympathize with others?

His next task was to deal with the notices and formal invitations, which had to be read, however cursorily. Like all public men Patrice was a member of numerous societies which demanded his support; and since 1936 he had learned to expect many communications, addressed to him in familiar terms by people he did not know from Adam—these he invariably classed as 'political' and threw aside.

While he was irritably engaged in his work of sorting Patrice hummed a tune he had heard the night before, a tune which certainly had nothing whatever to do with the job in hand. This dual capacity of the brain he used to call 'polyphonic intelligence.'

Occasionally he referred to his address book, an ancient affair that was by no means up to date.

Turning through it, he thought: 'A cemetery! A prison! A hospital! A mental home!' He began to strike out the names of those who were dead, but it promised to be a long job and, seized with frenzy, he had a desperate impulse to annihilate the lot, to be finished once and for all, as far as he was concerned, with everything and everybody that involved him in this insoluble riddle of the universe.

He went back to the mountain of papers and glanced through the newspapers and periodicals. Among them were various organs of propaganda. The successful ones, fat and well illustrated, inundated the worlds they hoped to conquer, while the lost causes replied with little multigraphed bulletins, usually illegible; unhappiness breeds unhappiness, misery walks hand in hand with misery. Insistently Patrice thought: 'Whoever is on the side of the under-dog cannot be in the wrong.'

Patrice often came across his own name in the papers. 'That's not true,' he thought, frowning. 'Judging the rest by what I actually know myself, it's all a pack of lies. I was not born in 1879, but in 1881. I did not marry Germaine Lemarchand but Clotilde Demoncelle. I have not seven children— I have only four. I am not professor at the College of France but at the Sorbonne. Incidentally I know nothing about the reservoirs of the Central Massif. The silly fools think that the gall bladder is part of the water system of the Central Massif! No, my sons are not registered members of the Communist party, nor are the registered members of the Communist party my sons. . . .'

Whereupon Patrice opened another paper, hit upon

a vitriolic article which he read and re-read, heaved a sigh, and threw the corrosive pages into the waste-paper basket, murmuring: 'It's appalling! What on earth is he getting at? But there's at least one thing to be said for these diatribes—I don't have to answer them.'

At that point in the professor's meditations he heard a knock at the door. Before he had time to answer, the door opened and Hervé came in.

'Father,' he said, 'you don't seem to realize it's half-past twelve.'

'Good heavens! Is it really? No, it never even occurred to me.'

Like his brother and sisters, when they came to see their father, Hervé sat down on the sofa on which Patrice used to stretch himself when he wanted to read. The young man looked preoccupied and worried, and kept on moving his extraordinarily mobile ears. Watching this performance Patrice could not help thinking: 'My brother Gustave is the only one I know with a similar development of the muscles of the pinna. This anatomical peculiarity marks Hervé as a Périot; in other respects I am not so sure. How extraordinary are the by-products of heredity!'

'What do you want, son?' he asked, still in a dream.

Hervé did not reply immediately. He was biting his nails.

'You might be a Member of the Institute,' said Patrice.

'How do you mean?' Hervé was obviously annoyed.

'Because of the way you bite your nails. At least three of my colleagues do it—and certainly they ought to know better.'

52

Hervé shrugged his shoulders and went straight on: 'Christine is stupid and wrong-headed, but I am not to blame for that.'

'No, of course not.'

'Nevertheless she gets me down, with her domineering ways.'

'I understand, exactly.' Patrice looked exasperated. 'Outbursts of this kind remind me of a well-known quotation—I can't remember the author—"Families, I hate you all," or something of the sort.'

The young man jumped nervously to his feet and said: 'Father, I don't hate you.'

'Just a moment, boy. I have it now. It's by Corneille.'

'Please don't make fun of me, dad, but listen to what I have to say.' Hervé went over to his father, and then almost turned his back on him. 'Dad,' he said in a low voice, 'give me a hundred thousand francs.'

'What's that?' Patrice retained his self-possession.

'A hundred thousand francs,' Hervé went on in hollow tones. 'It's absolutely essential.'

There was a noticeable pause before Patrice spoke again. 'It's an extraordinary thing, but whenever I break a tooth it's not when I'm chewing nuts, but eating stewed apples.'

'What do you mean by that?'

'It's difficult to explain, son. I mean that things often work out very differently from what I anticipate —and that in this case I was expecting an ordinary family row.'

'Listen to me, father,' said Hervé. 'You try to be a little friend of all the world, and yet you forget your own children and their troubles.'

53

Hervé was twenty-four, but at this moment he looked like a child in distress, and his face was distorted by tics.

'Now listen, father,' he went on. 'I'm going to do you a good turn. You remember the document they brought you to sign the other day—Christine was there, I know all about it, calling herself Vera for the occasion—well, you will read it in the newspapers. They have added two lines to it; I know what I'm talking about.'

Just then the door blew open and Christine came in. Without any preamble she said: 'I have heard every word.'

Patrice looked overwhelmed. 'There's family life for you,' he said, 'and what a family! We can never even tell whether someone will be listening behind the door.'

'I was not behind the door.'

'Where were you then? You've only just come in.'

'I turned up just at that moment.'

'And yet you had time to hear everything we said? What an amazing contraction of time, Christine.'

'I have asked you a hundred times to stop calling me Christine. I am not a Christian.'

'Be that as it may, it's a nice name, and it suits you. Besides, it's no easy matter for me and my friends who have known you since you were an infant.'

'It's lunch time,' said Christine obstinately. 'Hortense is being kept waiting and she's beginning to get nasty.'

'And Edwige? And her husband and children?'

'They are coming over in relays.'

Patrice Périot rose wearily and whispered to Hervé:

54

'A hundred thousand francs, old chap! You must be crazy! I haven't got that much.'

'You could sell the house at Jouy-le-Comte.'

'You are completely mad. Come and eat.'

Patrice went into the dining-room where the table was laid for the Sunday meal. Edwige, the oldest of the four Périot children, had just arrived with her three babies.

'Isn't your husband in yet?' asked Patrice anxiously.

'No, father. You know he plays tennis on Sunday mornings. It's his only chance of exercise.'

'All right, all right.' Patrice refused to be put out.

Edwige was a good-looking woman of about thirty. She was not in the least like her sister Christine. Whereas Christine, the younger by four years, was a doctor of law, Edwige had made it obvious very early in life that she had no intellectual ambitions. She had married an industrial scientist, Maurice Ribeyrol, a determined young man who, although she had already borne him three children, accused her of flirting, and staged daily scenes of jealousy. She used to complain of him to her sister and brothers, and they all took sides against Maurice, the stranger. Edwige was not a coquette, but she was full-blown, sensual, and occasionally peevish. Her comely breasts moved gracefully beneath her white, pink, or orange silk blouses. She used vast quantities of lipstick, leaving traces behind her on table-linen, curtains, fountain-pens, door-handles, and all sorts of household objects. She was one of those women with tearful voices who cannot enter into any conversation without embarking on veiled yet unmistakable references to the functioning of the anatomical apparatus peculiar to their sex, a

55

habit which roused Christine-Vera to cold fury. But Patrice Périot was especially fond of her, partly because she was the eldest of his four children, and partly because she never bullied him, which his other daughter, the lawyer, the little witch-doctor, as he called her, did not hesitate to do at moments of crisis.

Sunday dinner was begun forthwith, primarily because Mme Hortense had given the word, and secondarily because Patrice had declared once and for all that they would not wait for late-comers. The meal began in an atmosphere of bickering, which was the normal family climate, even when the emotional temperature was low and the day comparatively calm and peaceful. Patrice took no part whatever in the conversation, and could not have done so had he wanted to. Most of the arguments flared up over one or other of Thierry's various pronouncements. Christine looked daggers and talked dialectical materialism. Hervé took no interest in politics, but would discuss some ultra-modern abstract school of poetry, in which all the words had to be sustained by labial consonants within lines of five syllables. Edwige's little ones greeted the arrival of each dish with cries of: 'I won't have that! I don't like it!' Patrice smiled at his memories, and mused: 'How many times have I told them not to put their elbows on the table when they are using a spoon, or not to hang their arms under the table as if they were fiddling with their shoe-laces. And now they are grown-up men and women. Yes, women! I'd give anything in the world to see Christine married, but I have no influence over her now. On the other hand, a husband might have a very bad influence on her. . . . Now they've started

56

talking biology, and it will all be rubbish. And here comes our absentee—I wasn't expecting him till the cheese.'

Maurice Ribeyrol had just come in, and as soon as he sat down the dispute was augmented. Patrice went on with his dreaming. 'Clotilde liked her own unusual christian name, and she wanted to give them all uncommon names. Edwige's husband, Maurice, thought that this was all very absurd, and insisted on very common names for his own children. They're nice kids, I must admit. Now they're on the subject of my Louis XV sideboard. They might at least wait till I'm dead. They can have it now, as far as I'm concerned, but I can hardly cut it into four. . . .'

After a brief passage of arms in which the sideboard was at stake the conversation reverted to science. For a moment the name of Pasteur floated like a straw on the eddies of the quarrel. In a tired voice Patrice said: 'What's this about Pasteur?' Under his breath he added: 'Now for the massacre. And starting on Pasteur of all people!'

Maurice Ribeyrol forged ahead without so much as a glance at his father-in-law. 'There is nothing to be gained by chewing the rag over Pasteur. He is completely out of date in his own field. It is true that he discovered certain microbes, but the world would have discovered them without his assistance. He failed to make due acknowledgment to Claude Bernard who forestalled him in the discovery of the virus. I've read all the books about it. Let's change the subject!'

Edwige adored her difficult husband. Every weighty utterance of his was endorsed with a childishly admiring intake of breath. Thierry sprang to his feet and asserted that Pasteur was a saint. They nearly came to blows when Maurice said he was a royalist, which everybody knew, and Christine-Vera began to make enigmatic insinuations in her cutting voice. By this time Patrice was exhausted and nearly in despair. Each week he looked forward to Sunday dinner as a time of happiness as well as of refreshment, only to be disappointed.

By half-past two they had all finished eating, and the party broke up. Patrice put on his overcoat and made it obvious that he was going out without saying where.

He took the metro, as usual, to the other end of Paris, reached a rather shabby house in the boulevard Arago, walked up to the fourth floor, and rang the bell gently at one of the doors.

There lived his brother, five years older than him and a bachelor in poor circumstances. He was a rather depressed type of man, who had missed everything in life; neither natural gifts nor good fortune had come his way. Patrice used to go to see him twice a month. He would find him in bed, disgruntled and bitter. Patrice always handed him an envelope containing a small sum of money, and this was the most difficult part of his short visit, demanding considerable tact.

'I see!' said the invalid. 'You've come to bring me your money again.'

'I have indeed, my poor man.'

'What's the idea of the "poor man"?'

'It's only a figure of speech. I talk to you as I would to myself. I often call myself "poor man" in a friendly way.'

The sick man opened the envelope with shaking clumsy fingers. 'Always the same amount.'

'If I didn't give you this money,' said Patrice in conciliatory tones, 'you would write me reproachful letters, and you would be quite within your rights.'

'You could easily send it to me by money order. That would be much less humiliating for me.'

'You would say then that I was neglecting you.'

The sick man swallowed some imaginary saliva, and said in a peevish voice: 'Those friends of yours are making you sign all sorts of rubbish. Yes, they are. Look in the papers for yourself. The fact is, you don't read what you sign.'

'You're mistaken.' Patrice spoke like a tired man. 'I only sign what I have read, and I am prepared to stand by what I believe to be true.'

The conversation lasted a few moments longer, and then Patrice, murmuring vague excuses, hurried away, glad to return to the fresh air and the city streets. He walked alone among the Sunday crowd, and told himself sadly: 'What an uncomfortable place this world is! I am ill at ease at home and a misfit in my own generation. People who like me for selfish reasons give me up as a bad job, and those who like me for my own sake get on my nerves and bore me. I must do some work this evening. Work is my only source of happiness, the only thing that does me any good. But I no longer have time to work at the things after my own heart. The fact is that life's waste products interfere with its functioning. That is biologically true. Age, work, fame, all these things poison life and cripple productivity.'

Absent-mindedly he prodded with the end of his

walking-stick at a little knot of blonde hair-combings that must have fallen from a window and was being blown along the pavement by the wind. Around this delicate clue he wove a dream of life, love, and passion.

'Bah,' he said, walking on again, 'I shall feel better to-morrow! I am not always in the blues, and I have no idea whence comes the gleam of hope. But come it does, or nearly always. Fundamentally I ask only one thing—that people shall not be unhappy. What a forlorn hope!'

Then suddenly a remark came back to him from the talk he had just had with his sick brother, a remark which linked up with one of the hints dropped by Hervé that very morning, before Christine had butted in. 'What do they mean when they talk about my being made to sign things? I only do what I intend to do. I am nobody's tool. And even if the unhappy masses did turn out to be mistaken I would still stand by them in their error, pointing out of course where they were wrong! For ultimately, truth, truth . . .'

CHAPTER IV

PATRICE PÉRIOT was in the habit of pausing at the foot of the staircase of the Institute, whenever he found himself alone there, in silent admiration of the statue of Minerva.

The goddess as represented there is something less than life-size. She is a handsome and decorous virgin, with purity expressed in every line of her. Not a young virgin, but a woman of well over thirty with small breasts set far apart. She inspires respect and admiration and the passer-by might be tempted to seek her advice and help, were he not drawn upwards by the staircase ahead. Where Minerva stands the staircase divides into two branches, offering a choice between right and left. Patrice Périot recalled that he always took the left-hand branch, and smiled to himself under his greying clipped moustache. 'If my worthy colleague Ponthieu could see me now,' he thought, 'he would undoubtedly read a symbolic meaning into this and would label me an intellectual fellow traveller. But to be strictly accurate is it ever possible to indulge in any thought or action that does not involve some degree of choice or selection? My dear Minerva stands immobile at the junction of two routes, but if she had to get into action herself and climb the stairs, she would then have to make her choice between them like the rest of us. There is a lift, it is true, but that is for the weary ones, for those in fact who want to go up without having to make either choice or effort.' A little way up the stairs he murmured: 'We must not let our imaginations run away with us. Broadly speaking, those who take the left-hand route do so because they are going to the secretary's office; those who choose the right are on their way to a certain little room where they can make themselves comfortable before the session. . . . Ah! Ponthieu is behind me. Side-step! Dodge him!'

Ponthieu was a scholar who did not conform to the ordinary pattern. No single book, no one piece of original research, could be attributed to him. He published articles here and there devoted neither to theories, nor to new methods, nor even to new ideas, but exclusively to personalities. For many years he had edited a publication called *The International Science Review*, which enjoyed an inexplicable reputation, and for this reason, no doubt, he had been elected a Member of the Institute, where he wielded considerable influence, directed the elections, and gave decisive rulings on the awards of prizes.

Patrice Périot, after his slight detour, entered the conference hall to find the assembly at work. It may be remarked that the atmosphere in which this work was being carried on would have caused a stranger no little surprise; but Patrice had a long experience of the place and its occupants, and was inclined to be indulgent. So he signed the members' book and took the first empty seat he could find. The hall looked very fine with its tall panelling, statues, busts, and gold-lettered inscriptions. Facing the assembly was a blackboard and a narrow platform on which someone was making a speech, standing chalk in hand like a schoolmaster. The words of the speaker were lost as soon as they were out of his mouth in the tumult of conversation going on here, there, and everywhere among members congregating in pairs or small groups. A few old men, hands cupped among the tufts of white hair behind their deaf ears, made obviously vain, almost desperate, attempts to catch an occasional word and trace some interest in the lecturer who was holding the floor. The rest got up and moved about, laughed and coughed with every sign of complete inattention. Some of them went for a moment to the next room, not as might have been expected to talk more comfortably, but because they caught sight of a friend there whom they wanted to meet. The journalists grouped near the blackboard listened spasmodically and shook hands with the academicians who were walking up and down casually in the main gangway. The hubbub rose and fell, flowed and ebbed, now in one part of the hall, now in another, and a newcomer might have been reminded of one of those synagogues or chapels where, although God is present, the faithful come to talk over their affairs rather than to pray.

Most of the men there, seated at the green baize tables, had worked for years in seclusion, observing natural phenomena, creating and verifying daring hypotheses. Some of them had discovered new laws, invented new methods and techniques, and thus profoundly affected the spiritual or material lives of their

fellow men. Yet they behaved like unruly school-
boys, partly because they knew that anything likely
to excite their interest could always be looked up later
in the books and periodicals, and partly because they
reserved their serious attention for their own special
subjects. Twentieth-century science has grown too
big and too complex, and each must choose independently his own pasture on the slopes of its chaotic
mountain.

Patrice Périot sat down and took a few deep breaths,
as was his wont, to put himself at ease and relax.
Nevertheless he kept his colleagues under constant
observation. Those who were neither talking nor
listening appeared to be lost in deep reverie. Some
were exploring their nostrils with a searching finger,
and withdrawing small mucosities which they would
disintegrate by rolling them slowly between thumb
and forefinger, all this with a thoughtful, artless air of
confirmed ineffectiveness. Some were turning through
the magazines lying on the tables. Others were
drowsing under the strain of digestive effort. Others
again, inquisitive, observant, and restless, were casting
a roving eye round the assembled company. Patrice
showed his preoccupation as usual by doodling,
drawing boats, animals, and Noah's arks. Sometimes
he tried, without much success, to make sketches of
his near neighbours.

The man on his right suddenly leaned over and said
with a smile: 'Tell me, Périot, you haven't much
sympathy with the Government, have you?'

Périot was surprised. 'How do you mean exactly?'

'Come on, Périot, you know well enough. You and
Eymonnet and Rebufat signed that protest. We were

all talking about it amongst ourselves in the court-yard only a little while ago.'

Patrice Périot, with an expression of weariness rather than firmness, looked him straight in the eyes for an appreciable time. Pierquin was a mineralogist, whose fixed wry smile masked a mind that was at once bitter, flexible, elusive, and obstinate. In any group of distinguished men unanimity is never more than a lucky accident, and when such a company have signified their agreement by silence or by some such device as a show of hands, the mere suggestion of a vote by ballot will immediately shatter the fragile harmony. Unexpected or indecipherable votes and blank papers come pouring in. The momentary pause forces them to make up their minds individually, and the inattentive and the deaf interpret in their own fashion the question that has been put. Some systematically and methodically refuse to make any decision, others are consumed with a burning desire, which they subsequently rationalize, to mark their independence by being different from the rest. Matthew Pierquin was in the latter category. One had always to be prepared for the unexpected from him, so much so that Romanil, with his usual grudging good sense, used to say: 'I only know one thing for certain about Pierquin, and that is that I know nothing about him.' Pierquin had a curious nervous tic; he moved his head ceaselessly from left to right and from right to left. His loosely hung jaw amplified these oscillations, and on the rare occasions when his mouth said 'Yes' his head went on obstinately saying 'No.' Nevertheless intelligence shone from his irregular features. His expression gleamed with malice.

'What exactly were you people saying outside?' asked Patrice Périot, with as much calmness as he could muster.

'We were discussing the fact that you are employed by the National Educational Service. . . .'

'And that I am therefore not a free man?'

'Oh, we didn't go quite so far as that! We were merely asking ourselves whether a professor on the active list has the right to criticize the Government that employs him, that is to say to criticize and publicly condemn the acts of that Government.'

Pierquin had a folded newspaper in his hand. He turned his attention to it, and read, deliberately articulating each word:

'We the undersigned, being of the opinion that the French Government, in refusing entry to Seretti and Montecolla when they tried to cross the French frontier, bear in some measure the responsibility for a trial and sentence against which all friends of freedom will protest, consider that this Government has cast a serious slur on our ancient traditions of hospitality. . . .

'You may be within your rights in holding such opinions. But if you should find yourself sent for, to-morrow, by the higher education authorities, you would have no cause for complaint. I'm telling you this because we're old friends, and besides, cases of this kind concern us all.'

Patrice Périot knit his brows in concentration, and rubbed his chin, making a noise like a scrubbing-brush. 'Thank you, Pierquin. I have thought a lot about these problems, as you may imagine. I love my country, but I am not a servant of the nation, although it may appear so. Neither am I a servant of humanity, although my heart is full of sympathy for its sufferings. . . .'

'To whom then, or rather to what, do you owe your allegiance?'

'I am first and foremost in the service of pure knowledge, just as you are, Pierquin.'

'I agree with that.'

'I am in the service of truth and justice.'

'My dear chap, you are sublime! All this presupposes that you have an infallible definition of what you are pleased to call truth and justice.' At this Pierquin shook his head, in his usual fashion, and then added: 'I must say I admire you. Of course, you will realize that none of this matters to me either way —I am not interested in politics.'

Having delivered himself of this, he turned deliberately to his other neighbour. Patrice went back to his elephants and giraffes, but inwardly he felt very uneasy. The thought of a reprimand had not even occurred to him. If it had, he mused, it would only have confirmed him in the stand he had taken. It struck him that he could not remember very accurately the drift of the document he had signed at his house the other evening in the presence of Romanil. Had he really read the piece about the official refusal of entry, ten months ago, to the two revolutionaries who tried to cross the frontier? Or had his attention been wandering at the time? If the government had refused asylum to two hunted men, there was no harm in pointing it out. The real difficulty was to be sure whether Patrice Périot had really read the document or not—and the fact that he could not be sure was very annoying, and a worrying symptom of over-tiredness into the bargain. Then there was the additional possibility that the wording had been altered after he had signed it.

Absurd as it might seem at first sight, this hypothesis tormented Patrice without respite. He was now drawing cats that looked like a cross between dolls and monkeys. Meanwhile speaker succeeded speaker at the blackboard, like voices crying in the wilderness. Then suddenly, in one of the seats in shadow at the other end of the hall under the rarely opened high windows, Périot saw Rebufat the mathematician, or to be more accurate Rebufat's bald head.

Rebufat was one of the signatories of the single-page manifesto entitled *Appeal to the French Conscience*. Patrice Périot abandoned his drawings of animals and arks, and made his way from group to group, resisting all interruptions until he found himself sitting next to Rebufat at the end of the room.

Noël Rebufat was a tall, thin man, and his permanently tense expression suggested a deep resentment, combined with the fear of fresh and inevitable affronts to come. One had only to look at Noël Rebufat to be sure that attack in any guise would fail to harm him, for it would be awaited apprehensively and with defences already alerted. He was completely bald, and year by year developed an increasing horror of hair. A hair on his clothes was a disgusting object in his eyes; one hair on his desk would put an end to any possibility of constructive thought. Although every one took him for a confirmed bachelor he was in fact married to a white Russian, whom he had met in Warsaw during his student days after the First World War. This lady was one of those Russian exiles who loathe the Bolshevists and at the same time remember with pride the day when the Polish troops were cut to pieces by Boudienny's cavalry, because the latter were still Russian despite being Red. Out of her love for Holy Russia, even while fuming against the Soviet system, she had gradually made it appear that her husband was mildly sympathetic to the Communists. All is asked from a party man—more than all may be expected from a sympathizer. Matthew Pierquin, mentally and physically a wobbler, once said to Patrice Périot grimly: 'Every French intellectual married to a white Russian is a left-wing extremist, either because he loves his wife, or because he hates her.'

And so Patrice Périot, sitting next to Rebufat, waited a little while before engaging him in conversation. He knew his man, and was feeling his way. Eventually, to master his nervousness in the presence of his cantankerous colleague, he went straight into the attack.

'Tell me, Rebufat, did you really read the text of that manifesto they gave you to sign the other day?'

The mathematician replied sharply: 'Do you imagine I sign everything that comes along, without looking at it?'

'As a matter of fact,' said Périot, 'I too read it very carefully. I cannot for the life of me remember that allusion to the effect of the French Government's action in refusing admittance to those two unfortunates.'

'The effect of their action. . . . You really are extraordinary! From the way you speak you appear to be in some doubt about the harm being done by the very men who, regardless of us, are blithely throwing away the country's chances.'

Périot was silent. Undoubtedly Rebufat lived up to his hostile-sounding name.

'The organizers of the appeal,' Rebufat went on, 'forgot to mention the Seretti and Montecolla business, and I asked them to make a brief reference to it. I felt quite sure in doing so that I should have your unqualified support. It never occurred to me that I could be wrong about this.'

'No,' said Patrice Périot, plucking at his waistcoat, 'I didn't mean it that way. You were perfectly correct in your facts. But——'

'But what?'

Périot made no reply. He was in the grip of a complex distress, compounded of weariness, anxiety, and an unpleasant sensation of losing control of his actions and possibly of his thoughts as well. He got up and returned to his original seat to escape from the cross-grained Rebufat. On his way Clement Romanil thrust a chit into his hand. Patrice unfolded it as soon as he was sitting down, and read the mystifying phrases: 'Beware of your left hand because it is clumsy. Distrust your right hand because it is generous.'

He shrugged his shoulders and waved to Romanil from a distance in a vaguely amicable way. 'That is the poet in Romanil,' he reflected; 'it is of no practical importance.'

Soon afterwards, seeing Romanil get up to go, he also left the hall and caught up his friend in the gallery. They went down the staircase arm in arm.

'Even if you have nothing to say,' said Patrice quietly, 'try to give the impression of talking to me, so that we shall be left alone. I have had enough of these gentlemen for one day.'

On reaching the courtyard Romanil paused on the steps, cast an angry eye over the rows of cars against the walls, blew out his cheeks, and said: 'I belong to the generation when scholars were poor men. In the old days, and I'm thinking of times more recent than my early youth, you would see very few cars here on the days of our meetings. To-day half our people are connected with business or industry. I don't blame them. I only say that science is a very different matter from what it was in my student days. I hardly recognize it.'

'Our special subject,' said Patrice, 'yours and mine, happens to bring us within the ambit of a great many associations—rackets if you like to call them that.' He felt himself blush and was surprised not because he had regarded himself as too case-hardened to do so but because he had believed that his arteries had lost the necessary elasticity. 'Besides, I should be the last one to talk, for they gave me the Gordon Pain prize. Did you know that my wife hit on the idea of leaving that money in America? Thanks to her foresight I have been able to help my family and keep the house in Jouy-le-Comte, though it is a heavy drain on my resources.'

Clement Romanil broke into a hearty laugh. 'Well, what do you know about that! Prize or no prize, my friend, you still remain, like myself, an unselfish scientist of the old school. Let me assure you that if I had the disposal of that prize again, I would have

71

given it to you. Out of the lot of us—us biologists, I mean—you are still the one who most deserves it.'

Instead of answering, and to hide his emotion, Patrice Périot grasped the fat man's arm and tried to shake it, without much success, however, because of its enormous size.

Romanil smiled and said : 'Now you're pinching me! You remember what old Nicolle used to say—Charles Nicolle, I mean, I scarcely knew the brother—"Biology in its present state does not appear to lend itself to evil doing." Of course he hadn't envisaged the possibility of bacterial warfare. I'm afraid our friend Nicolle was wrong. Anything can be put to evil purpose, even pledges of peace and love. And in saying that I'm not getting at you and your band-wagon. . . . Come on, let's go along to the Sorbonne together to hear the report of the Committee of Studies for the standardization of measuring instruments, etc. . . .'

'No,' said Patrice firmly. 'I am a member of a whole host of commissions, and I am president of endless committees. More than half the time I haven't the faintest idea what the business in hand is. I don't put my name forward—they conscript me. I don't mean to suggest that these committees are entirely valueless. There's usually some bright spark among them who knows what he's after and manages to persuade the rest of us to play. But I'm not going to the Sorbonne meeting. I intend to work this evening. It's time I put my work in order. No, I won't go.'

'Nor I!' said Romanil violently. 'After all, you and I are both still capable of doing creative work. And I'm not saying this to try and wean you away from your public speaking—I promise you I'll never say another word on that subject. Look! Your bus! Are you going to catch it or not? You are. All right then, it's good-bye for now.'

At home again Patrice Périot found his son Thierry standing on the one-armed chair in the study. 'What are you up to, Thierry? Catching flies?'

Even in winter there was always a solitary fly in the study, silently doing the rounds of the ceiling. This fly, mysteriously re-born from year to year, was a family institution. Every one respected it, even the supercilious Mme Hortense. If the fly was missing for a minute, someone in the house would always notice its absence, but it invariably turned up again to carry on describing its melancholy circles.

'Catch the fly? Our fly! No fear,' said Thierry. 'I am asking its advice. Besides, I feel so pleased with myself this morning that I must stand on something.'

'So you're feeling happy? That's good news, Thierry.'

'Yes, I have just had a row with Christine.'

'And that makes you happy—a quarrel with your sister?'

'But it was such a splendid quarrel, dad. Christine, who knows everything there is to be known—she is terribly intelligent—told me that scholars like you and Cuénot are straying into finalism! Straying! From Christine of all people! I asked her to tell me who Cuénot was. She made fun of me. Then I began to sing the *Magnificat*, which led to a bit of an argument.'

The young man jumped down and impulsively seized his father round the waist. 'You'll come over to us, dad! You'll end by joining us, and on that day

73

there'll be rejoicing in the world and in heaven too. Then you'll really be a great man.'

Patrice Périot shrugged his shoulders. 'My dear boy, you bandy the word "great" about, like the rest of your generation, though I know it's not your fault.'

'Daddy,' said the young man, eyes shining, 'I love you, and I admire you too. . . .'

'That's all very well, but it doesn't make sense. . . .'

'One day God will whisper in your ear, and that day the trumpets of heaven will sound for me.'

Patrice Périot had thrown himself into the damaged arm-chair, and was idly cracking his finger-joints. 'Taking it all round,' he thought, 'Thierry gives me the least trouble of them all. Nevertheless he's a bit mad, like the other three.' Aloud, he said: 'Considering that science is your subject, Thierry, you don't display much curiosity. Don't take this as a criticism. But the truth is you have never read anything of mine.'

'You don't understand, dad. Such is my trust in you that there is no need for me to read what you write; my heart tells me, and I absorb it inwardly. The mere thought that you are "straying into finalism," as Christine says, makes me want to climb the furniture and make acts of thanksgiving. *Magnificat anima mea*——'

'Calm yourself, my dear boy. I'm beginning to wonder what is going on in this house, and whether we are all going off our heads. For the time being let us leave the question of my relation to finalism— we can discuss all that later, when you know more about life. Now leave me to my own devices, will you, Thierry?'

Thierry went out, singing, and Patrice heard him for a little while exercising his lungs along the corridor. Patrice's expression clouded. He was thinking: 'The Government was wrong to refuse entry to those two unfortunates. All the same, Rebufat might have given me a ring on the phone. The whole thing was too high-handed.'

CHAPTER V

EASTER-TIDE came round, and a miraculous
peace descended on Patrice Périot's soul. Each
year, for more than twenty years, he had made a
habit of going into retreat in the early spring. He
used to leave Paris and escape to the house at Jouy-
le-Comte, which had been bought out of Clotilde's
money and kept up by dint of prodigies of economy.
It was an old house, undistinguished looking, but full
of antique furniture which the children laughed at
indulgently, and regarding the ownership of which
they used to argue amongst themselves even in the
presence of their father. An elderly couple acted as
caretakers. The house was surrounded by an unkept
garden leading to a field overlooking the valley of
the Oise.

And so each year Patrice would leave his best
students in charge of the current experiments at the
laboratory, and accompanied by Mme Hortense take
the train from the Gare du Nord. At first he tried
travelling second-class, as in the days when Clotilde
was alive. But he gave it up, saying to himself: 'The
third-class passengers are a more natural crowd. The

second-class people talk a lot of rot, and in the first-class they don't talk at all. I must say I like the third-class best.' This decision was interpreted by Mme Hortense as a regrettable measure of economy. 'The professor doesn't seem to consider what people will think,' she used to say.

The train plunged into the spring breezes and Patrice was intoxicated by the thought of soaking himself in the blessedness of solitude. Occasionally Mme Hortense would take him to task in her firm masculine tones. 'The professor did not let me know that his trousers were nearly worn through. I cannot attend to everything. The professor should pay more attention to his dress.' Patrice would mumble excuses, thinking: 'When it isn't Hortense, it is one of my own children pointing out my shortcomings, or else Gérin-Labrit, or Schlemer, or maybe the impeccable Rebufat. They're all the same. And on the rare occasions when they forget to blame me for something, I blame myself. Life is very extraordinary. . . .' Whereupon he turned his attention to the April countryside and the advantages of a hermit's life.

Mme Hortense soon brought him back to reality by insisting that the windows should be tightly closed. The instant a window was found to be slightly open anywhere in the neighbourhood of Mme Hortense she could be heard sneezing ostentatiously. Mme Hortense was at all times a personification of queenly dignity except when she sneezed. In that reflex act she appeared to lose all self-control. And so Patrice Périot had to close the window, with a mute appeal for the indulgence of the other passengers. In a tone that brooked no argument Mme Hortense said: 'The

77

professor feels the heat. He's lucky. I'm numb all over with the cold. I've lost all sense of feeling.' Patrice Périot did not doubt her insensibility. For many years he had given up making any reference to his own minor complaints. He well knew that if he so far forgot himself as to complain of a chill on the kidneys Mme Hortense would reply inflexibly: 'And what about me, professor? With your good health you can't have any idea of what I have to go through.' On such occasions, Patrice Périot would think to himself: 'I suppose it's her peculiar way of showing sympathy. Were she to reply to my complaints by saying she felt perfectly all right, I should be no better pleased. So what am I going on about?'

Mme Hortense said in a hard, school-marm voice: 'We will have a very light meal this evening. I am not feeling quite myself, and the professor eats too much and takes too little exercise.' Patrice nodded his approval. He knew that if he raised the slightest objection Mme Hortense would make it a pretext for one of her moods, and that next morning he would be given the stalest dish of butter, on the excuse that it was more economical to use it up before the fresh. From then on till the end of the journey he tried to keep up a running conversation about trivialities, for fear that a stony silence might have been interpreted as sulkiness. He was especially careful not to enthuse about anything or anybody, because on these occasions Mme Hortense liked to be the object of his exclusive attention. At last the train pulled up at Parmain station, and Patrice Périot congratulated himself on having accomplished the journey without any serious complications. Helping the old station-master

78

to put his cases on a hand-cart Patrice Périot thought to himself: 'I am soon bored in the company of intellectuals, and am only too glad to escape among simple folk. I often think that the so-called simple folk are really more complex than the others, for any one who can see beneath the surface. Unfortunately for me they are off my usual beat, and so I find myself resorting again to the intellectuals, my brothers, and my equals; my detestable brothers, the intellectuals. Life is not a unity. I ought to have learned that lesson, I of all people. . . .'

The house again; the quasi-religious joy of finding things waiting faithfully in their places; the happiness of lighting a wood fire in the hearth; the intoxicating, poignant smells, awakening sweet memories.

His hands in his pockets Patrice strolled in the garden, which was beginning to put on its spring green. He recognized each flower and shrub with an overflowing heart, and eagerly counted over the trees. Every year one of the trees died and Patrice Périot used to think: 'Children and young folk do not realize that trees die. One must be well on in life to grasp the fact of the solidarity and interdependence of all living things.' And suddenly his thoughts took a familar turning: 'One of these days Thierry will tell me that he is going to be a priest or maybe a monk. The mere thought of it turns my heart over. But it is not for me to dissuade him from the life of contemplation. They say I'm a party man—that may be so. But it would be truer to say that I am a solitary condemned to live in the crowd. Here, in the silence of the countryside, everything looks simple and straightforward, even the mind behind the laws of nature, which has nothing in common with our human intelligence.'

Patrice Périot paused in his walk and gazed long and earnestly at a slug, which had emerged prematurely from the depths. He knew well that in the wet climate of the valley the slugs were enemies, but to tell the truth he did not relish the idea of celebrating his first day of philosophic solitude by a minor murder. He passed the slug by. 'Not to-day!' he said; 'but to-morrow you would be well advised to keep out of my way.'

Patrice felt for his pocket-knife, to cut a hazel-switch. To his amazement the knife, which he always automatically put in his right-hand pocket, was now in the left. This was serious. For a minute he was badly shaken. Then the biologist in him gained the upper hand. 'Who was it who said that Nature makes no sudden leaps? Leibnitz, I think. What an idiotic statement! Nature works entirely by fits and starts. I am no out-and-out mutationist. Certainly there are such things as mutations—I should know that, seeing that I can make such a mistake over my pocket-knife —but Nature can also make mistakes. Every now and then she forgets old habits, and the result is a monster. . . . How peaceful I am here, on my own! How restorative the silence is!'

He spent two whole days in this state of peacefulness. On the morning of the third day, while shaving, he said to himself: 'Every day the same routine. Wash, shave, eat. It's becoming monotonous. There's not much satisfaction in merely looking after the daily needs of this old carcass of mine. I find that I experience a mild thrill if I have a new razor-blade or toothbrush. How childish!'

On the very first day of his retreat he had given strict instructions: 'If any one rings up, I'm not here.' On the third day the telephone rang and Mme Hortense replied firmly that the professor was not at home. Patrice held out for a few minutes, and then asked: 'Who was that on the phone just now? Luckily no one knows my number.'

'I said that you were not at Jouy-le-Comte.'

'Yes, but who was it?'

'I think he said he was the secretary of the Association of Free Minds.'

'A pity,' said Patrice Périot. 'Please take it that I am out except to them. There is something I want to talk to them about.'

'Next time,' growled Mme Hortense, 'I shall say that the professor is in, but that he has asked me to say that he is out.'

'No, no, you could say that you will go and see if I am in.'

'And what if they say they will call you again?'

'You must use your judgment,' said Patrice Périot awkwardly.

This day, the third of his holiday, Patrice began to wonder whether any of his children were likely to honour him with a visit. He grumbled at them, strutting up and down his study. 'My children are what they are, and of course they have their faults. But in a sense they share my solitude, and I should be pleased to see them here. I would go further and say that if they come they will not break my cherished solitude. Besides, I am used to working in a noise, not to say an uproar.'

He cracked all his finger-joints one by one, and

before long he found himself philosophizing about his troubles without exactly admitting to himself that he had any. 'I am not enjoying this period of quiescence so much as I should. Probably I shall appreciate it later, in retrospect. The experience will grow richer and riper with the passage of time.'

He was beginning to yawn over his blank sheet of writing-paper when he heard the purring of a car. It was Edwige and Maurice Ribeyrol, calling to deposit their three children before going on to Brittany for an engineering congress. As it happened they had brought their domestic help along with them, a listless girl whom Mme Hortense hated, and of whom she volunteered the remark: 'This girl comes to help me; the only result is that I shall have four extra people to look after instead of three.' Patrice Périot gave his grandchildren a heart-felt welcome; but he glimpsed Mme Hortense's reaction and thought: 'Peace! And I am the man who is demanding world peace! I would much rather first establish peace between Mme Hortense and—what is this girl's name? I can never remember. They change their staff so frequently.'

The Ribeyrols spent two hours at Jouy-le-Comte— just long enough to have a meal and get back into their car. In the middle of lunch Christine arrived from Paris. Luckily there was still some food left. A conversation sprang up at once, in which Patrice Périot took no part.

Ribeyrol said: 'I don't suppose you have read the article in the *Occident*. You should have done. Lavernède says that when a scholar turns to politics he is finished.'

'Always excepting the right-wing people,' Christine-Vera hissed. 'Your boon companions . . .'

They went on discussing this thorny subject for some time, but Patrice was not listening. He had insulated himself from the outset by thinking privately: 'There is something in what Maurice says. Take the case of Rebufat, in fact of mathematicians as a whole. And in my case, well, of course I am not a politician.'

Immediately after lunch the Ribeyrols drove off in their car. Patrice satisfied himself that his grand-children were being properly fed and looked after, and then took a stroll round the garden with Christine before retiring to his study.

'Can you stay on for a few days?' he said diffidently.

'No. But I will come down again on Sunday for a longer visit if I can get away from my work.' Christine did not close her mouth, and Patrice realized, from her unusual expression, that she had come to discuss some particular thing with him, and that she was hesitating to start. He waited, humbly and apprehensively.

Suddenly the little witch-doctor said: 'Father, keep an eye on Hervé.'

'You are an extraordinary girl, Christine. You know perfectly well that Hervé is as slippery as an eel. What have you found out now? What's the trouble?'

Christine's voice was like a knife. 'Hervé is mixing with a crowd I can't very well describe. They'll drive him off his head in the end.'

'Tell me, Christine, what sort of people?'

Through her clenched teeth she said: 'Blackmailers, gamblers, inverts——'

'In——'

'Yes, inverts. I believe that's the word. I am not an authority on such things.'

'This is terrible news,' faltered Patrice Périot. 'Are you sure of what you say? Have you any proofs?'

The little witch-doctor regarded her father compassionately. 'Daddy, if we wait till we have what you call proofs, it will be too late to do anything.'

'Christine,' moaned Patrice Périot, 'Christine, where are you going?'

'Back to Paris, daddy. I only came to have lunch with you.'

'And to tell me——'

'And to tell you what you ought to know. That's all I have to say.'

A moment later Christine-Vera was driving through the garden gate in the little car that she handled so skilfully. In his distress Patrice made a tour of the garden. He had wanted to see his children, and behold they had come and gone like a tornado. He had thought that Hervé was certain to come down during the holidays, and that there was no need to be precipitate; but now he was seized with anguish, and the lovely spring countryside suddenly lost all its charm. He went up to his room and sat at his desk, plunging into his work as an escape. On the margin of the reverse side of one of his folios he wrote, for his own relief, a phrase that had nothing to do with the book he was writing. 'It is not wear that destroys the shirt, but washing. It is not illness that ruins the constitution, but our half-baked remedies. It is not work that burns us up, but pleasure. In which case,' he added below, 'I shall live to be an old man. So much the worse for me!'

At dusk he went out into the garden again because the children were being bathed, and that was a noisy business. He was amazed that he had been able to concentrate on his writing, so black and clouded were his thoughts. 'Hervé! Hervé! My poor little Hervé! I can't believe it.'

Pacing the garden, now freshened by a shower, he soliloquized: 'I believe that my children hold me in respect; but they behave as if they don't. I believe they are fond of me, yet their affection is extraordinarily like indifference. When they're away, I miss them, and when they're here I miss—how shall I put it?—not them, but the picture of them I carry in my mind when they're away.'

That night Patrice Périot went late to bed. Sleep did not come to him, and he rose and resumed his work. Towards dawn he thought: 'When I am happy I can sleep and idle away my time. Therefore happiness cannot be productive of good work. I must see what the historians and biographers have to say on this point, though it wouldn't necessarily apply to people like me.'

Having washed and shaved, and while Mme Hortense was dusting his desk, he went to see the three children playing in their bed. The dispirited little nurse was helping in the kitchen. Patrice took one of the babies on his knee and scrutinized him with a mixture of perplexity and despair. 'There are people,' he said to himself, 'who have convinced themselves that childlessness is the best solution to life's problems. What they must suffer from lack of suffering! What they must suffer from having nothing to think about except their own precious bodies and souls!'

The child caught up the last words, and said: 'What did you say, grandfather? Eh?'

Patrice settled the child in bed again and fled to the garden, the only place where he could find some respite. He thought of his old friend Romanil, who had never married, which was strange considering that he was very fond of other people's children. Romanil had an elderly mistress; he did not live with her, but he went to see her once or twice a week at the end of his day's work, and they would spend an hour or two talking and arguing. These occasional visits had satisfied his need of feminine company for a period of over thirty years. Romanil called her his 'calm sister.' But the good lady had never read her Mallarmé, so that she did not resent the allusion to the freckles that heightened her complexion before the onset of the darker tint of old age. Patrice Périot walked to and fro under the cherry blossoms and thought: 'I wonder if Romanil has chosen the better part? I don't know, I'm sure. Having no children doesn't worry him, but there are a good many things he knows nothing about—I can't help thinking that, in trying to approach the great biological problems of life, which are my particular study, it is a help to have begotten life oneself, to have given hostages to fortune.'

Patrice Périot was interrupted in the midst of these reflections by an unexpected visitor, a man who ten years before had asked Périot to find him extra-mural work at the university; no easy matter, but by dint of considerable efforts, Périot, out of the kindness of his heart, had fixed him up successfully. This good man, no sooner provided for, came back for more. Every two or three months he turned up again, always with some fresh demand. His tone was impudent and dictatorial. 'My future is in your hands,' he would say; 'but I know how good-natured you are, and I have no hesitation in coming to you again. Do for me what you would do for yourself. You must know the ropes, to have got where you are.' There was no answer to these very unwelcome arguments, and Patrice Périot used always to give way with a feeling of complete defencelessness. Although he was exasperated by this visit he could not very well send the fellow packing to Paris after a minute's conversation, seeing that he had spent an hour on the journey. He received him in the garden, walking up and down The visitor came straight to the point. Some friends of his were putting him up for the cross of the Legion of Honour. He was sure that Professor Périot, seeing how much he had done already, would not refuse to write personally to the ministry and the chancellory and various other influential people who must be numbered among the acquaintances of such an eminent man as the professor. Périot reminded him gently that he himself was only an ordinary member of the Order, but his visitor, smiling obstinately, would not be deterred. 'You have so many other distinctions, professor, that you have no need of this one. For me it's entirely different. Professor, you have never deserted me in my times of trial. . . .'

Patrice looked his visitor up and down. The word trial was no exaggeration, for the man was indeed in the grip of a fixed idea, his brow a mass of wrinkles and his eyes gazing at the garden path. In the end Patrice, against the grain, asked the importunate beggar into his study, and wrote a letter, then another,

87

then a third. 'Moral and financial credit are very similar,' he thought; 'I am now committing an act of wild extravagance.' Satisfied at last, the visitor allowed himself to be shown to the gate.

Returning to the house, his fists clenched with exasperation, he encountered Mme Hortense. 'You should have told that chiseller I was out, or ill.'

'I never know what to do,' said Mme Hortense angrily. 'You always seem to be pleased to see the gentleman, so how can I tell where I am?'

Patrice Périot sat at his desk and groaned inwardly. 'I am on the point of putting the finishing touches on ten years of hard work, and this wretched fellow must barge in and ruin the entire day for me. Where can I find peace?'

He drew several deep breaths, felt his muscles relax, and followed his usual practice of writing a few phrases on the left-hand page of his note-book, phrases that had nothing to do with the work in hand but served the purpose of setting his natural processes in motion. He used to call the left-hand page 'the outlet,' and therein he wrote: 'The chief function of professional philosophers is to embalm contemporary truth in hermetically sealed words, to mummify living truths.' As he wrote he had in mind Eymonnet the philosopher, who had countersigned the *Appeal to the Conscience of France*, and he put the words on paper to relieve his feelings, thus symbolically sacrificing someone else on the altar of his wrath. Having done which he worked for several hours on end.

In the late afternoon Patrice Périot heard a car draw up to the garden gate. The window of his study was closed because of the threatening weather, but he thought he could distinguish Hervé's voice. His impulse was to run to the staircase and hurry down to the garden, but he managed to restrain himself and penned a few more lines. A moment later the door opened, and since there had been no preliminary knock Patrice thought: 'It must be one of my children. It's Hervé. . . .'

Hervé it was, wearing a flower in his buttonhole. Patrice noticed that there were stains on the lapels of his coat and that several of his waistcoat buttons were missing or undone. He exhaled an odour of Virginian cigarettes and frangipani. He came up to Patrice's arm-chair and kissed his father lightly on the forehead.

'What you, Hervé?' said Patrice, affecting surprise. 'How did you get here?'

'By train.'

'Why must he lie to me?' thought Patrice, in a flash. 'What makes him do it? I should not mind his telling me that a friend had brought him down.' Aloud he said: 'Are you intending to stay for a few days?'

'No,' replied Hervé. His manner was preoccupied. 'No, I only called in to say hallo.'

'Good enough, Hervé, we'll have tea together. Ask Mme Hortense to lay another cup for you.'

Patrice drank his tea at his desk. Hervé smoked as he sprawled on the old sofa, and Patrice watched him while he was off his guard. 'Very like his mother in feature,' he thought, 'but not in expression. Clotilde is accountable for that. She was the slave of us all. How self-denying she was! During her last illness, after the doctor had gone, she had said: "I am glad to think it is serious. I should hate you all to be upset over a mere indisposition. . . ." If only she were here now she would know what to say. But I don't. My work occupies my mind to the exclusion of everything else. I shall never be any good as a father, and I cannot forgive myself for that.'

This thought must have weighed on his mind, for he finished his tea and said: 'If your mother were still with us, she would be able to talk to you.'

Hervé shrugged his shoulders. 'I'm not in need of being talked to.'

'What do you need then, son?'

Hervé leaned over his father, and whispered urgently: 'Give me a hundred thousand francs. I assure you it is urgent.'

'Not those hundred thousand francs again! I had completely forgotten them.' Patrice heaved a sigh.

'That's where you were wrong, father. This is a very serious matter.'

'You have the nerve to come and tell me that I'm wrong to forget your wild ideas! My son, I am not a rich man. You know all my resources. I have to provide for your bed and board, and pay more than five thousand francs a month for your education and pocket-money—altogether a huge sum. Yes, I pay your fees and you do not even trouble to attend the lectures. When I run into your professors at the university I have to look the other way, for I dare not discuss your progress with them.'

'Father, I implore you, give me a hundred thousand francs.'

'I have not got that amount. You are torturing me needlessly.'

'Sell this house. It's of very little use.'

'This is no time to sell real estate, when we're in the middle of inflation. At least that's what your brother-in-law Maurice says, and he knows what he's talking about, not to mention what the house means to me personally. What do you want this money for?'

The youngster shrugged his shoulders and dragged himself to his feet. 'I'm tired,' he said, yawning heavily. Then he turned a wild look on his father. 'You will live to regret this.'

'That may be, my son. You children seem to do nothing but sit in judgment on me, all the lot of you; Maurice in the name of monarchism, Christine in the name of Karl Marx, Thierry in the name of religion, and you in the name of your eccentricities. If only your mother were here perhaps she would understand.'

'You are always saying that.'

Patrice Périot made no reply. He happened to have his pen in his hand, and on the virgin whiteness of the 'outlet' left-hand page he wrote: 'What man is there who does not talk nonsense to his nearest and dearest?'

Hervé yawned again, wiped his lips with the serviette that Mme Hortense had put under his cup, and left the room without uttering another word.

Patrice Périot resumed his work and succeeded, contrary to his expectation, in fixing his attention on it. Soon he heard a car drive up. A door banged. He took no notice.

It was dark by the time Mme Hortense came in to clear away the tea-things. She was just folding Hervé's serviette when suddenly she exclaimed:

'This was a clean serviette.'

'What of that?'

'There's a mark on it now.'

'What sort of a mark?'

'It looks like lipstick.'

'Impossible, Mme Hortense.'

'Impossible maybe, but it's the truth.'

The housekeeper swept out, tray in hand, with Olympian tread.

Next day Thierry dropped in, suit-case in hand, his face shining with good health. He went from room to room, and the house rang with his cries of pleasure and snatches of song.

'How wonderful it is here! I love it all. Hosanna! Dad, I want to stay with you till the end of the holidays.'

This was more than Patrice had dared hope for. It was his dearest wish come true. Instantly the house sprang to life again, as in happy days gone by. Thierry sang so much that he had to apologize for the noise he was making.

Patrice did not mind. He put his head out of the window and said: 'Don't stop. The stupidities and vulgarities of the radio interfere with my work, but your songs are fine, and they don't bother me at all. They soothe me.'

In the evening Thierry put away his text-books and called his father from the garden. 'Dad! Let's go as far as the outskirts of the forest. It's uphill, and it will do you good. You need some exercise.'

Patrice made a formal protest, and then grabbed an old hat and his blackthorn stick. Thierry chattered all the way as they climbed the slopes.

'You will come over to us, dad, I know you will. I'm not asking you, I'm telling you. And that won't prevent your being the man you are; on the contrary. There are plenty of left-wing Christians, even extremists. We are free under our own light.'

Patrice shook his head. 'We change as we grow older, but there is very little chance of my ever reaching the point you have reached now. I am held back by the habits of a lifetime. However, my relationship with God is by no means bad at the present time. I am entirely in sympathy with your idea of God, I assure you.'

Arm in arm father and son fell into step. 'I am an ungrateful old man,' thought Patrice Périot. 'I classify my children as this and that, but in reality Thierry is entirely different from the others. He may be a bit foolish, like the rest of them, but his is a lovable folly. I expect he will end up as a monk, or as a priest in some out-of-the-way country village, and although my dreams for his future have been so very different his happiness is all that matters. What better fate for a human being than to be within the security of an all-pervading faith? What is the best thing I could wish for Thierry? Happiness! And I really believe he is happy.'

By now father and son had reached the top of the ridge. Thierry grasped his father's hand, and said ecstatically: 'Dad, I saw the flame on your countenance. You are one of us.'

Patrice wiped his face, heated by the exertion. 'Not at all. I am in a muck-sweat, and that's what you saw. Let me get my breath, Thierry. I may not know all you seem to know, but you certainly have no idea of what goes on in my mind.'

They went down the hill again on good terms with

each other. On the way Patrice said: 'Christine paid me a visit the other day. I feel that if I stop calling her Christine I shall break the impalpable tie between us, that if I call her by the name she wants it will make all the difference in the world. I told her this one day, and her answer, reasonably enough, was that we shall soon see big differences in the world anyway.'

A little while later he added: 'How much do you know about Hervé's affairs?'

'Hervé is unget-at-able. But I shall get at him one of these days.' Thierry smiled calmly.

Patrice Périot did not dare to pursue the subject any further, and they finished the walk in silence.

Next morning, still in his dressing-gown, he was glancing through the daily papers when he gave vent to a sort of groan:

'Ah! This is too much! It is unbelievable.'

He hurried down to the telephone on the floor below, and struggled for a long time to obtain the number he wanted. At last he got through and shouted furiously: 'Mademoiselle, if M. Gérin-Labrit is in Paris tell him that I shall be there myself this afternoon and that I beg him to come and see me at my house, on a very serious matter, at about four o'clock.'

An hour later, having said good-bye to Thierry with a promise to return the same evening, he was boarding a train at L'Isle-Adam station. The week with Thierry, dedicated to peaceful work and recuperation, was ending in a raging fury.

CHAPTER VI

THE part of the flat that Patrice Périot reserved, or rather tried to reserve, for his own use looked both dark and dusty. Patrice threw open the shutters to dispel the darkness, whereupon the dust proclaimed its presence more strongly than ever in the bright April daylight. Patrice Périot hated dust, or perhaps it would be truer to say that his beloved Clotilde and Mme Hortense between them had firmly implanted in his mind the idea that he hated dust. He cast a glance round his study, picked up a feather-duster which was lying on the book-case and dusted his desk perfunctorily. Breathing like a mastiff to persuade himself that his rage was not dying down he sat in the broken-down arm-chair and systematically cracked the joints of his fingers, always a symptom of indecision with him.

He had lunched across the way with his daughter, who never took a holiday, for the simple reason that her husband would not take one. Maurice Ribeyrol, turning an inhospitable eye on his father-in-law, had dropped various general remarks with very specific application, such as 'a man can be a brilliant scholar and at the same time a fool in politics,' or 'For my part I would not venture to express an opinion on the colonial question unless I had personally visited the various countries concerned.' Patrice watched Edwige's face and saw her mute distress, but he set his own jaw grimly, partly because he did not want to be the first to throw down the gauntlet and partly because he had no intention of dissipating energies that he would certainly need later in the day.

After lunch he had visited his brother at the other end of Paris to take him the usual envelope. There, too, he arrived without any offensive designs in mind.

Gustave Périot was flourishing the newspaper spread out on his bed, with a malicious look in his eye. 'I must say it is by no means a pleasant experience being the brother of Patrice Périot. One never knows what to say to the people one meets.'

'But you never go out, Gustave.'

'That,' the invalid replied balefully, 'may be the very reason why I never go out. And I might add that my illness is largely due to you and your excesses.'

Patrice had returned immediately by metro. At home again, he aired the study and dusted his desk, cracked his finger-joints, and set himself to read the newspaper he had just taken out of his pocket. It was an extreme left-wing paper, which often gave him its approbation, and yet made him supremely uncomfortable whenever he opened it. He put on his spectacles, and read for the tenth time: 'The undersigned, in view of the present state of the world, of the time-honoured French tradition, and of the current trend of thought on the subject of colonial development, invite the peoples of France to demand the evacuation of territories conquered by force, and the immediate liberation of subject races. Signed Ludovic Eymonnet, Member of the Institute; Bertrand Recordeau, ex-minister; Patrice Périot, Member of the Institute; Joseph Mousselon, Deputy of Paris; Pierre Gérin-Labrit, author . . .' A list of other less distinguished names followed. It was stated, moreover, that the manifesto could be signed by all free-thinking men.

Patrice Périot pulled out his watch, and saw that his visitor was due to arrive at any moment. He forced himself to collect his thoughts and marshall his arguments. There were two separate questions to be considered; the first was his signature, and on that he would admit of no compromise. . . .

When Mme Hortense was away at Jouy-le-Comte, the concierge used to look after the Paris flat. Patrice could hear her wandering about the passages, knocking her broom against the skirting-boards. . At a quarter-past four the bell rang, and Patrice reflected that his caller was not unreasonably late by modern standards, in an age when civility and punctuality counted for little.

Gérin-Labrit came in and Patrice Périot rose to greet him. Intermittent sunlight shone in the empty room and Patrice had a chance to observe his man closely. The worn, handsome face and long features of the writer were set in an expression of lassitude mixed with proud disdain. Just as Patrice was offering him a seat he suddenly noticed a large spot on Gérin-Labrit's trousers, of the type that doctors call 'suspicious' when they cannot diagnose the cause. It made Patrice feel physically sick for some reason that he did not want to examine. Gérin-Labrit had a reputation for loose living, which was clearly nobody's business but his own, so long as he never took it into his head to . . .

This train of thought was bidding fair to side-track Patrice Périot from the main point at issue when Gérin-Labrit himself brought him back to it. Surprisingly enough it was Labrit who took the offensive with his opening words, and that on a front that was both unexpected and inadequately defended.

'My dear professor, when my secretary informed me of your wish for an interview I was just about to ask for an appointment. I realize that you are bound to hold specialized views on this problem, but you must remember that it is of extreme interest to all men of our creed. Otherwise I would not have the temerity, as a writer and a man of letters, to tackle you on questions of which you are an acknowledged master. But your friends are seriously troubled. The Russian scientists, whom you received so amiably some thirteen years ago, and who still have a good opinion of you, share with us our—how shall I put it?—our distress at your recent findings.'

'My recent findings?'

'Your findings about the organs under the control of the voluntary nervous system. The argument is not about the facts, but about the interpretation of those facts. Apparently if your former conclusions are closely examined, for example, your theory of the natural reservoirs. . . .'

By now Patrice was beginning to recover from his astonishment. 'Tell me, honestly,' he said, 'have you ever read my book on the functions of the natural reservoirs, or my recent findings on the organs controlled by the voluntary nervous system?'

'That is not the point,' Gérin-Labrit replied. 'They say that only a dozen people in the world can fully understand the work of Einstein, for example. Nevertheless, the world is perfectly entitled to hold Einstein responsible for a theory which from now on will profoundly affect both individual and social life. The same thing applies to the splitting of atoms, whether heavy or light. The man in the street does not know the difference between a neutron and a proton; but since he may die to-morrow, burned to a cinder, he is entitled to take an interest in what the scientists are doing and thinking. We Communists, professing as we do a rigid doctrine, are in duty bound to examine the work of the scientists, and if it so happens that their work threatens to disturb what we hold to be the order of things, then we must issue a warning. We must do what I am now doing, my dear professor.'

Patrice Périot half closed his eyes, as if to aid reflection, and then said in a steady voice: 'I was prepared for almost anything except this fantastic warning. We will discuss these points some other time. For the moment I want you to understand clearly that nothing will prevent me from disclosing and publishing what I believe to be the truth.'

'Even when you know that the truth will undermine the confidence of the masses in those who are leading them towards better living conditions?'

'Yes, definitely. For me better living conditions based on blindness, falsehood, or ignorance would not be a better life. As I told you, we can discuss all this some other time. I can assure you it was not for such a discussion that I asked to see you.'

'As you wish. In any case, I have said most of what I have to say.'

A short silence fell. Then Gérin-Labrit took up the conversation again, as if he were anxious to retain the initiative in both matter and manner.

'I notice that you have been re-reading our manifesto. You must admit that it is moderately phrased, while at the same time being firm.'

'I have not been re-reading it,' said Patrice Périot, springing to his feet to give full play to his annoyance. 'I have not been re-reading it; I have just read it for the first time. Now do you understand what I am getting at. By what authority did you append my signature, without having asked me, or advised me, or submitted the text to me? The Germans used to do that during the war, no doubt, for those who would not collaborate; but you, my colleague, with whom I have worked hitherto in complete confidence——'

Gérin-Labrit made a gesture of impatience. 'You were away in the country. That's reason number one. We did not know how to get hold of you. Furthermore I remember telling you that we must have four or five reliable signatures we could depend on in cases of urgency.'

'Signatures you could depend on!' Patrice Périot was outraged. 'Signatures——'

He got no further. Gérin-Labrit motioned him to sit down, authoritatively, and proceeded to spring more surprises.

'My dear professor, you do not appear to be aware of the power and value of your name. Do you realize

100

VICTORIA COLLEGE
LIBRARY
VICTORIA, B. C.

that Seretti and Montecolla have not yet in fact been executed? Probably they never will be. The preservation of the lives of these two heroes is your doing and you are not apparently aware of the fact. You lent your signature and a miracle was accomplished; a miracle, and you have forgotten it already. But this fame, which enables you to weigh the scales of destiny so effectively, does not belong to you alone. It is not your exclusive property—a man's fame never is. Pétain did not grasp this point and de Gaulle seems to be falling into the same error. You may have earned your fame, but it is we who have given it to you.'

'You?' queried Périot, overwhelmed by all this eloquence.

'Yes, we, the people. You can work prodigies and discover what you call truths. Granted. But only the people can make you famous. For this fame you are indebted to those who have enthroned you. That is the view of all of my way of thought, of all of us who regard ourselves as committed to the greatest adventure in the world. You apparently are not committed.'

'I should like to know,' said Patrice with a supremely innocent air, 'exactly at what point a commitment is made, in your eyes. Half my friends accuse me of being a fellow traveller.'

'Half your friends!' Gérin-Labrit's every wrinkle expressed scorn. 'Half your friends! Really, professor, you keep very bad company.'

Unsmiling, without turning a hair, and leaving his opponent no time to recover himself, Gérin-Labrit plunged into a welter of pompous and uplifting sentiments.

'My dear professor, he who genuinely joins a party

and is loyally associated with the members of a party, does not change his opinion on a matter of detail, even if his comrades make mistakes. A party is like a country. Would you consider changing your nationality because France dropped a brick? If so, you would have done with being a Frenchman long enough ago. A party is like a religion. A true Christian may think what he likes in his secret heart about the doctrine of the Trinity. He is no Christian if he parts company on a point of detail. A man must look squarely at all the faults and crimes of the group he allies himself with and give his opinion courageously inside the group, but always without betraying them or being false to the trust placed in him.'

As a man of science and a recluse Patrice Périot was not used to this sinuous dialectic. He realized that he was losing his advantage in the argument, and began to suspect his own position, becoming more and more irritated.

'I am ready to discuss the improper use you have made of my name. But I give way to no one in my sincere love of my fellow countrymen.'

'For heaven's sake, do not drag that in.'

'And why not?'

'People like you love their fellows only so long as their physical or moral well-being and their precious habits are not threatened.'

Patrice rose to his feet and paced the room, hands in pockets. 'I can be for the people,' he grumbled, 'without joining your party.'

'Make no mistake, professor, if you are not prepared to act with us you are an enemy of the people, a renegade from now on.'

Patrice Périot felt his anger rising. 'People like me, to use your expression, may be human beings, but are essentially non-political.'

'Obviously,' said Labrit coolly.

'What do you mean?'

'I mean that you are a man of impulses. Noble impulses certainly—but they do not make the world go round. One word more, professor. Remember that nothing gets done without us.'

'Without you?'

'Without us, the working class.'

'But you are not a working man, Gérin-Labrit.'

'You seem to forget that I am here as the mouthpiece of the working class.'

There was silence between them. Then Patrice Périot, in a changed voice, said: 'You must understand that nothing will deter me from taking the side of those I judge to be the under-privileged.'

'This is sheer folly.' Labrit's voice was icy. 'We are not the "under-privileged," as you call them. We are the strong.'

'Very well then. Since the people you claim to represent here are the strong, then you have no need of me.'

Gérin-Labrit shrugged his shoulders. He looked exasperated and frustrated. After a long pause Patrice went on deliberately: 'You dazzled me somewhat just now with your flood of words, your disturbing phrases, your facility in controversy. But you have not succeeded in making me forget what I wanted to say to you. It is quite simple. I have no personal knowledge of colonial affairs—on them I cannot make a judgment, although in the eyes of the world I have just made one—I have acted out of character, because you have forged my signature. Possibly others permit you to do this—in that case I am sorrry for them. As far as I am concerned you will never do it again. I hope that I have made myself clear. Never again. As a first step you will publish a statement rectifying my position.'

'You cannot mean this seriously, professor?'

While Patrice Périot was hesitating, Gérin-Labrit went on: 'I have too high an opinion of you and your work and of all that you stand for in our eyes to publish a conversation which would damage your reputation irreparably with the working class and the free peoples of the world.'

Having said which he made his exit, leaving Patrice Périot in the throes of rage, astonishment, and consternation bordering on despair.

CHAPTER VII

HIS Easter holiday was definitely over. Patrice Périot returned to Jouy-le-Comte merely to pack his bags and bring Mme Hortense, his grandchildren, and Thierry back to Paris. No sooner were they re-installed in the flat in the rue Lamarck than he began to regret having left his rural sanctuary. He forced himself to put Gérin-Labrit's visit out of his mind, but he was in a state of anxiety that had no relation to the actual facts. He had said what he had to say; he had stood up, if somewhat inconclusively, to this difficult, unpredictable man, the very thought of whom set his nerves on edge; in short he had behaved courageously. Why then the gnawing anxiety?

While he was trying to introduce a semblance of order into the papers on his desk he heard the telephone ring. He threw open the door and called out: 'Madame Hortense, don't touch the receiver. These telephone calls are a pest.' Instantly the thought flashed across his brain that his children were still on holiday, and that one of them might be stranded somewhere. 'I'm sorry, Madame Hortense,' he shouted;

'please answer the phone. It may be one of the children.'

Soon the ringing ceased in the room below, and Mme Hortense appeared at the door. 'It's that fat man,' she said in a gloomy voice.

'Which fat man?'

'The gentleman who smells of sweat and is always shouting at you.'

This short description left Patrice Périot no room for doubt. 'It must be M. Schlemer. . . .'

'Yes, I think that's his name. I told him you were away.'

Alone again Patrice Périot felt more strongly than ever the urge to escape. He lunched tête-à-tête with Mme Hortense and decided to go along to the laboratory, half hoping that his colleagues would be away. Surely as professor he would be able to get some peace in his own department. As he was leaving, carrying his portfolio under his arm, he said to Mme Hortense: 'Do not answer the telephone unless it is one of the children.'

Mme Hortense threw him a pitying glance and said reproachfully: 'How on earth can I tell whether it's one of the children without lifting the receiver?'

This relentless logic so exasperated Patrice Périot that he made for the stairs without giving any coherent reply. By the time he reached the concierge's office he felt calmer. The staircase must have worked its usual miracle, bearing out his dictum: 'Stairs are good counsellors.' The concierge was in, and he greeted her courteously: 'Good day, Madame Vidrequin.'

Had he spoken too quietly? Was Mme Vidrequin getting deaf? Or was she in a bad mood? She was usually so kind and nicely spoken, and yet she had not answered his greeting. On the pavement he thought: 'What can I have done to upset Mme Vidrequin?'

The incident, which would have had no significance another day, was enough on this occasion to shatter Patrice Périot's serenity, already wearing thin. He felt that the people of the street, all of whom had known him by sight for many years, were taking no friendly notice of him. Not, of course, the shopkeepers seated either at their cash-desks or at the back of their shops, but the casual passers-by on the pavement and the street vendors. They all seemed to be so cold and reserved. Since he was in no hurry, he elected to walk until he began to feel tired. On such occasions he used to follow a series of byways, like crevasses, which led to the opera, and from there on, whenever he felt energetic, he would head for the university quarter by following the general direction through the Halles district, inhaling on the way all the smells of city life.

But to-day his uneasiness, far from being dispersed by the soothing muscular exercise, grew on him steadily. This could not have had anything to do with the attitude of the passers-by, because he was in a quarter where no one recognized him; it must be attributable to inner unhappiness, to some psychological mal-adjustment. Patrice Périot experienced the mounting torture of a man who has something with which to reproach himself and whose conscience will not leave him in peace.

In the hope of shifting his anxiety he considered taking the metro, to stun himself, as it were, by impact with the crowds whom he loved and from whom he had so often drawn inspiration. But he was restrained by a fear or scruple, comparable to the state of a Christian who goes to the communion rails when not in a state of grace. And so he made his solitary way along the pavements, until suddenly a word spoken by his visitor of the evening before came back to his mind. He realized that this word was at the root of his trouble, that it had sunk deep into him until it had touched a sore spot, and that, at whatever cost to himself, he must cast out this word and all it stood for by association. 'The dirty swine,' he said; 'he hasn't the guts to treat me as a renegade, but he takes care to let me know that in his eyes I could be one. The whole thing is absurd and hateful.'

He tried desperately hard to remember the previous day's conversation phrase by phrase. He could not but admit that the 'dirty swine' was a clever orator and that many of his arguments were too powerful to be answered on the spur of the moment. And so Patrice Périot, still walking the streets, thought up effective answers in his mind, alas much too late in the day. But the word 'renegade' remained a stumbling-block, and clear thinking yielded to unhappiness and anger.

Although he had never plunged into the whirlpool of politics, he knew plenty of men who could be labelled renegade in the sense that they had quitted their parties and let their friends down. With few exceptions they lived thoroughly unhappy lives, a target for insults from all quarters, left and right, east and west. Patrice Périot had nothing in common with these men who had lost their sense of direction. He had made no oath of allegiance to any political party. He was not even a Communist sympathizer. His mind was open, and he wished neither to lose his freedom of action, nor to abandon the cause of the great working class, for whom he had a sincere affection totally different from the mixture of fear and dislike that characterizes so many of the well-to-do. Under the pressure of events he had gladly given proofs of his goodwill, and had lent his name to the people's cause; he had declared himself; in other words, he had been ready to play his part. And now he was being pushed around and ordered about. They were abusing his signature, and he was not even given the right to complain. One complaint, and the shameful term renegade was held over his head like an axe.

He reached the Halles neighbourhood, where the streets in the early afternoon are still a mass of litter. He was stooping as he walked, a prey to anxiety— when he slipped on an orange-skin and fell full-length on the pavement.

'Watch your step, grandad,' called a porter with a loaded basket.

The familiarity comforted him and soothed him. In the eyes of this honest fellow Patrice Périot was not a 'renegade,' but a brother of the street, a fellow sufferer. He thanked the porter with a glance and pursued his way, his equanimity restored. Never would he lose his affection for these men, but as for the talkers and the agitators, the masters of the social order of the future, the Gérin-Labrits of this life . . .

The Sorbonne came into view. He had walked for more than an hour to shake off his malaise and at last he had succeeded. Frowning and smiling into his thick moustache he said: 'If they think they can make me toe the line, I'll show them where they're wrong. Nothing shall deflect me from what is the right road for me, Patrice Périot.'

The Sorbonne was almost deserted. In the laboratory only one of Périot's pupils, assisted by a faithful lab boy, was at work. The professor listened to a brief report, inspected the graphs and notes, and then went into his office, changed into his white coat, and sat at his desk.

The room lent itself to quiet concentration. Through the high window Patrice could see the buildings and roofs of the Louis-le-Grand school. The street noises were neither continuous nor disturbing. From a courtyard within could be heard the barking of the dogs kept for experimental purposes. Patrice had been well advised to escape from the household, the querulous children, and the unexpected and unwelcome callers, to the comparative peace of this little dusty ill-furnished room, where he could at least dream creatively.

His reflections were interrupted by a knock at the door, and the lab boy announced that a large, fat man was asking to see the professor for a few minutes.

It was Schlemer. Patrice Périot could see him through the half-open door, climbing the stairs and mopping the sweat from one chin after another.

'Show M. Schlemer in.' Patrice sighed inwardly.

Schlemer came in and settled himself comfortably in a chair with the air of a man who is in no hurry and who intends to stay until he has said all that he has to say and done all that he intends to do.

Patrice Périot was on the point of hazarding a discreet reference to the telephone call reported by Mme Hortense that morning, but he was given no opportunity. Schlemer ran his handkerchief round the inside of his collar and said : 'I just dropped in by chance. I happened to be in the neighbourhood, and, knowing the way, I took the liberty of coming up to your room. I guessed I would find you working as usual.'

'He is lying,' thought Patrice Périot. 'Why won't he admit that he has been trying to get hold of me since first thing this morning, and that he has at last succeeded in running me to earth in my office?'

Schlemer was a clever and popular journalist. He had begun his career as an art critic, with *Comoedia*, along with Léon Blum, who at that time was a sort of dramatic critic. Both became interested in Socialism, and later Schlemer, feeling that the Socialist party was losing ground and in danger of being outmoded, joined the Communist party with a considerable fanfare of trumpets. He again set himself up in the left-wing press as a judge of artistic problems of every kind, and he did not hesitate to write political articles and make any number of public speeches, at which he excelled. Aesthetically he claimed to preserve the French tradition and to interpret in his own way the rulings from Moscow. He was partial to the latest forms of abstract art, such as algebraic and crystallographic sculpture and the painting of symbols instead of real objects.

Having satisfactorily mopped up and dried off his huge face Schlemer pulled a paper out of his pocket and began to fan himself with it.

'My dear professor,' he said, 'I have come to ask you to do me a service; one of those services that redounds to the credit both of him who gives and him who receives.'

Patrice Périot, taken off his guard, waited anxiously for what was coming next. Schlemer went on: 'As you probably know, we are getting up a one-man exhibition of Ramachoff's pictures, and we thought, if we could arrange for a leading modern scientist to write a signed introduction—one typewritten page would be enough—that such a tribute from science to the most modernistic, and incidentally most philosophic, form of art might be a very significant event. A sort of marriage between advanced science and modern art.'

Patrice Périot could hardly restrain a sigh of relief. He was expecting a renewal of the bitter quarrel of the evening before, and behold, it was nothing of the sort. Actually Schlemer's visit appeared to be entirely fortuitous and free from any evidence of what journalists are so fond of calling collusion.

Schlemer was still talking. He outlined a panegyric to Ramachoff, the Bulgarian artist who early in his career had established himself in France, and on whom France, with her usual generosity, had bestowed first proofs of kindly interest, then more tangible proofs of success, and finally fame.

Patrice Périot, as was his wont, stood up and paced the room; he always did this when his imagination began to carry him away. Thus he immediately expressed in his own person the old psychological maxim that the mental image is the motivating power.

He had the concentrated expression of a man who is watching the birth of an idea in himself. 'I cannot pretend to enjoy Ramachoff's latest work at all. I belong to a different generation, and have grown up with other ways of thought. But I am faithful to the principle of research and experiment in the arts and in science alike. Incidentally, it is my opinion that photography has ousted painting in some respects. In the old days it was the painter's job to give us faithful representations of man, of animals, of concrete objects, and of natural scenes. Nearly all these subjects have been snatched away from the artists by scientific processes. Therefore it docs not seem to me surprising, though formerly I should have been shocked, that the artists are forced to look around for new canons and new methods of self-expression. . . .'

Schlemer's expression was one of unqualified jubilation. 'My dear professor, in a few minutes you have composed, in front of my eyes, the essence of the very message we are wanting from you.'

Rather late in the day Patrice Périot realized that he had been caught once again. He was now bound to give in to Schlemer's request, which would cost him a whole day's work, and worse still would create a precedent. He was thus, as always, the victim of his own too vivid imagination, whereby he risked the loss of his precious time, his solitude, and his personal liberty. However, he had the reward of knowing that Schlemer, who was one of the extreme left-wing spokesmen, was no longer thinking of him as a future 'renegade,' seeing that they had counted on him and on the unlikelihood of his refusing their request. At this point the big man put the paper back in his pocket with a heavy sigh and said: 'I cannot tell you how thankful I am to have your approval and your promise of help, and I am especially pleased to think that nothing has been irreparably damaged between us by your recent outburst, which I understand well enough.'

A cloud passed across Patrice Périot's brow. So he was right in the first place. This business of a message and an exhibition was a transparent ruse to test him out, and Schlemer's casual approach had concealed a carefully calculated plan.

He sat down again, and said: 'Nothing irreparably damaged . . . my recent outburst . . . I don't know what you're talking about.'

'My dear professor, you astound me. Last night, quite by chance, I met our mutual friend Gérin-Labrit, and he was obviously so genuinely affected by a conversation that he told me he had had with you at your house during the afternoon, that I cannot believe . . . do you really mean that you have no recollection of a conversation to which the rest of us, your friends in the party, attach the very greatest importance?'

Schlemer was now on his feet, striding to and fro as he did on the public platform. He shot his cuffs like a conjurer preparing for a difficult trick, and held out his hands appealingly.

'Surely you must see that this dispute was more than sufficient to cause us dismay! At this very moment we are thinking of giving you striking proof of our confidence in you by offering you the editorship of *Science and Freedom*, recognizing you as one of the leaders of popular thought, indeed of thought in general, and you must choose this particular time to turn your back on us and say things which are entirely out of keeping with what we know of you.'

'Wait a moment!' said Patrice Périot. His expression was stubborn. 'Not so fast. I have not yet accepted the editorship of your review. What do you want from me, Schlemer? What exactly are you and your friends asking of me? Hard work and research? Or is it to be propaganda, for which I am entirely unsuited, and to which I refuse categorically to devote my time?'

'Forget about the review for the time being,' said Schlemer genially. 'Put it out of your mind. We can discuss it later. Until this wretched dispute broke out, and you'll admit yourself that it's utterly un-important——'

'No! Emphatically no! I do not admit that the dispute is unimportant.'

'Until this dispute broke out, Professor Périot, nothing has clouded our friendship. As you know, we have the highest respect for you as a man and as a scientist. In our eyes you have nothing in common with men like Anatole France, who join us because they would rather ride than be taken for a ride. We have shown you our respect and admiration in a thousand different ways.'

'One moment. Do you consider that to make use of my signature without consulting me is a mark of respect?'

Schlemer remained unperturbed. 'We have never put any pressure on you to join the party. We have not even particularly wanted you to——'

'So as to leave me the freedom of a decoy-bird?'

'I need not even reply to such an unworthy sug-gestion. I wonder if you realize that the day you join the party will be a day of rejoicing for us. By your delay you are showing how little you understand us.

You completely disregard all our rules and regulations. But we do not mind; we take you as we find you, and all we ask from you is to do the same for us, making allowances for inevitable defects. In return for our tolerance——'

'All the things you are saying I have heard a dozen times before.'

'But these things are worth repeating and thinking over. With all deference, professor, I am talking to you as man to man. Listen to reason. Communism is the thing of the future, and you know it.'

'A little more of this, I warn you,' cried Patrice Périot, 'and we shall part company altogether, which is not what you're aiming at, I take it. Communism loses all its interest for me from the moment that it becomes a commercial proposition. For example, if you were to come along with an offer to name one of the main streets in Ivry or Villejuif after me, I should merely laugh in your face.'

No more was said for a few moments and Patrice Périot, utterly exasperated, opened a book and pretended to read it.

Schlemer's musical voice broke the silence. 'I am filled with dismay. We have learned to expect friendship and trust and understanding from you, professor. Ah well! Regrettable as it may be, we shall have to carry on our work without you.'

'You are dismayed and I am dumbfounded,' Patrice Périot replied. 'I did not expect people to take advantage of me to the extent of embarking on something very much like blackmail.'

'You are too free with your speech, professor. Blackmail is a very ugly word, and should not slip off the tongue so glibly. All your old friends will be deeply wounded. What will your own colleague M. Rebufat say, for example?'

Patrice Périot spat an imaginary cherry-stone over his shoulder.

Schlemer went on in an unctuous tone: 'M. Noël Rebufat is a man of genius.'

Patrice Périot had reached the limits of exasperation. 'Maybe he is, Schlemer, but there are times when all men of genius can go to hell as far as I'm concerned.'

No sooner had Schlemer closed the door behind him than Périot felt his anger subside. He was within an ace of running after his visitor. Certainly Schlemer had been clumsy in the extreme, and had done everything in his power to enrage Patrice. But what of it! Schlemer was decent enough in his way. He had bungled a difficult mission, but Patrice could certainly take no credit to himself for his own behaviour.

The solitude that was so dear to him was shattered, both in the laboratory and at home, and he put on his hat and raincoat and went out to the street. Beneath his irritation he felt unhappy and disillusioned. Everything seemed to be conspiring to deprive him of that atmosphere of mental freedom which was essential for his work. And his work was his chief reason for going on living. My work and my children—these words set the rhythm of his walk along the pavement of the rue Saint-Jacques. Once again he experienced the vague uneasiness of the evening before, which had led to the realization that he might well be taken for an untrustworthy, narrow, self-satisfied, egotistic man. Soon he felt his thoughts soar above the welter of self-criticism, and began to see another side of himself.

'It was I who in all sincerity urgently demanded that those two Italians should not be shot. But I should like also to intercede on behalf of the firing squad, the ignorant masters of the moment. Their need is as great as that of their victims in this vale of tears. Intercede! Intercede with whom?'

He could not help laughing at himself for his next inward admission. 'There's a question I must be careful not to ask Thierry. He would give me the answer without the slightest hesitation. Thierry never does hesitate.'

CHAPTER VIII

THE week following these conversations was notable for a number of minor incidents, fortuitous on the surface, yet significant enough to keep Patrice Périot in a state of suspense and anxiety. Seen in retrospect they had the quality of an absurd, or even crazy, prelude to some vivid dream.

Early one Monday morning, looking through the free copies of the papers that were sent to him, Patrice Périot happened to notice an article entitled 'The Intellectual at the Cross-roads.' He knew instinctively that the article was expressly directed at him, and he ran his eye through it. Actually it was quite a good article, clever and forceful, and the whole argument was summarized in the closing sentences:

It goes without saying that the mass of the working class needs scholars and artists and authors; but nowadays it is generally realized that such men must be drawn from their own ranks. The average working man is too sophisticated to accept anything the intellectuals may think fit to hand out to him; and men like Patrice Périot, for example, of whom we had such high hopes, will never rid themselves entirely of class prejudice and will never be quite proof against subtle or violent reactionary temptations.

'Amazing!' grumbled Patrice. 'Absolutely amazing! My father was a tailor, and he worked in a basement at the Bon Marché for thirty years or so. All my education was paid for by means of scholarships and grants. And it is common knowledge that Gérin-Labrit is the son of Gérin the joiner. Equally every one is aware that in 1910 the firm of Schlemer and Valdelaude was one of the richest perfumiers in the Place Vendôme. Where does the working-class angle come in? The whole thing revolts me. It's unfair.'

Gradually his twisted self-criticism began to turn into positive rancour. At the beginning of the dispute he had had the feeling that his own conduct was not altogether above reproach and that on two occasions at least he had been unnecessarily cutting. Now the balance was beginning to swing the other way. The realization that his old friends, whom he must now think of as his enemies whether he liked it or not, were attacking him made him more determined than ever to maintain his complete independence.

He dressed hurriedly, took the first metro to the other side of Paris, and ensconced himself in his laboratory. He spent a soothing, and to some extent productive, morning there. Then he remembered that he had a date for lunch with Clement Romanil, just the two of them, in a quiet little restaurant near the Odéon.

At half-past twelve the two old friends met on the pavement of the rue Racine.

'Magnificent,' cried Romanil, 'we are the last of our species——'

'The last? How so?'

'The last to observe the rules of punctuality.'

'True,' said Patrice. 'In my case it's even more praiseworthy than in yours, because my children, much as I love them, are never in time for anything. I believe they would think they had lost face if they failed to keep me waiting. It is an unexpected triumph for East over West, and one which I find rather disquieting.'

'It would be good news for some of your old friends,' said Clement Romanil, 'to hear your disavowal of the East . . .'

'Yes?'

'Forgive me, I undertook never to refer to the subject again, especially at the very moment when your pals are out to trip you up.'

'You must have been reading the papers. You seem to know the score, old man.'

The two men of science were now seated opposite each other in the little room like a hat-box on the first floor of the restaurant. Romanil stretched his hand across the table and grasped his friend's.

'I know the score because I know you, and because I am very fond of you.'

'There you are,' cried Patrice, his voice charged with emotion, 'there you are, you old sceptic, you love your fellow men after all.'

'Not at all. Far from it. I am fond of you, Patrice Périot, but not of men in general. Occasionally I feel sorry for them, but that is as far as I can go. Look, Patrice, I'll tell you, I am a pessimist by nature, and an optimist only by accident. I look at it this way: I always presuppose that my fellow cads are ready and waiting to strip me, rob me, bind me; it follows that when they omit to indulge in these edifying pursuits

I am in heaven. What a happy surprise for me! There you have my recipe. As for that blighter's article, I must confess that I was expecting it. There will be more like it.'

Patrice Périot bowed his head. 'They will do as they wish, and say what they like. Nothing will deflect me from my course. I will not allow myself to be separated from my countrymen, even when they are in the wrong. . . .'

Patrice had a suspicion that he was repeating himself, that he had said all this before, possibly even to Clement Romanil, and that Clement Romanil with his needle-sharp mind would begin secretly to think of him as a bore.

'Even when the country is in the wrong,' echoed Clement brusquely. 'Now you're talking sense. At any rate you are admitting that the people can be wrong.'

'You know as well as I do, Clement, that fundamentally the people can make no lasting mistake.'

'In which case,' growled the old bear, 'you might remind them, since you have their ear, that they have never had a more glorious opportunity of *not* making a mistake.'

Sparring thus, as they had loved to do ever since their younger days, the two old friends ate their lunch, washed down with a bottle of Arbois—in homage to Pasteur, as Romanil said—and Patrice Périot suddenly felt more at ease, almost light-hearted. Seeing that his opponent, in his enjoyment of the occasion, had apparently laid down his arms, Patrice said sententiously: 'I am no visionary, but I see that a Communist experiment cannot *not* be made. It will be made, and on a very large proportion of the human race. You will see. . . .'

'No I won't,' Romanil grunted; 'too old.'

'It will be made, and afterwards humanity will turn to other dreams.'

The conversation followed these lines for a while and Patrice was not a little surprised to find himself talking like Gérin-Labrit or Schlemer, much to his own mortification. Romanil stuck to his guns obstinately:

'Don't believe a word of it. Nor do you. Too long in the tooth, both of us.'

The conversation came to an abrupt end and the two scientists left the *bistro* arm in arm, discussing old age with the ease of men who see it coming on but are not yet suffering its sharpest pangs.

Romanil's breath smelt pleasantly of cognac. 'Old age,' he said, 'is a secret, which is taken down to the grave by its discoverers without their being able to reveal it to any one. Young men—and there's something I want to say to you about them in a moment—young men talk about old age with an understanding air of pity or sarcasm. If they had any idea of what old age is really like they would lose all their zest for life. They would commit suicide on the spot. Patrice, you are five years younger than me—which makes you a young man in effect. I tell you, watch out! Old age does not creep on gradually, as all the poor devils believe; it strikes, like a bird of prey.'

They went on discussing old age on their way down to the river, and Patrice completely forgot that Romanil had something to say to him on the subject of young men in general, or of one young man in particular.

The talk veered to the question of fame, on which great subject Patrice had ideas of his own.

'Fame is fleeting, in a man's lifetime. An energetic and determined chap—and I have known such myself —can hold the stage for twenty, or maybe twenty-five, years. But sooner or later the crowd gets tired of hearing Aristides labelled "the Just."'

All this was in the nature of table-talk, the sort of pleasant, superficial talk that raises no disagreeable problems and helps the digestion.

Romanil raised his harsh voice above the din of the traffic. 'Speaking for myself, I have no ambitions.'

'It is ambitious in the extreme, old man,' Patrice Périot replied, 'to expect to be free of ambition.'

Walking along the narrow pavement of the rue Mazarine, Clement Romanil went on: 'For men like us there is no solution to the political problem; we have to transcend it.'

An anxious expression came over Périot's face, and he paused in his walk. Romanil continued: 'Suppose, for example, that you want to drill a tunnel and you know that you will have to spend all your energy, and the rest of your life, to do it. In such a case you may have to resign yourself to going over instead of through the mountain. Listen, let's go round to the back gate —it will save us a few minutes and there are fewer people about. Wait. This isn't what I really want to talk to you about at all. We were discussing young men just now. I didn't want to upset you, especially after our enjoyable couple of hours together; but I've been hearing things about your boy Hervé. It's no use my telling you the names of the people concerned —they're a crowd you know nothing about. I have no children of my own, so that in a sense I am an ignoramus; but I strongly advise you to keep your eye on that boy. That's all I have to say. I have heard rumours of deplorably bad company—watch out, I say—I've told you all I know. Now come on, Périot, I can see your old comrade Ludovic Eymonnet —he's one of the bunch that is demanding the evacuation, pure and simple, of all the French colonies, as if it were merely a matter of emptying a bottle.'

Patrice Périot smiled and turned his head so as not to see Eymonnet. In silence they climbed the stairs and Patrice took a seat near the back while Romanil, puffing and blowing, hands in pockets, made his way among the benches.

The session was in progress. In front of the blackboard a man with a long beard was reading a paper on soil erosion throughout the world. No one apparently took the slightest interest in this serious problem. As for Patrice Périot, he experienced a sort of contraction of the heart; a moral contraction, as it were, not of the blood-filled muscles but of that part of the being which even the mechanistic scientists, like all the rest of the world, are still forced to refer to as the heart. For the millionth time he thought to himself: 'My dear Clotilde left me too soon. Am I really a bad father? Alas, it is quite on the cards. At best I am a negligent one. But then I cannot be expected to do everything. Study the laws of nature, write books, educate! Poor Hervé! I do not take him nearly seriously enough. And even on the rare occasions when I could devote myself to him that crowd is round me like a swarm of bees, stealing my time for their messages, their prefaces, their speeches, their everlasting platform-strutting. But I'm definitely finished with all that now. I must seize my opportunity.'

Just then Patrice Périot heard a voice in his ear, above the din of the meeting. It was Pierquin the mineralogist with his fixed and bitter smile. 'According to Ponthieu,' whispered the eccentric, 'you enjoy addressing these revolutionary meetings—Communist meetings, I suppose they are called. According to Ponthieu it's a sort of habit, almost a vice.'

Patrice Périot looked exceedingly angry. 'Let me tell you, Pierquin,' he said in a low voice, 'that what Ponthieu says, or doesn't say, is not of the slightest interest to me. I have other things to think about.'

Matthew Pierquin chose that moment to do a simple but surprising thing. He put two fingers in his mouth, withdrew his denture, cleaned it carefully, scrutinized it through half-closed eyes for a time, and then went on in a sepulchral voice: 'I'm telling you this for your own good. There is no doubt that in the depths of his heart Ponthieu would like to see you join the Communist party.'

'For heaven's sake, why?'

'Because under a new government he could make you resign your chair at the Sorbonne.'

'I see.'

'Apparently it's quite on the cards. Incidentally, he has a candidate, ready groomed, in his pocket. One of the old staff of the *International Review*.'

Having said this the mineralogist opened his mouth, carefully replaced his teeth, reassumed his smile and said: 'He's terribly long-winded.'

'Who?'

'This speaker. Our friend the geographer. You know his name as well as your own.'

'And you?'

Pierquin raised his eyes to heaven. 'Why, I have known his name for twenty years, only I've forgotten it for the moment.'

'Evidently amnesia is contagious.'

Patrice got up, suddenly utterly disheartened. Had he used up his day's ration of happiness over that pleasant lunch with his dear old friend Romanil? And what was he to think of this curious warning about his son Hervé? Was there something seriously wrong that he had failed to see? Was he behaving like a blind idiot? He would get to the heart of it, and that very evening.

At about four o'clock he left the Institute and crossed the river in the mood of a man escaping across a frontier from the society of his fellows, only to realize when he reached the right bank that he had no option but to go home. He dismissed the idea of returning to the Sorbonne—he would inevitably run across his colleagues there, and would be dragged into discussions and arguments with them. Unlike Romanil he had no mistress to whom he could go for a friendly gossip. He did not frequent the cafés like Eymonnet who could always be found on the terraces of St. Germain-des-Prés. The library of the Institute was quiet enough, but he would probably meet someone he knew there. The only course was to go home, which was his firm intention, his strict duty moreover. He would go home and learn the truth about what he had to know. In the meantime he was not tired, and he might as well walk, even though it was uphill to

Montmartre, seeing that walking was the only suitable exercise for an arthritic like him, and since the noisy streets were his surest refuge from the crowd.

He set out, musing, sometimes talking aloud to himself. First he had to provide himself with good reasons for going north instead of south. 'My current experiment at the laboratory is a tedious piece of verification. It will be enough for me to supervise it. Joubert and Tilly are promising students. My primary duty is to get on with my writing, and I can safely leave it to Mme Hortense to send the callers packing. Research workers like us run up against, say, three or four basic theories in the course of our lives—and that's a generous estimate. Once a theory is proved and established, it is up to us to erect the superstructure.'

A mood of sweet idleness stole over him, and he gazed into the shop windows. Not that he wanted anything, but for the sheer pleasure of gazing. 'Life goes on! During the years of struggle we were so poor that I was dominated by one thought—how to feed and clothe my children. When there was only one biscuit left in the tin, and they used all to watch me out of the corners of their eyes to see who would have it, I was at my wits' end, and I would gladly have made biscuits out of my own old bones if I could. All this sounds very like a bird providing for its young. Actually Romanil always used to call me "the pelican." It's good to see food and clothes in the shops, but it's a false plenty; most people haven't the money to buy the goods.'

As a scientist he was fortunate enough to be simultaneously well known and unknown; well known to the few who were interested in his work and ignored

by the rest of the world; in this dual role of famous
and obscure person he felt genuinely sorry for the
potentates of this world who dare not walk the streets
alone—dare not because they are afraid, or because
the regime they represent keeps them in a glass case,
like a precious object, for their symbolic value. He
was thankful to be able simply to wander at will,
hands in pockets, without being surrounded by a
crowd of motor-cyclists, police officers, and armed
men. His mind went back again to the chicanery of
the day before. 'Gérin-Labrit often told me, in the
days when we saw eye to eye, that I think and speak
like a bourgeois. What is the bourgeois mentality,
and what does it mean to me? When I was a child
the aim of the Government, whatever any one may
say now, was the steady raising of the standard of
living of the people. Nowadays Gérin and his crowd
think not of exalting any one, but of laying low the
mighty, as in my Thierry's beloved *Magnificat*. But
if I breathe a word of this I'm labelled a back number.
So I must plough a lonely furrow. I dare say that the
root of Hervé's trouble is one of those mysterious
vitamin deficiencies of which we know next to nothing.
No doubt genius and subnormality alike depend on
diet as well as on heredity. A chronically starved
nation shows no sign of its former genius.'

By half-past five Patrice Périot was walking up the
stairs of his own house. He let himself into his flat
with his private key and found it marvellously quiet
and peaceful. Through the window of the dining-
room he could see the Ribeyrols' house opposite.
Edwige's children were playing on the balcony to which
the aerial conveyor cable was attached. No worry

seemed likely from that quarter, and besides, Patrice knew that in any emergency Edwige would cross the road and ring the paternal front-door bell. He went out to the landing and listened. Not a sound from any of the rooms. A faint odour of freshly smoked Virginian cigarettes assailed him in the half-light.

Out of a sense of duty, Patrice Périot went into Thierry's room without knocking. The room was empty and by no means tidy, but its untidiness was of the innocent kind that suggests moral health. A lamp was burning in front of a statue of the Blessed Virgin. Patrice could not restrain a smile—Thierry would do without oil at table in order to keep this little flame alight, and if his father were to make any comment, he would reply: 'Even if you double the oil ration, I shall not take any with my meal. The sight of this little flame does more for me than any amount of food. Physiological science needs thoroughly revising —honestly, dad.'

Patrice shut the door and pursued his investigations. Christine's room was locked, by tradition. Christine, in her calm and lucid voice, used to say: 'My brothers cannot leave anything alone. If I leave my room open, I shall lose my papers, my books, and even my clothes. I shall not have a pen or a pencil or a paste-pot that I can call my own. Therefore, I keep my door locked.'

Again without knocking, Patrice went into Hervé's room. Hervé was sitting there alone, smoking a cigarette.

'Sorry,' said Patrice, 'I didn't expect to find you in or I would have knocked.'

Hervé smiled faintly, and his manner expressed complete indifference.

Patrice Périot sat on the end of the divan bed, and said in a friendly voice: 'I hope I didn't disturb you, Hervé?'

'No,' said the young man phlegmatically; then gazing at the darkest corner of the room, he added: 'Thierry is never bored. How can any one not be bored?'

Patrice Périot did not know the answer to this question. Much and cruelly as he had suffered during his lifetime he had never known what it was to be bored. He gazed long and earnestly at the twenty-two-year-old boy—how quickly he had grown up!—twenty-two, and it was more than likely that he knew things about life that were entirely outside his father's ken. To Patrice Périot boredom was an unknown world, an unexplored continent, an abyss which held no temptations for him. Like every one else Patrice had his own private hell, but it bore no resemblance to the chasm yawning at Hervé's childish feet. For Hervé was little more than a child. In the half-light Patrice noticed the downy freshness of the boy's cheeks. To break the silence, or perhaps to overcome his own shyness, he said: 'Is there anything you need specially, son?'

Hervé raised his eyebrows. 'No, nothing, thank you.' He looked his father in the eyes, a thing which he rarely did, and smiled. Patrice had a fleeting impression that there was something queer, almost disruptive, about the smile, but it was growing dark in the room and he could not trust his eyes. 'He smiled,' he told himself; 'that is the main thing.' He went out to the passage, closed the door behind him, and paused there in the gloom. A phrase of Descartes came to his mind, a little phrase which had long worried him because of the irony he could detect in it. 'It only remains for me now to prove that material things do in fact exist.' What a generalization for a philosopher! Or what muddled thinking! For Patrice Périot had been trained in an austere and exacting school, to whom metaphysics were but a pipe-dream. With the reckless pride of a twenty-year-old Patrice Périot had thought: 'It only remains for me to prove that immaterial things do in fact exist,' and now, year by year, he sensed more and more in himself and in life all around him the power of the indeterminate, the rule of what the father of pure sciences would call 'immaterial things.'

That evening Patrice dined alone with Mme Hortense and Thierry, who was in a mood of lyrical joy so eloquent that it could not fail to be contagious. After dinner he retired to his study for four fruitful hours. All was quiet in the house. As he went to bed Patrice Périot thought: 'There is nothing to be gained by worrying about what may never happen. On the whole things are not too bad.'

The next morning, as he was writing, clad in his dressing-gown and surrounded by a huge pile of manuscripts, notes, brochures, and unread letters, he saw Mme Hortense come in. His frown failed to halt the advance of the dragon.

'There are two of them,' she announced.

'Two? Two who, two what, Madame Hortense? How can I be expected to guess?'

'Two gentlemen.'

'Quite. I am out. You have told them so, of course.'

'I cannot tell a lie, professor. You are always

urging me to lie, but I cannot do it. And besides, the gentlemen said it was very important, and that the life of someone or other was at stake.'

To his own surprise Patrice Périot realized that he was pleased by Mme Hortense's news. Logically he should have thought: 'Gérin-Labrit and his gang again,' but logic is apparently contrary to human nature, for he found himself saying: 'I knew they wouldn't be able to get on without me.'

Trying to look like a very busy man he threw up his arms and said: 'Show them in.' A moment later Mme Hortense announced them, and Patrice Périot directed a keen glance at his two visitors. They were strangers to him, well dressed, one wearing the rosette of the Legion of Honour.

'I must apologize, gentlemen,' he said, 'for receiving you in this way. You have taken me unawares. Please sit down.'

Each took a chair, and the older of the two introduced them both. 'My name is Armand Riboulat,' he said, producing two visiting-cards, 'and I am a mining engineer; my friend here is M. Otokar Nagy. We are respectively vice-president and secretary of the Franco-Transylvanian committee, whose untiring efforts on behalf of an autonomous Transylvania will not be unknown to you. We stand for the independence of this noble and unhappy country from the claims made on her by Rumanians, Hungarians, Germans, Poles, Walachians, Ruthenians, Greeks, and of course Moravians.'

Patrice Périot inclined his head in such a way as to suggest that he was not unaware of the problems of the Transylvanian people, whereupon the speaker found his second wind. 'One of the members of our society, Miron Geisenko, the well-known sinologue, deported from his native city of Kolozsvar on account of his revolutionary activities, had to return there under an assumed name to attend to personal affairs. While there he was denounced, thrown into prison, and then transferred to Bucharest where he has been sentenced to death by the Communists. The execution will probably take place next week unless we can succeed in rousing world opinion. We are now collecting signatures—we already have Mgr Mortier, Pastor Müller, ten from the Institute, ten privy councillors; and we thought that perhaps . . .'

Patrice Périot appeared to be lost in thought, his head sunk on his chest.

'We can guess what you must be thinking, professor,' went on M. Riboulat; 'you are well known for, shall I say, your left-wing tendencies. All right, it is for that very reason that we decided to make this approach to you. Should you be generous enough to support our cause by countersigning the petition we are going to put before you, then the authority you enjoy in Communist circles will lend great weight to your intervention. I might add that His Holiness Pope Pius XII, who cannot, of course, sign a near-political document, let it be known that he approved . . . even that it would be among his intentions . . .'

Patrice Périot hardly paid any attention to the last part of this little speech. At first he had thought, privately, that this was only another machination, this time from the right wing, and that there was probably no such person as Miron Geisenko, the famous sinologue, who had been created merely to dupe him, just as he had been duped by the opposing camp. Geisenko? Miron Geisenko? He could not remember ever hearing the name mentioned by the hieroglyphists at the Institute. Then it occurred to him that to sign such a text at the very moment when he was in conflict with the left-wingers would suggest a definite rupture, which he did not want, and moreover, that far from doing any good with the Bucharest people, who would have been kept informed about what was happening, he was much more likely to annoy them. He could impart none of the thoughts that were thus running through his head to his visitors. In the end there came to his mind the old arguments he had used a hundred times in debates, at the Sorbonne, at the Institute, and elsewhere, which could be summed up in phrases such as: 'It is better to intercede on behalf of ghosts and puppets than to allow one innocent creature of flesh and blood to be condemned to death. In politics the death penalty brands the regime and shames the civilization that imposes it.'

Seeing that the professor was no longer paying any attention, being apparently in the throes of some complicated thought process, the two strangers waited, with eyes glazed and mouths half open. Eventually Patrice Périot looked up and held out his hand. 'Let me see the petition,' he said.

As if in answer to Périot's unspoken thoughts the vice-president of the Franco-Transylvanian Society offered him a parchment, saying: 'The names of the signatories are published daily on the front page of *The World of the Future.*

Patrice Périot made a non-committal gesture, intended to indicate that his mind was made up. He laid the parchment on his desk, read the text which was not at all offensive, asked some questions about the other signatures, and appended his own in a free corner.

As soon as the two men had gone he tried to recapture his train of thought, with frequent reminders to himself that he was a man of independent path, only asking that people should not be put to death for following their own line of thought. 'That is the essence of my philosophy. Now, to work!'

Finding it difficult to concentrate again, Patrice Périot went to the bath-room for a shave. Shaving was always a clumsy performance with him, resulting in minor cuts and scrapes. Then he went to his bed-room to dress. He had the impression that someone was moving about the house, and thought that the children must have come home early for once. When he was ready at last he made his way to the kitchen to talk to Mme Hortense about various domestic matters. Over her shoulder Mme Hortense threw him a caustic glance.

'So you have company?' she said.

'What on earth do you mean, Madame Hortense?'

'I mean, as you well know, that your lady friend is waiting for you in the study.'

'My lady friend! What are you talking about? I am not expecting any one.'

'The lady tells a very different story. She told me that you were expecting her, and she came in as if she owned the place. She said that she was on very important business. They all say that.'

Patrice Périot was beginning to wonder if he had forgotten an appointment he had given someone. That did happen occasionally, much to his subsequent annoyance, although he was always careful to make a note in writing. 'She's probably the lady from the Distressed People's Aid Society,' he suggested cautiously.

'You're telling me,' replied Mme Hortense darkly, and went on with her work.

So Patrice Périot had to tread once again the seemingly interminable passage-way to his study. He opened the door and shut it behind him without attempting to disguise his ill humour.

She was a girl, no longer in her first youth, of some twenty-five or twenty-six years of age, and she was strikingly beautiful, tall, well built, and rounded of figure. She was wearing a spring frock which was elegant, although no longer new. Despite his surprise at a visit from such a person at such a time Patrice noticed that her corsage was unstitched, possibly torn, at the line of the arm-pit, and that the skin with its dark hair was visible. The girl was standing behind the desk, looking at him with a strange smile, in which even the most inexperienced onlooker would have discerned a mixture of ingenuousness, pride, and a shade of fear.

'Who are you, mademoiselle?' the professor asked her. 'You claim to have an appointment with me, but I do not know you.'

'You do not know me, professor, but I know you, very well.' She spoke French with a slight foreign accent, in a musical voice which had some indefinable relationship with her mysterious smile. 'Yes, I know you very well indeed. You cannot possibly know who I am. I am a student at the college at Nancy, a pupil of Professor Martz. My name is Anna Boëff.'

'Did Professor Martz send you to me?'

'Yes.'

'Are you sure?'

The strange young woman burst into a peal of laughter at this question, put so quietly yet sternly, and Patrice Périot was completely taken off his guard, for the laugh was neither bold nor vulgar, but simply young, and possibly a bit anxious and nervous.

'Did Professor Martz give you a letter for me?'

'No. He advised me to come and see you, because I am writing a thesis, and I need to consult you personally about one of your own books. Look . . .'

Patrice Périot was by now sitting in the old arm-chair with the missing arm. The girl pushed a large portfolio across the desk, which he opened mechanically. He began to turn through the leaves.

The pages were covered with manuscript notes, many of them illegible. With difficulty Patrice Périot deciphered quotations from various contemporary biologists, several from his own works being marked with a cross in red ink. He was beginning to grasp the meaning of this scrawl when he suddenly realized that the young lady was on her feet, that she had come round the desk, and had taken up a position beside him so that she could read over his shoulder. For a moment he felt something warm against his right side, which was probably either her thigh or her hip. He was more than a little irritated, and at the same time he was anxious to know the significance of this gibberish, on every page of which his own name occurred. He began to feel his exasperation rising, and as he breathed heavily he realized that the air of the room had changed its quality and was charged with the animal and chemical perfume of this extraordinary and un-expected visitor. . . . Suddenly he realized that the girl had put an arm round his neck and was leaning so close that he felt her hot and urgent breath in his ear. At this point he pulled himself together, pushed back the arm-chair, and sat on the edge of the desk, looking pale and agitated after his flush had worn off.

'What is the meaning of all this, mademoiselle?' he said.

The girl was so placed that the light from the window shone full on her, and what he saw filled him with pity and astonishment. Her teeth began to chatter, breaking the silence in the room. She made an attempt to open her pretty, well-moulded mouth, and he saw that her tongue was trembling against her lips. By now he had largely recovered himself, but there was still a note of surprise in his voice.

'I think I understand . . .'

'There is nothing to understand,' the girl declared. 'I admire you and I was looking for an opportunity of telling you so.'

Patrice Périot was now himself again. 'You can hardly expect me to believe that! I assure you that I understand. But what an extraordinary choice on your part! It is hardly credible. How old are you?'

'You are a great man and I am full of admiration for you. I am twenty-five.'

'Allow me to tell you that the affair is over and that there is no point in your going on with it.'

The girl flopped into the old arm-chair, pulled a handkerchief out of her hand-bag, and began to cry. She spoke disconnectedly. 'I did come from Nancy . . . I swear I did. Professor Martz is always talking to me about you. . . . I am extremely interested in your work on conscious control. . . .'

'It's no use. None at all.' Patrice Périot spoke calmly and decisively. 'Leave Professor Martz out of it, or I shall have to speak to him on the telephone while you are powdering your nose. It's useless, young lady. I understand completely. Actually you are the third, in the last three years to—to—— Now look at it reasonably, as I do. I am an old man, weary and careworn. I have not the least desire for you. No, I am not coming round to your side of the desk—you can console yourself well enough. You are clever, I admit, but you are still very young. I am not saying that you are not a student. I am not even saying that you are not a pupil of my friend Professor Martz of Nancy. Now, be sensible. As you see, I am not angry with you. All I will say is that you deserve better of yourself. This is no sort of undertaking for a girl of your age. Now listen! You will tell them that I was ill. On no account let them know that I saw you. Say that my door was locked, bolted, and barred. So now that you have restored your usual good looks there is nothing to stop your going. I will show you to the door myself—it is better that I should do so.'

The girl walked towards the door, and while Patrice Périot stood there to see her off she took hold of one of the buttons of his waistcoat in a gesture that was both childish and graceful. She was trembling no longer, and she even managed to raise a smile, like a good player who has lost the game and admits it. She pulled at Patrice's button two or three times and said: 'What a pity!'

'There's a good girl—and nicely said.' Patrice's voice was soft. 'So no ill feelings! And no regrets! I shall not breathe a word to any one. Good-bye, now!'

He saw her to the top of the stair. On his return he noticed that the kitchen door was ajar. 'Madame Hortense,' he called, 'we will have dinner at the usual time, with any of the children who happen to be in.'

Mme Hortense appeared in the doorway, imposing and severe. She sniffed, and said in her gloomy and accusatory voice: 'I am going to air the rooms.'

CHAPTER IX

MME HORTENSE and the Périot family, including Patrice himself, were in the habit of classifying certain types of people as 'Monday visitors.' This week, from Wednesday onwards, the Monday visitors were coming every day and all day, and Patrice Périot realized, with secret uneasiness, that all these visitations had some connection, either directly or remotely, with the recent dispute, of which the reverberations were still threatening his precarious peace of mind.

Thursday began well. Patrice Périot had worked since dawn, having first resolutely disconnected the telephone. Four times he had heard the door-bell ring, and on each occasion Mme Hortense must have been able to contain the aggressor, because no one had succeeded in penetrating as far as what Christine, in her icy voice, used to call his 'holy of holies.'

Shortly before midday Patrice heard someone knocking on the lintel.

Before he had time to say 'Come in,' the door opened and a young man entered the room. He was wearing a tartan shirt with most of the buttons missing, and his appearance was at once elegantly shabby and aristocratically poor. Without waiting for any questions to be asked, he said: 'My dear professor, I found all the doors wide open, and since no one answered my repeated calls I found my way to this room. My name is Odilon Leméténier, and I am the editor of *Hope* and *The Bikinist*. At the moment I am conducting two questionnaires, which in my opinion would be incomplete, I might say falsified, without your replies.'

Giving Patrice Périot no opportunity to collect his thoughts, he proceeded to propound his questions. There was nothing new about them. 'Should an intellectual stand aside from politics, or should he proclaim himself in word and action?' Question number one. Question number two was no less indiscreet, and it ran: 'Who, in your opinion, is the greatest thinker of the twentieth century?' The young man had already taken the opinion of more than forty famous people on this question. Ten had plumped for Einstein, and most of the remainder had voted for Eliacheff, the astronomer and mathematician whose works were not yet available in translation, and whom some three or four people in the whole world might claim to understand to some extent.

Patrice Périot all but lost his temper, upon which the young man announced calmly that such discussions enabled eminent men to give unobtrusive help to struggling young authors.

Flattered, against his better judgment, Patrice Périot referred to *Stello* for the first question; the second he refused to answer, saying that he would need to put forward fifty names or more, and that even then he would probably be doing someone an injustice, because scholarship in so many countries was in the hands of anonymous teams without any obvious leader.

Patrice Périot was about to show his importunate visitor to the door when Thierry bounded into the room, in a manner that appeared to disregard the laws of gravity, and more nearly resembled a bird, a flame, an arrow, or a gust of wind than an ordinary biped.

'Daddy,' he urged, 'daddy, I must have five minutes with you. Your full attention and sympathy. Just five minutes, daddy, please!'

Patrice Périot thought of handing the journalist over to Thierry, to be conducted to the staircase, but he changed his mind. Thierry, the young scatter-brain, might say something extremely private or indiscreet to the editor of that weekly illustrated paper, *The Bikinist*. And so Patrice accompanied the intruder to the door himself and then returned to his study.

The little saint had calmly taken the place of the head of the family. He pulled a letter out of his pocket, rose to his feet with a bound that nearly hit the ceiling, and said: 'Daddy, do you know the Abbé Broche?'

'No, I do not, son.'

'He is a Catholic progressive. He's absolutely super. We argue about everything, but he's smashing! Yesterday he asked us all to sign a manifesto protesting against the use of the atom bomb. It's terrific! Complete outlawing of atomic warfare. I didn't sign.'

'What did you say?'

'I said I didn't sign. I have a great respect for our name and I know that if I go and put my signature,

144

a little nonentity like me, people won't look at the initials and they'll think it's you.'

Patrice Périot stroked the boyish cheek with his finger. 'Well, well! So you thought of that—you, my own son. You will never know just how right you were!'

Thierry glowed. 'I think of things a thousand times better than that. You'd be surprised.'

'That's good enough to go on with, old man. You've made an excellent start.'

'Wait a moment, dad. Not so fast. I haven't told you the whole story yet. I refused to sign for the reason I have just given you, but at the same time I am entirely in favour of Abbé Broche's resolution, and I think you should sign it, daddy.'

Patrice Périot shook his head pensively, weighing up Thierry. '*Tu quoque, fili!*' he said.

'What makes you say that, dad? I know you, and I am sure that you must disapprove of the atom bomb.'

'Only a little while ago I resolved to sign no more manifestoes, appeals, or what-have-you, to sign nothing unless I have written it myself. Nevertheless, since I can refuse you nothing, Thierry, my resolution will have to take effect as from midday. Give me the paper.'

'I knew you'd do it! I had no doubt of it! Thank you, thank you, daddy!'

Thierry was about to dart off as he had come, when Patrice detained him for a moment with a gesture, then released him. 'It's no use,' he thought to himself as Thierry made his escape; 'if I talk to him and the others about Hervé we shall only manufacture a Hervé situation. Better say nothing.'

He sat down again in the damaged arm-chair, muttering: 'I've been had again,' and then wrote a phrase on the left-hand page of his note-book that must have been the result of various random thoughts. 'To think that we shall be the ones to witness the end of the world betokens an excess of pride. Besides, that would be much too simple a solution. No, the world has not yet reached the end of its suffering.'

Next day Patrice Périot gave his lectures to his band of faithful students. The fact that nothing out of the way had happened during the morning first surprised, then alarmed him, and he reached home positively upset that no demands had been made upon him. He remembered the story of the Romanoffs who used to receive daily a large number of petitions, and who were filled with dismay when they had no more to deal with. The comparison made him smile. The rest of the day, however, was to prove that the hour of solitude and oblivion had not yet struck for him.

Early in the afternoon one of his best pupils, Gaston Tilloy, who was working at the laboratory for his thesis, came to see him. Tilloy wore gloves to indicate that his call was in the nature of an official visit.

'What's on your mind?' Patrice asked him. 'I saw you this morning and you said nothing.'

Tilloy had an orator's voice, strong and flexible. He took a bulky package out of his case. It was the manuscript of his thesis, and he asked the professor to be kind enough to glance through it and give him an honest opinion. Seeing that he made no attempt to leave, Patrice Périot began to scratch his chin. Then Tilloy pulled another exhibit out of his case; a letter addressed to the Research Centre asking for a subsidy, for which he wanted a sponsor. In drafting the letter of recommendation Périot thought: 'He is presuming on me, and he is interfering with my work, but at any rate it's nothing to do with politics.'

Just then Tilloy said deliberately: 'It has been suggested to me, professor, that you will certainly be able to enlist the support of your friends, M. Noël Rebufat and M. Ludovic Eymonnet on my behalf.'

'Um, they're my colleagues rather than my friends,' Périot growled, and then thought: 'It's shocking. Politics seep into everything.' Whereupon Tilloy pulled another exhibit out of his case which really enraged Périot. It was a box of sweets.

'You really are crazy, Tilloy,' he said, red with anger. 'I am only doing my job; why should you make it positively painful for me?'

'I meant them for your grandchildren,' said Tilloy tactfully.

Périot shrugged his shoulders. He might as well give in with a good grace, and he untied the parcel, trying to think of something pleasant to say. 'Tilloy, you know my opinion of you—really there was no need . . .' Opening the manuscript at random he murmured, amiably but without conviction: 'It all looks very interesting. . . .'

At first glance he had seen that the manuscript was illegible and badly spelt, and plastered with erasures. He took Tilloy to the hallway and helped him on with his overcoat. The young man was apparently so preoccupied that he completely forgot to say thank you.

No sooner had he gone than Mme Hortense opened the kitchen door and, putting her finger to her lips, whispered: 'That's not the lot. There's still another one to come.'

She pointed to the door of the drawing-room, which opened to disclose a personage clad in velvet jacket holding a roll of papers in his left hand.

'Professor,' he said, 'in a curious sing-song accent that Patrice could not place at first, 'I ask but one single hour of your time.'

'My dear sir, it is quite out of the question.' Patrice Périot was now thoroughly upset. 'I don't even know who you are. Have you an appointment with me? No! I'm sorry, but it's impossible for me to see you.'

'Half an hour, or a mere twenty minutes, I beg of you, professor. You will not regret it, I can guarantee. I am assured in advance of your interest and assent, indeed of your whole-hearted collaboration.'

Hounded, pushed around, buffeted, Patrice Périot soon found himself in the study that he could no longer call his own, inexplicably in conversation with this stranger who was undoing his roll of paper and saying simply: 'I am the inventor of a system for stabilizing currency, arresting inflation, ending the price war, and re-establishing social harmony. I am acquainted with your humanitarian views and I am going to read you the first chapter of my work. It is entitled *A Plea for a Subjective Currency*, and it is in five chapters. I claim, through my researches, to have discovered the solution to all the problems of our unhappy age. Chapter One begins as follows.'

'Stop, stop,' cried Patrice, 'I am not an economist.' To prevent himself laughing he had opened the box of chocolates.

'But I know where you stand in relation to the present social tragedy.'

'No, it's useless,' Patrice went on; 'it's absolutely impossible for me to listen to you. I have urgent work of my own, and besides . . .'

Just then Patrice noticed that the gentleman of the velvet coat had ceased holding forth and was staring fixedly at the full box of chocolates. Suddenly advancing a finger and thumb, and with a glint in his eye, the visitor said: 'May I? Just one? Or maybe two, professor?'

He took the sweets and put them in his mouth, then, his lips black with chocolate, he launched out on fantastic schemes for raising a mere hundred and fifty thousand francs, to defray the printing costs of his system. Unfortunately he was poor, so poor that he had had nothing to eat for two days.

At first Patrice had thought that he must be a mystic, then he had put him down as an inventor. Several times a week he interviewed people in the throes of invention. Eventually he arrived at the obvious explanation: 'He is a cadger, no more and no less.'

He gave the man a hundred francs, allowed him to take four of the chocolates intended for his grandchildren, and pushed him firmly to the door. The stranger's eyes filled with crocodile's tears and he said: 'I tell you, professor, I'd do anything in the world to stay an honest man—to achieve that end I'd even be mildly dishonest if necessary!'

At the last moment Mme Hortense appeared on the scene, and gave as her verdict: 'The professor is too kind to all these wastrels.'

Patrice Périot felt thoroughly played out. 'We live in a diabolical era,' he thought. 'We are surrounded by lunatics. I am going to clear out of it all and turn Trappist. Then they'll talk about my conversion in their gutter press. Are they trying to drive me mad too? Are they determined to turn me against my chief interest in life, which is my work? I am losing my ideas and my gift for words. I have to note everything down. I have to grab at thoughts, painfully acquired at great cost to myself, to prevent myself from throwing them into the rubbish pit. I could make great progress, like any young student, at the Sorbonne Library, or at the library of the Institute, but I am not there ten minutes before someone buttonholes me. The world is becoming uninhabitable.'

It was undoubtedly a week of utter chaos for Patrice, and the days ahead were to offer no respite. On Friday morning, notwithstanding all his precautions, he was attacked from an unexpected quarter. He had to interview a woman, who made such a scene at the door that she could not be got rid of and who turned out to be a fleshy, aggressive female, of the type that the people of the street call *rombières*, possibly because of some devious and forgotten connection with solid geometry. She was apparently engaged in praiseworthy social work, though she looked more like a barmaid. She came straight to the point by reminding the professor that the society she represented had already contributed to the subscription being raised by various groups for the presentation of his sword of membership of the Institute. Without further preamble she went on to say that her society was getting up a gala for the benefit of children with whooping-cough, to enable them to go up twice a week in aeroplanes for an altitude cure over the Paris suburbs.

The lady had a powerful voice, and she used it to proclaim opinions which she called 'advanced,' while at the same time referring to Patrice Périot as 'citizen.' In the end all she asked of him was to accept the honorary presidency of the gala. Patrice was cornered, and dared not refuse. The *rombière* made her departure, leaving a trail of scent behind her. His head in his hands, Patrice thought: 'Never again will I accept a favour from any one. In future I resolve to pay for everything. Money was invented to simplify material life.' No sooner was this resolution made than Patrice realized that although he had never asked any favours for himself he had in fact been obliged to ask them for others and sometimes even for his own children. This thought undermined his heroic mood.

The same day, early in the afternoon when Patrice was finishing a cup of coffee, he heard sounds of an argument in the corridor and realized instantly that Mme Hortense was in full retreat before an enemy better armed and more resolute than herself. Three seconds later Mme Hortense came in, holding the corner of her apron in one damp hand and with the other presenting a visiting-card. Patrice Périot had barely time to glance at the card and take in the words 'Carlos Winterbach, member of the Oscar Wilde Academy,' before the man himself was in the room, and in full spate.

'Our society,' he said, 'is not yet officially recognized, but with your help, professor, it soon will be, and I shall shortly be publishing my life-work, to be entitled *In Defence of Sexual Inversion*; needless to say the work will be copiously illustrated. . . .'

'What's that?' Patrice Périot felt himself blushing.

'Of course. We shall print portraits of all the famous men who have practised or advocated sexual inversion. You must know better than I do that almost all the philosophers, poets, and artists whose work is the glory of mankind have condoned homosexuality. The opinions of writers like Janet and d'Antheaume on this great subject are biased and of no account, just as the German theories are absurd, despite the fact that Germany has given the world some notable examples of inversion. I intend to prove by means of documents, tests, and a series of graphs that paederasty is a factor in the conservation of good health. Most homosexuals live to a happy old age because they practise a wise economy of their emotional energies. Crimes of passion are very rare in the circles they frequent, and in times of stress and moral disorder sexual inversion makes its appearance as a guarantee of the future of humanity. My colleagues and I have been hoping that some eminent biologist will preface my work in the way it deserves.'

The man stood during this speech, toying with his monocle. He was dressed with extreme care, and it would have been practically impossible even for an acute observer to guess the age of this unique academician. Taken right off his guard, Patrice shook his head and was surprised to find that he could not even look at his visitor without acute embarrassment. Eventually he said : 'I must admit that I know little or nothing of the strange problem in which you are interested. We scientists include very few paederasts among our numbers, and to people of my way of thinking sexual inversion appears to be a literary cult or a pathological freak——'

'A cult! A pathological freak! My dear professor, can it be that you are making the same mistakes as Moll and Kraft-Ebing? I must say you shock me.'

Patrice rose to his feet. 'Be that as it may, I'll tell you one thing for certain, and that is that I will on no account write the preface you want. I will not do it. I hope that I am making myself clear.'

The stranger picked up his light grey felt and his lace-edged gloves. For a few moments he looked at Patrice Périot intently, and his lip curled with anger. 'I must tell you that I came here with every reason to expect a very different reception from you. In taking my leave, professor, I tender you my respects, not unmixed with regret.'

On the spur of the moment Patrice Périot resolved not even to see his visitor as far as the door. Painful thoughts assailed him. 'Reason to expect a very different reception.' What on earth could the fellow mean? Patrice dared not recall certain hints he had heard recently. He dared not, and he would not. But he was suddenly very unhappy. The house in which he lived and worked inspired him with nothing but weariness and disgust. What possible value could there be in his disintegrated life? What had he to offer all these lost sheep, given over to conflicting passions, to fixed or unpractical ideas, to anger, error, ambition, and vice?

To cleanse himself, and also to abase himself completely and touch the rock bottom of his misery, he made up his mind to shut up his study for at least an hour and pay his usual Sunday visit—though it was only Friday—to his brother Gustave on the other side of Paris.

In the metro he read the heading of an article in the evening paper over his neighbour's shoulder. IF WE ARE ABANDONED BY OUR INTELLECTUAL LEADERS IN THE HOUR OF PERIL, WE SHALL BUILD OUR NEW WORLD WITHOUT THEM. The entire phrase, of three lines, was printed in half-inch capitals. 'Without a vestige of a doubt,' thought Patrice Périot, 'this drop of poison is meant for me.'

His motive in going to see his invalid brother was to reach his lowest ebb, so that by the law of life he would inevitably find himself on the upgrade again. He reached the boulevard Arago and climbed the dingy staircase. His fingers closed round the envelope in his pocket, and at the same time his mind thought: 'What was that disgusting creature insinuating in talking to me as he did?'

Unexpectedly the invalid greeted him with a grimace that almost amounted to a smile. 'So you've come to see the dying man! You don't stay long, and you never tell me anything of any interest, but at least you come and see me, which is more than your children ever do.'

'You must make allowances for them, Gustave—they have their own worries and their own lives to live. Even I, who live with them, see very little of them.' And he added under his breath: 'I see neither my children, nor my closest friends—nor myself.'

'Eh?' The sick man's hearing was suddenly more acute.

'Nothing. Just dismal thoughts.'

'So you see no one?'

'I couldn't say that, unfortunately. Put it rather that all the people I see are seen against my will.'

Gustave coughed interminably and then said: 'Hortense.'

'What about her?'

'She doesn't care about me. She never comes to see me.'

'She is thoroughly overworked, like the rest of us.'

'That has nothing to do with it. She neglects her duty. Remember what I told you when Clotilde died —I was still on my feet then—and Hortense was laying her out. It may sound a very small point, but Hortense never put any brilliantine on poor Clotilde's hair. They always use it on female corpses; it's the custom; you know that without my telling you.'

He changed the subject abruptly and went on in his habitual bitter style: 'Patrice, you are surrounded by a crowd of mediocrities. Oh, I know it gives you the illusion of being a somebody, but as with everything else in life it's a question of comparison. That crowd you waste your time on wouldn't amount to a row of beans but for their dirty politics. To think that my brother, my own flesh and blood . . .'

Patrice felt that the visit had lasted long enough. He grasped his brother's hand, mumbled an apology and fled down the stairs. Turning the dark corners he said to himself: 'If I ever feel myself getting swelled head I have only to come and see Gustave. Anyway, that's over for the moment. Of all my acquaintances, I am the only one who knows when to go. I may be guilty of pride in saying that, but it's true. The knowledge of when to take one's leave is a lost art.'

On her way to the metro station he noticed an open manhole, wired off by a little metal fence. A watchman was in charge, sitting with an acetylene lamp between his gum-boots. Patrice glanced down the iron ladder disappearing into the depths from which rose a nauseating vapour.

'What's the idea?' asked the watchman aggressively.

Patrice threw up his hands. 'Every day,' he said, 'I have to look into depths more murky than that, and leading nowhere at all.'

He continued on his way, crossed Paris by the underground, strap-hanging in the crowd, and arrived home. 'I wouldn't mind betting that at least half a dozen people have called. My life is a misery. As likely as not I'll find some maniac sitting on my desk. . . .'

As it turned out, a young girl was waiting for him. Mme Hortense greeted him with the news, adding in a whisper: 'A terrible case, this time. No other word for it.'

It would indeed have been impossible for any one to look upon the girl sitting in Patrice Périot's study with feelings other than of pity and dismay. She could not have been more than twenty years old, and her face had the pallor, not of the dead or of someone in the last stages of cancer, but of a ghost. When Patrice Périot took his accustomed seat she did not rise from her chair, but merely made a sign of recognition. There was a long silence while the girl, tight-lipped, stared at the corner of the room and Périot played with the paper-knife his children had given him for his birthday the year after the liberation. He took a grip on himself and said: 'What can I do for you?'

The girl opened her mouth and said dully: 'My father is sentenced to death. He will be shot any day. Next week. To-morrow. I couldn't tell you.' After

a long pause she added: 'My name is Louise Delavanne, daughter of Raymond Delavanne. He has been
found guilty of being an enemy agent.'

Patrice Périot could not have failed to hear about the
long and painful trial, concluded in Paris a few weeks
before. Scarcely able to control his emotion, he said:
'And what do you suppose I can do?'

'You are a world-famous scientist, respected everywhere.'

'Alas, no.'

'Write a letter. Write to the President of the
Republic or the Prime Minister. You would know
best. No one will help me. But write—you cannot
refuse—you must do it!'

Patrice Périot took some note-paper out of his drawer
and began to write. He had to tear up the paper
several times, and start over again, such was his
clumsiness and inability to find the right words. In
the end he wrote quite a short note, saying how the
most insensitive of men could not fail to be moved by
this girl's character and plight. He handed the letter
across the desk to the girl, who said: 'Excuse me, but
the truth is I can hardly read. I have implicit faith
in you.'

He slipped the letter into an envelope, addressed it,
and gave it to the girl, thinking, as he bowed his head:
'In this unhappy girl's eyes I am an accomplice of
those who have judged her father, though I know next
to nothing about him. That is why she has come
to see me.'

Sad thoughts, excluding the possibility of any useful
work, occupied him for the rest of the evening. He
thought up terrible physical and moral sufferings and

wondered how he would be able to endure them. For these imaginary woes he sought the consolations of philosophy.

In order to apply the closure to his mental gymnastics he made himself a cup of tea and took a sleeping-tablet. The night, far from being refreshing, was made hideous by nightmares, absurd in themselves yet degrading in his eyes. Patrice Périot had never found the slightest relief in attempts at dream interpretation.

By a strange stroke of good luck it seemed as if this hectic week was going to end peacefully. Feeling exhausted to the point of illness Patrice Périot telephoned the laboratory to tell them that he would be at home all day, and having given the necessary instructions to his students about the experiments in hand, he turned his attention to his writing in the certain knowledge that he would make no useful progress. But he worked the greater part of the day in solitary state with complete success. From time to time he would exclaim: 'It's amazing! Almost too good to be true! Evidently the trouble-makers and the scandal-mongers observe the forty-hour week. There's something to be said for regular hours!'

Late in the day there was a ring at the bell, and a familiar voice echoed in the corridors. It was Romanil. With a good day's work behind him Patrice Périot felt that he had earned a break and was delighted at the thought of the visit.

The old man came into the room with the delicacy of a buffalo, puffing and blowing and knocking over chairs. The greetings over, he slapped his chest.

'I am ashamed and disgusted to admit, old chap, that I have come to ask a favour of you. And what makes it worse,' Clement Romanil went on, 'is that it's a very trivial and humiliating affair. It's about the Legion of Honour.'

It flashed across Patrice Périot's mind that Romanil, who must be an officer of the Legion of Honour although he never wore the ribbon, had come to enlist his, Périot's, support for further promotion in the Order. 'I would have preferred it otherwise,' he thought; 'it is an extraordinary thing for him to do. How a man can change as he grows older!' But Romanil was speaking again and Patrice had to admit that he had guessed wrongly.

'I want to talk to you about Vigroux,' the old man went on, 'the conference master and our near colleague, if I may so call him. He is still only a chevalier and I fancy he is developing a grievance about it. Like old Lepreux of the P.C.B.—I dare say you remember him. He had never even thought of the Legion of Honour, and he must have been well over sixty when someone or other put the idea in his head. He became obsessed by it, and could think of nothing else. He made approaches to all and sundry, badgered everybody, and in the end literally worried himself to death about it—those six months broke him up completely and naturally his name was never put forward. Anyway, it has struck Vigroux that he has been chevalier for twenty years, and that he is being unfairly treated because everybody of his seniority has the rosette at least. He is getting thin and querulous. I am doing my best, but I have very few contacts. Now I have written a letter to the minister—will you sign it with me? Two members of the Institute—one a Gordon Pain prize man—that will make the sparks fly, and we shall achieve our aim.'

Patrice Périot was immensely relieved and pleased. Romanil was still Romanil, and when he asked for something it was not for himself. Life, after all, had its altars of repose and its compensations. Patrice Périot signed the letter with enthusiasm, whereupon the two old friends fell to discussing freely and openly the thorny question of honours. Romanil gave expression to some home truths in his usual style.

'For most men it's much better to pin up any gong that comes their way. We never know but that one of these days we may get swelled head and curse ourselves for having missed chances when we were young. Did you ever know Léon Resillod? No? He was an amazing chap. . . .'

There was no time for Clement Romanil to tell the life-story of Resillod, because at that moment Christine-Vera came into the study. In her flat voice she said: 'Oh, I'm sorry. I thought you were alone, daddy. I'll come back later.'

'I'm just going,' cried Romanil, struggling to get up from his chair. 'I must go—I'm late already.'

He spoke but made no further efforts to move. For a moment Patrice Périot became aware of a definite feeling of anxiety. Without fully admitting it to himself he wanted to cross-examine his old friend about that mysterious reference to Hervé, dropped some days ago into the smoky welter of their conversation. Suddenly he heard himself saying: 'Tell me, Christine, will Hervé be in to dinner this evening?'

Christine seemed to want to avoid the question. She took one or two steps across the room and then said: 'You must have noticed, like the rest of us, that he hasn't been home for three days.'

'Three days?' echoed Patrice Périot. 'Three days! Didn't he tell any one? Why haven't you said anything to me about it?'

'It's not my job to look after Hervé.' Christine's expression was obstinate. Then she added a phrase without appearing to realize its time-honoured significance: 'Hortense has just told me that Hervé left a letter on your desk.'

Patrice Périot threw up his hands. 'A letter! I have seen no letter. How can I hope to find it in this rubbish heap?'

Christine came up to the desk and rummaged among the papers with her thin, cold, little hand. In a couple of seconds she found a white envelope, neatly sealed down, on the outside of which was written 'For Father.'

Patrice Périot took the missive and muttered anxiously: 'You were talking about Resillod. . . .' All the time he waved the letter in the air, between trembling fingers.

'Read it,' said Romanil quietly.

Patrice Périot opened the letter and read it, once rapidly and then a second time. Romanil and Christine watched his colour ebb slowly. He got up and said: 'Excuse me one moment. I must make a phone call.'

The telephone was in the next room. Christine and Romanil listened to Périot hunting through the leaves of the directory; at last they heard him dial a number, and scraps of the conversation reached them. 'Hallo, hallo! Is that the Medico-Legal Institute? Yes.

This is Professor Périot, Member of the Institute, speaking. Ah! You were going to telephone me. . . .'

A rush of confused words followed which apparently had something to do with the Billancourt bridge. Then the two listeners heard Patrice Périot drop the receiver without troubling to replace it properly. The door opened and Périot came in. He walked heavily to his chair, sat down, and raised his head; his face was ravaged and unrecognizable.

'Forgive me, Clement,' he said, 'my son Hervé is dead. I have just heard the news. There is no doubt about it.'

He said no more and fell face forward among the litter of papers on his desk.

CHAPTER X

CONTRARY to Clement Romanil's first fears, and even to the secretive and silent Christine's, it soon became apparent that Patrice Périot was not seriously ill. He had definitely not had a 'stroke' or whatever the doctors call it in Latin. There had been no paralysis, and his heart and arteries were going to stand up to the shock. He had merely lost consciousness as a result of a shattering emotional trauma, and was evidently to live to drain the cup of anguish and bitterness to its dregs.

All the time he was unconscious the letter he had found on his desk remained clenched in his right hand, and no one tried to take it away from him. The combined efforts of Romanil, Christine, Mme Hortense, and Edwige, summoned to the scene, lifted him on the divan, and after a few minutes he regained consciousness, muttering inconsequent phrases which presumably meant something to him alone.

Romanil had immediately sent for Dr. Chabot, faithful family doctor and friend, who for thirty years or more had witnessed all the memorable events in the Périot clan. Dr. Chabot soon reassured every one about Patrice's condition, and this done he had a private conversation with the invalid, the gist of which was disclosed to no one. Emerging from this talk the doctor simply announced that Périot should spend the evening in bed but would probably be able to get up as usual the next day, which would be Sunday, and that since the Medico-Legal Institute would be closed he would make use of his right of entry and go along personally with one or more members of the family to identify the body, and attend to the other formalities; he added that it was late and that he was a busy man.

At this juncture Edwige's husband, Maurice Ribeyrol, displayed qualities hitherto unsuspected in him. Arriving on the scene soon after his wife, he gave her a chance to have her cry, then with a manner that was in keeping with the seriousness of the occasion put himself at Dr. Chabot's disposal. Mme Hortense, who had watched poor Hervé grow up from childhood, retired to the kitchen. Her expression was one of mortification rather than suffering. With a glassy stare she said to Christine, who had fled to her for comfort: 'He must have been blind! I have been expecting this to happen every day, for over a year.'

Through the half-open door she watched Maurice Ribeyrol talking in a business-like way to Dr. Chabot and Professor Romanil, and nudged Christine with her elbow.

'He's in his element now. A death in the house is right up his street. Give him two deaths in one house, and he would still be ready for another!'

In the days that followed Maurice Ribeyrol was in fact to prove himself the perfect organizer of funeral ceremonies. He wore gloves continuously, and gave

164

all the necessary orders with an authority which none dared to question.

Thierry turned up late on the evening of the tragedy, and hurried to his father's room. He wept as he kissed the old man's hands. Christine saw him from the doorway and said: 'You are doing more harm than good. Dr. Chabot recommended quiet.'

Patrice Périot made a sign that he wanted Thierry to stay with him. The young man squatted on a hassock near the divan on which his father was lying. Every now and then Périot's hand would grope for Thierry's head and stroke his hair. Christine rejoined Edwige and Mme Hortense in the dining-room, and a sort of torpor descended on the house. Edwige sent a message by the cable conveyor to her domestic help, telling her that there had been a serious accident and that she was to put the children to bed.

At about ten o'clock Dr. Chabot came round, with Maurice Ribeyrol and Clement Romanil.

The body, found by boatmen floating in the Seine near the Billancourt bridge, where the two streams join, was unquestionably that of Hervé Périot. Ribeyrol, Romanil, and Chabot had identified it immediately, although it was already decomposing and bloated as a result of its long immersion in the water. The unfortunate young man's note-case, containing money and an identity card, was found in his pocket. The staff of the Medico-Legal Institute had been about to break the sad news to Professor Périot when he had telephoned himself. There were apparently a few points still to be cleared up, for Chabot asked for a few words alone with the professor, which seemed to offend Maurice Ribeyrol. Thierry stood up, and left the room, sniffling and walking unsteadily. Chabot closed the door and sat by the head of Patrice Périot's bed.

'Will they let me have my boy's body?' the professor asked.

'Of course,' replied Chabot; 'but he cannot be brought home.'

'Why not?'

'It is against the rules. In any case the burial permit can only be issued if the officials are satisfied that the death was voluntary and not criminal, that is to say if young Hervé committed suicide and was not murdered.'

A long silence fell, and the doctor went on: 'No doubt you yourself would wish that an investigation should be made, and if it turns out to be a criminal affair that the guilty parties should be brought to justice and punished.'

Once more a long and heavy silence. In the quiet room the sound of whispering could be heard, through the partition, and occasionally a voice was raised and instantly controlled.

'There's no need to look for criminals, I mean for people directly responsible. My boy killed himself.'

'How do you know that?'

'He wrote me a letter, but I opened it too late. Even had I read it sooner I doubt whether I should have been able to find my Hervé in the ant-heap that is Paris.'

'So he gave you warning?'

'Yes, and before writing this particular letter he had often threatened that it would come to this. But in the end I gave up worrying—I did not even let it bother

me. He was what you doctors would call an anxiety
case and a melancholic, possibly he may even have had
a persecution complex. I do not know, I cannot say.'
Patrice Périot made a gesture of grief and despair.

'Can you let me see the letter?' the doctor asked
patiently.

Patrice Périot's expression was a mixture of acute
suffering and fanatic determination. 'My dear old
friend, do not ask me to let you read my boy's letter.
You would learn nothing from it. It is a sorry affair
that concerns him and me alone.'

The doctor looked thoughtful. 'We must get the
burial permit as soon as possible—the corpse certainly
shows no signs of violence. Of course you remember,
Périot, that I am attached to the Special Infirmary,
and that I know personally many of the people connected with these curious institutions—at police head-
quarters and at the Medico-Legal.'

'Quite.'

'If you don't want to show me the letter could you
let me have a written statement to the effect that
Hervé had announced his intention of committing
suicide?'

Patrice frowned deeply. 'One moment, before you
go on. I do not on any account want to ask you to
commit an irregularity, but I do sincerely wish that
an inquest could be avoided. I have no fear for my
own memories of my unhappy child, but I ask for
silence, for the repose of his soul, and for oblivion—
yes, oblivion. I give you my word, Chabot, that it
was an absurd suicide, terribly sad and trite. I would
be very much obliged to you if you would use your
influence to ensure that the officials concerned behave

discreetly, and that the formalities are carried out quietly and decently. We are all quite miserable enough as it is.'

'Write that letter,' said the doctor. 'You are well known, and your evidence will suffice. Let me help you to your desk. To-night it is late, and to-morrow being Sunday all the offices will be shut, but on Monday I will do what is necessary. Meanwhile you must get some sleep. You have some gardenal in the house? Good. Take it and I will call to see you to-morrow.'

With many corrections and erasures Patrice Périot wrote the required letter, then made a fair copy and put it in the envelope which the doctor slipped into his note-case.

Périot, standing up to walk over to the divan, suddenly looked hollow-eyed and shrunken, and twenty years older.

'Excuse me, old man, I can manage all right, but I must get used to my trouble by looking it in the face until I can accept it. If only the outside world will respect my sorrow! That is all I ask.'

'Do not stay down here. Go to bed, and let merciful sleep come to your rescue.'

Dr. Chabot went through the library to the dining-room where the family were assembled with Mme Hortense and Clement Romanil.

'He'll probably sleep now,' he said. 'Madame Hortense, you might take him up a cup of tea. To-morrow I will go and see one of my friends, if he happens to be available, about a burial order for Monday. For the moment the body is in cold storage, but we shall have to act quickly when it comes out.'

Maurice Ribeyrol said: 'Set your mind at rest,

doctor. No time will be lost in carrying out your instructions.'

Christine gave her brother-in-law an icy glance, and Thierry, covering his face with his hands, went off to his father's room without uttering a word.

'Come with me, Romanil, if you will,' said the doctor. 'My car is outside and I can drive you home. It is getting late.'

The two men departed, and Mme Hortense addressed the three young people in mournful tones. 'It is nearly eleven o'clock, and none of you has had anything to eat. Now I am going to get something for you all. I have some cold meat and sausages in the larder.'

All three affirmed that they were not hungry, but Mme Hortense went out and came back with the plates. They all sat down and began to eat the cold meat and sausage. Periodically Edwige was shaken by fits of sobbing, from which she recovered and resumed eating, at the same time protesting that she was not hungry. Maurice Ribeyrol began officiously to make up a list of people to be formally notified.

Christine looked on with overt distrust. Nevertheless she ate a slice of cold meat.

Patrice Périot drank his tisane and went to bed. Thierry pushed the *chaise longue* alongside his father's bed and curled himself up in it. The lights were turned out and silence reigned. Hearing his son tossing and turning in the darkness Patrice Périot suddenly whispered: 'Your unhappy brother has done nothing blameworthy—do you hear, Thierry?'

'Yes, dad. I understand.'

Patrice Périot let his imagination wander, and waves of sadness now soothed now exacerbated his suffering.

'To commit suicide like that when you have a brother
and sisters is a terrible thing. What a bad example,
what a temptation for the others in moments of
despair! But it's all my fault. As a father I am weak
and indulgent; I am not a good father. I have never
learned how to discipline them. I and my crowd
renounced metaphysics, but in our generation we still
had our moral armament. My poor children have had
to trust to luck, and then their mother left them when
they were at a critical age. I am only a care-worn
old man. Is it sensible for an overburdened man, a
man with a mission in life, to procreate children—
especially in these accursed times? Anyway, it's too
late now and there's no use in going back over past
deeds and misdeeds. I felt myself in duty bound to
devote part of my time to my ideas of justice and
charity and the welfare of mankind. As a result my
own children's welfare has been thoroughly neglected.
What would have happened to Hervé if he had learned
a rule of life? Would it have saved him? Is there
now any room for discipline in this lost and restless
world of ours, where no light shines and no voice
speaks from the infinite spaces? We are living in a
dead world.'

Patrice Périot gave way to sadness and sleep would
not come to him. A little later he thought: 'Absurd
as it may seem, I shall have to get up. My wretched
body is making its needs felt—and I shall probably
wake up my little saint, Thierry! Just to think that
not long ago I was filled with anxiety at the thought
that, in a moment of exaltation, he might turn his back
on the twentieth century and go into a monastery.
May he do it, may he withdraw into solitude if that

170

will spare him from suffering . . . and may he pray for me, and for all of us for this generation which has lost its way in life! Rationalist though I am, I have never doubted the efficacy of prayer. One of these days the scientists will discover that mental forces are capable of a remote action that can alter the train of human destiny and possibly even the organic structure of the world! No contingency can be ruled out—we have already seen men deny almost everything, including their own denials. . . . But I must get up. Not a moment to spare. How ridiculous!'

Patrice Périot got up, and heard Thierry whisper: 'Are you ill, dad, are you in pain?'

'I'm in pain, but I'm not ill. I shall be back in a moment.'

He groped his way through the darkness. A faint gleam of light from outside, filtering through the curtains, sufficed for his manœuvres. He avoided switching on the light, partly because he did not want to rouse Thierry completely, and partly so as not to catch sight of himself in the wall mirror.

He got back into bed and lay on the extreme edge, so that he might feel his son's breath among the tufts of grey hair in his ears. He held his breath, realizing that Thierry was not asleep, and heard the almost imperceptible sound of two lips opening and shutting.

'What are you doing, son?'

'You know well enough, dad.'

'Yes, indeed. Thank you, Thierry.'

The minutes passed slowly. At last Patrice Périot, with his head over the edge of the bed, heard the faint sound no longer. 'Now he is asleep,' he thought. Just then the young man coughed lightly, as if to signify that the soul was still on guard. Patrice Périot found himself whispering things which were a surprise even to himself.

'You see, my child, I do not talk the same language as you; but maybe we are no more apart in eternity than we are now in the darkness of this night of suffering.'

'No, father,' breathed Thierry, 'we are not apart, and we shall never be separated in eternity.'

'In my wretchedness,' continued Patrice Périot, 'I cry to God my need for rest, security, and forgiveness.'

'Yes, father! Exactly.'

Another long silence ensued. Thierry answered clearly each time, but for all his burning emotion he seemed to be taking care not to interfere; he allowed the distressed old soul to make its own way through the shadows.

'Undoubtedly I am unbeliever, and have been one so long that I can hardly recall the enthusiasms of my childhood. But you know I love Christ, Thierry. Jesus is called the "Son of Man" because He is humanity's finest creation. Would humanity to-day be capable of producing a Christ, or even of imagining such a God? That is the question I ask myself, and I think that the answer is "No."'

In the darkness the young man seemed suddenly to have stopped breathing, but he made no attempt to reply. Perhaps he was anxious not to make this tottering journey through the valley of the shadow more painful. He took his father's hand and pressed it gently. Time passed. Suddenly Thierry realized that the old man's hand was relaxed, and that it responded no longer to his grasp. Then he heard his father breathing noisily but rhythmically like the breaking of little waves on the seashore. The gardenal must have done its work. He made a few more silent prayers, and eventually fell asleep himself.

It must have been nine o'clock in the morning when Patrice woke. The first thing he knew was the bitter taste of sorrow in his mouth. His first waking thought was that despair was lying in wait, ready to strike, like a beast of prey sure of its victim. Thierry was still asleep on the sofa, with the complete physical abandon of childhood.

While Patrice Périot was making ineffective attempts to shave himself in the bath-room with a blunt razor he heard a slight noise at the end of the corridor. It was not Mme Hortense on her usual domestic occasions. Someone was talking, and Patrice could hear that one of the voices was urgent and insistent. He had the feeling that the nocturnal interlude was well and truly at an end, and that the drama was once more taking its course. Probably someone wanted his opinion, or his signature, or one or other of the formalities that were the undercurrent to his daily life. He dried his face, put on his dressing-gown, and walked stealthily through the library to the dining-room door. Mme Hortense was speaking, not angrily, but quietly and stubbornly.

'No, sir. The professor is not at all well.'

'I guessed as much, madame, and it is for that reason that my collaborator and I have called.'

'The professor is very much upset. He will not see any one.'

'Quite so, madame,' the voice went on obstinately, 'but he will see me, if only for two minutes. The suffering of a great man is a remarkable sight, and it is important to put it on record. Two minutes only, and there's no need for you to warn him. We come inside, click, and it's over. I want to photograph the famous scholar in tears. I want to be the first photographer of the grief of Professor Patrice Périot.'

Patrice Périot's heart beat wildly and his hands trembled with rage as he listened through the door to this surprising conversation. Then realizing that Mme Hortense might give way and that he could not master his temper much longer he turned the handle, crossed the dark corridor, opened the landing door and went up the stairs waving his arms furiously.

At that moment a magnesium flash illuminated the interior, disclosing the two men with their photographic apparatus. They both followed him through the door on tiptoe, saying effusively: 'Thanks a lot, maestro!' As they crossed the threshold a second magnesium flash blinded the professor.

He slammed the door, and fled down the corridor with a roar of anger. The tidal wave, miraculously arrested during the hours of the night, was in spate again, sweeping away all common sense in its fury.

CHAPTER XI

THANKS to Dr. Chabot's urgent intervention and to the respect which the name of Patrice Périot commanded in official circles the burial permit was issued on Tuesday. Maurice Ribeyrol, for his part, had taken various steps and had arranged for Hervé's body to be placed in a leaden coffin at the Medico-Legal Institute. After much hesitation Patrice Périot decided not to view the body. 'I would prefer always to carry in my memory the last picture Hervé left me of himself,' he argued. 'It was a sad and sorrowful picture, but it was not an ugly one and it was not disfigured or sodden with water. I must now learn to find a way of living with the shade of my departed son.'

Maurice Ribeyrol, always on the spot at crises of this sort, had let it be known that he would take care of all the funeral arrangements. From the first it had been necessary to give up any idea of the family tomb in Montmartre Cemetery. There was only one vacant place, to which the Demoncelles, Clotilde's side of the family, were entitled, and to which they uncompromisingly pressed their claim. At the special request of Patrice Périot, who was anxious to escape the noisy crowds during these trying days, a concession was obtained without difficulty in the little cemetery at Jouy-le-Comte. In accordance with Patrice's wishes no notice had been given to the press. He took it on himself to inform his own relatives and a few close personal friends. Reporters who had got wind of the affair from some unknown source began to arrive on Sunday evening at the rue Lamarck. On Monday they came in such numbers that a barrier had to be put at the foot of the staircase. The concierge dealt with the advance guard. She gave them a hot reception to begin with, but gradually her temper improved, and she volunteered all sorts of intriguing inside information, although she really knew nothing of what had happened. From Tuesday onwards the Paris dailies began to publish little articles under various titles, all carrying the implication that young Hervé Périot had met his death under mysterious circumstances. Some of them printed a portrait of Hervé Périot which no one in the family could recognize. It was just a portrait of any young man among a thousand. Some of the press notices said that the deceased was a budding young scientist, already the father of three children, others that he was well known as a staunch Catholic who had only recently signed various peace appeals. There is always a germ of plausibility in misinformation, a fact which can be made use of by any one who is sagacious enough to disentangle root causes from confused conjecture and fact. One left-wing evening newspaper gave out that 'the son of the great revolutionary scientist Patrice Périot was, like one of his sisters, keenly attracted to dialectical materialism.'

Normally Patrice Périot read only the various journals that were sent to him free, but in the last few weeks he had stopped reading anything at all. All the same there was always someone around to open a paper and tap it with an exclamation of surprise, with the result that he would be forced out of his daydreaming to confirm that the simple truth had once more been violated.

It was the very end of May, and the weather had been hot and thundery for several days. The funeral had been fixed for Thursday. The body of the young man, in its leaden coffin, would be collected at the Medico-Legal Institute, and taken from there direct to Jouy-le-Comte in a hearse which could accommodate three or four members of the family. Those of the relatives who did not travel in the hearse would follow in private cars, among which would be Ribeyrol's and Christine's. Ribeyrol was leaving his three children at home in Paris, and proposed to take Romanil with him. Patrice had not informed any of his colleagues at the Institute or the Sorbonne. He yearned for solitude and silence. Although he held himself to be unprejudiced, the idea of going to fetch his son's body at the morgue filled him with shame and bitterness of spirit.

On the appointed day Patrice Périot and his children arrived early at the noisy Place Mazas. The sky was overcast by angry clouds coming from the south. Périot looked up from time to time, and found some consolation in the thought that the weather at least was in sympathy with his own heavy burden of trouble, with which a radiant spring morning would have been quite out of keeping. . . . Bare-headed he stood beside the hearse, his nearest of kin around him. It had been many years since he had wept, and he had forgotten how to do so. Perhaps he was never again to know the solace of tears. Edwige and Thierry made no attempt to control their sobs. He envied them. Christine, as secretive and cat-like as ever, was not crying. She looked at her brother-in-law, Maurice Ribeyrol, rigged up in a black coat and striped trousers, and with a curl of her lip murmured: 'He would have made a first-class undertaker.' Her spitefulness at such a moment filled Patrice with consternation, and he thought of reprimanding her openly. However, he was too tired, he who, on innumerable occasions, had gladly harangued crowds on the subject of a peace which he had never been able to establish in his own hearth and home. The modern age had no horizon, and all its outlets were blind alleys, except those which led to quarrel, resentment, hate, and unbounded distrust.

The cortège moved off. The heat was exhausting, even when they were in motion. Near the gates of Paris they ran into a traffic block, and Patrice Périot heard strange noises which seemed to be coming from the coffin and made him feel so odd that he dared not mention them. At first he had taken Thierry's arm, but seeing that they were both beginning to perspire and that his affectionate clasp would only lead to discomfort he withdrew his arm and retired into his own thoughts. He should have sold the house at Jouy-le-Comte, as poor Hervé had asked him; at all costs he should have given way, even at the risk of aggravating the boy's unstable and bewildered condition. Was it really this with which Hervé, in despair and on

178

the very threshold of death, had reproached him—
not to have given way, not to have handed over this
sum of money, large or small according to how you
looked at it, a sum which would have to be found now,
willy-nilly, to pay for the funeral? Was not the reproach rather for having given him birth, for having
pitchforked him into a world without light, unworthy
of redemption? Had he, Patrice Périot, any right to be
sorry for himself, even during these days of mourning?
In years gone by he had suffered a bitter blow—he
had lost Clotilde. But that was at a time of universal
tragedy, when all the world recognized a set-back or
a serious misfortune when they saw one. He used to
think that, despite disputes among themselves, he had
been lucky to keep his little clan of four while nearly
every family round him had lost one or more in some
tragic episode. Was it not excusable if the survivors
of this tortured generation, passed over by avenging
fate, lost their sense of judgment and direction in the
general darkness, to cling desperately to doctrinaire
life-lines. One old man's tears were he able to
squeeze them out of his dried-up glands, would only
be lost in an ocean of weeping. . . .

The sun broke through the clouds and its rays
poured down on the shiny black car. They had to
wait at the Domont level-crossing, and once again
strange noises came from the coffin. Thierry and
Mme Hortense obviously heard them too, but no one
said a word: Patrice Périot began to wander in his
thoughts again, while the sun blazed down. 'Taking
it all round Hervé made a peaceful and orderly exit,
despite the unwelcome attentions of the press. He left
this mad world with pitiful but exemplary discretion.'

His last letter, which still overwhelmed Patrice, was the letter of a child. There remained the problem of suicide. Patrice used to think, when he was a young man himself, that suicide was the ultimate manifestation of liberty in an aspiring soul. Later in life, having seen his children born and growing up, he renounced this opinion since it conflicted with his duty as a parent. Suddenly he wondered whether Hervé's deed might not be attributable to an hereditary trait, and whether his own old thoughts of suicide had been fulfilled in the person of his son. This idea activated his deepest pain anew. He was almost superstitiously afraid of the confused nightmares from which he sometimes suffered; and the thought of a waking dream in which he could no more control the working of his mind than of his liver or other similar organs, filled him with despair and disgust. He remembered an occasion in the early days of their marriage when Clotilde had taken him to the theatre, to see a play adapted from Dostoevsky. One of the characters had the line: 'Man is a thinker, and when he thinks there is no telling what shape his thoughts will take.' This phrase often came into his mind, and always left him with a curious sense of uneasiness. One strange thing about it was that it linked up by devious routes with some of his later discoveries in pure physiology which could be summarized in propositions such as the following: 'We have no control over our heart, kidney, or glands. We co-operate in the functions of these organs without being able to exercise any direct or effective control over them, except by encompassing their total destruction, e.g. by suicide. Is it possible to credit nature, that impersonal complex, with a will and a doctrine, with opinions and designs, while at the same time denying even to the higher animal the power of influencing the functions of the various organs of its own body, and regarding the latter merely as their trustee or more accurately as their untrained observer? What interest can this abstract conception of nature have in forcing living organisms to go on living?'

Even to the extent of excluding all other suffering, his mind was tortured by the thought that the power of reason, intelligent investigation, and invention might be no more subservient to the will than the action of the suprarenal glands.

He made an attempt to pull himself together and organize his pain. . . . After all, he was having it his own way. There was a pact within the family not to raise awkward problems, and to let sleeping dogs lie. One of these days, doubtless oblivion would do its work, submerging everything in the triumph of anarchy.

The little cortège was now passing through woodland. The foliage showed different shades of green, high summer not having as yet imposed uniformity throughout its kingdom. The fresh scent was soothing and the heat less thundery and suffocating. Patrice Périot's thoughts grew calmer, more objective, and more in accord with his early upbringing. In his secret heart he thought: 'And now I cannot even commit suicide myself! If I did they would call it retroactive heredity or something of the sort. Didn't that happen in poor Martel's case? My colleagues have an explanation ready for every emergency, and I am no better. What have I been doing all my life except to uncover the unknown in the hope of giving some meaning to this crazy world?'

The cortège crossed the Oise and a few minutes later came to a halt in the church square of the village of Jouy-le-Comte. As soon as he set eyes on the church Patrice Périot was extremely moved. For several days he had thought of absolutely nothing except his own distress, and he had left all the arrangements for poor little Hervé's funeral to his children and his friends. Would the body be allowed inside the church? On the one hand the thought that admittance could be refused offended Patrice, and on the other hand the prospect that the church would be opened shocked him by arousing vague but tenacious memories.

He was not left long in a state of indecision. A whispered consultation was held between the Périot children and the driver of the hearse. It was evident at once that the essential problem was whether the hearse should attempt the slope, which was steep and possibly too narrow for so long a vehicle to turn in. The bearers discussed the problem casually, and eventually every one got out and walked, leaving the hearse to make the ascent alone. On opening the coffin the bearers announced that the lead coffin, sealed before their departure, had bulged as a result of fermentation and had split some of the planks of the wooden coffin. They had to tie it up with rope to avoid more serious damage. This all caused distressing delays. At last they carried the coffin to the edge of the grave. Ribeyrol had arranged with the mayor for a vacant site in the north-west corner, alongside the wall. All the family were gathered together round this little excavation, dug by the hand of man but destined to engulf a man's mortality, when Thierry stepped forward. He took a book, bound in black cloth, from his pocket. Bareheaded, serious, his face inspired, he looked really beautiful at that moment, and his attitude seemed to imply: 'I can do what I am about to do, because I am not a priest and I have taken no vows as yet. I am simply a man whose brother is in trouble.' Then he opened the book and read aloud the prayers for the dead. Patrice Périot, suddenly released, broke down and wept.

Within a few minutes each in turn had leaned over the grave to make peace with the dead man or throw a flower on the coffin, and a brief family conference ensued. Patrice Périot expressed a desire to spend the rest of the day and the night at Jouy in his country house, which was always kept ready for visitors. Mme Hortense and Thierry immediately announced that they would stay too, and the three were left there, while the rest of the family scattered, returning to their various duties and responsibilities.

Patrice Périot refused to have anything to eat, and shut himself up in his room, where he fell into a profound reverie, interrupted only by the buzz of a fly or the siren of a tug, with its train of barges, approaching a lock gate in the Oise. Towards nightfall he tiptoed to the end of the garden and made his way to the cemetery.

Most of the village lies above the valley of the Oise, and the silence is rarely disturbed by traffic. Patrice did not meet a living soul on his way up. He felt the need to recover himself in solitude, to make contact with a departed shade who had left a number of questions unanswered and whom he must henceforward cross-examine to the end of his days. He pushed open the iron gate and pursued his course slowly among the tombstones. The grave was filled in and the grave-diggers had gone. But Patrice saw a head of fair hair among the crosses and wreaths, and he knew that Thierry was there before him, to get into touch in his own fashion with a soul in torment.

Thierry was on his knees on the stone footpath, praying with his head bent over the grave. He was so completely motionless that Patrice, accustomed to his usual hyper-activity, paused, unwilling to intrude on such concentration. Then gradually, a step at a time, as if drawn by this very immobility, he advanced towards the boy.

Against the wall there were five or six blocks of marble, jettisoned by the stone-masons. Tired out, Patrice went and sat down on one of the blocks. He took off his hat, and held his breath, thinking: 'What a miserable specimen I am! My suffering is disorderly and ineffective, while my youngest son, who is every bit as hard hit as I am, evidently knows what to do about it. He can put his sorrow into words and give it a sense of direction.' Just then the youngster raised his head, made the sign of the cross, and seeing his father, came and sat beside him without any embarrassment.

'I thought I would have the place to myself,' said Patrice Périot, 'and I find you here!'

'I knew you'd come.'

For a time they gazed at the landscape, which, without being unusually impressive, was nevertheless dignified and pleasing. The setting sun, no longer hidden by the clouds, was shining full on the beautiful Oise valley, which at this point is broad and thickly wooded. The forest of Tour de Lay comes right down to the floor of the valley, where lies the peaceful village with its graceful church tower, its cottages, and its gardens gay with flowers. This was no place for despair, but rather for calm meditation. Thierry did not apparently want to talk, and so Patrice began tentatively to give vent to thoughts which would stifle him if he tried to silence them any longer. From the outset he realized clearly that he was, unwisely perhaps, treading the edge of a precipice, and running all sorts of risks for which he was very ill prepared.

'I am very grateful to you, Thierry, for reading the prayers for the dead. Actually I thought that Maurice —well, I suppose I didn't really think about it at all, I was too tired, and too distressed—but I thought that Maurice had arranged for a ceremony of some sort in church.'

'I told him not to.' Thierry was frowning. 'It was my doing. You must know very well that it was out of the question.'

'Evidently that is so, but I was thinking of us all, and of myself, of course. I know what you're going to tell me, but the church is a resting-place in time of trouble even for those who do not listen to her teaching.'

Whenever Patrice, in all sincerity, ventured to discuss forbidden subjects, young Thierry, normally so talkative, would fall silent. In this case he listened wide-eyed, with an expression of anxiety rather than hope. Patrice spoke from the depths of his heart.

'You have probably heard what was said about your brother and the company he kept. I tell you again that he has done nothing you need feel really ashamed of, nothing truly blameworthy. He killed himself stupidly, and I'll tell you all about that some day.'

'Just a moment, dad, you have now told me twice that Hervé did nothing wrong. Poor Hervé! He has committed the most serious of all sins. And now we must win forgiveness for him.'

Strangely enough Patrice Périot, instead of being upset by this statement, heaved a sigh of relief. 'Yes, you are perfectly right, my child—I call you my child, though you speak with the wisdom and experience of a man, because to me you are, and always will be, my child.'

Instead of answering his father directly the young man said: 'I am by no means always anxious to go on living, but I have never had any wish to commit suicide.' Then he looked straight at his father and added: 'Mind you, I disapprove of it for a variety of reasons, and for one in particular, but all the same I sympathize and to a certain extent I understand.'

'You do?'

'Yes, because if one is to put up with life and the world, and to tolerate one's own inner conflicts, some help is needed. He who is not sustained can never hope to attain. And poor Hervé had no help. I am not blaming you and I am not excusing either you or myself—I'm simply wondering how it is that grace was denied him. He was cleverer than I, of that I am sure, and yet he hardly dared speak to you—at times he had to turn his back before he could talk to you. With me he was quite at ease; perhaps that superior intelligence of his was the cause of the trouble.'

'Alas,' thought Patrice Périot to himself, 'what use were his brains to him? Nothing is of any real value except what this young son of mine seems to have got hold of,' and he said aloud: 'Did he ever speak to you about his terrible project?' Thierry said nothing, and Patrice went on, his voice suddenly charged with emotion: 'He actually told me, two or three times.'

'Father! I can't believe it!'

'He did, but I came to the conclusion that it was a mixture of temper and youthful exaggeration. I persuaded myself that suicide is no easy matter, and that it was something which called for determination and the subjugation of reflex action.'

The silence which ensued was broken only by the loud and melodious song of a blackbird. When Patrice spoke again it was as if to himself. 'I thought you could all swim. Your mother used to take you bathing, and she told me so, unless I am mistaken. In any case, what does it matter now?'

'Actually mother must have told you that Edwige and Christine and I could swim, but that Hervé never learned properly. Besides, I doubt if it would have made much difference, once the decision was taken.'

'How do you know that?'

Thierry made an evasive gesture, and Patrice went on: 'I thought I was right to devote my life to the pursuit of knowledge; maybe I was wrong, maybe I have neglected my duty as a father——'

Thierry deftly forestalled the confession which he felt he was about to receive: 'Wait a minute, father. You speak of knowledge, but I too seek knowledge, though not in its academic sense. My search is for a knowledge of the absolute, and not of the relative.' He seemed inspired by an intense desire to get away from an excessively depressing conversation. With surprising firmness he went on: 'I refuse to believe that knowledge of absolute truth is beyond my reach. Christine is mistaken, but she is really after exactly the same thing as I am. That may sound surprising, but it's true. The only trouble is that she's on the wrong track.'

As Périot stood up to go Thierry pointed towards the grave. 'He will be forgiven, I am sure. I feel it in my bones. I knew a priest who committed the same sin and has been forgiven.'

'How do you know?'

'I can't tell you. I just know.'

Patrice, standing up, was showing signs of shakiness in his legs. 'Make the sign of the cross, father,' his son said firmly.

'You're making me feel embarrassed. I am not worthy. . . .'

'It doesn't commit you. It simply means that you are with me, with us, with yourself if you like, rather than with these poor lost sheep.'

Patrice Périot crossed himself clumsily and took his son's arm.

CHAPTER XII

THE first part of the night was soothing. Through the window, open on the lush valley, came a restless silence, and Patrice Périot felt as if he could hear the grass growing and the leaves shooting and the teeming life of millions of obscure creatures exhaling their hopes and their sufferings. The threatened storm passed over. Every now and then a puff of wind rustled the young poplar leaves.

Patrice lay on his back motionless and studied the functioning of his body. Apparently it had a fleeting consciousness of the achievement of the heterogeneous cells which for so long had worked for him to produce the sentient and rational being called Patrice Périot, who meanwhile ruled them with complete indifference. Now, in the dead of night, this same body was asking him, in his role of scientist, some very urgent questions and voicing the grievances of a weary and neglected populace. Regions of the body that Patrice had always taken for granted, and which had worked for him for years in humble obscurity, now began to ache.

He turned over to watch the intermittent shining of a star in the night sky and thought: 'I am not asleep, and yet I do not know whether I shall ever wake again. It would be pleasant to die, if only to dodge the reveille! Pleasant! What a word! However, its choice must signify that I am resigned to the idea of death.'

The thought of this tragic event inevitably revived the dominant problem of this dramatic week, and feeling himself slipping once again into the dark places of the mind he reflected that people who know how to pray must be able to face their hours of despair more calmly. He caught himself murmuring: 'Thierry! Thierry, my child, the baby of my family!' He abandoned himself to his thoughts. 'Am I to believe that faith alone could sustain one in such moments of agony?' He clenched his fists at the realization of what he was saying. 'Now I am talking like a pragmatist, and flirting with the idea of buying my peace of mind. Away with such cowardly thoughts! I will never yield to them, I shall never become a pragmatist. I am an agnostic, no more and no less, and a despairing one at that. I accept the light on condition that it is given to me when I am in full possession of all my faculties. It would be to my everlasting shame to give way for the sake of achieving mental peace, or simply because illness has reduced me to a shadow of myself, and what a miserable offering that would be to the Supreme Being who must be worshipped by no less than the whole personality in a state of self-mastery. If there is a God, I will not insult Him by treating Him as if He were a beachcomber.'

In the small hours of the morning, however, he fell asleep, murmuring: 'But does all this make good logic? Perhaps the real problem is to cross the threshold of death without having experienced the suffering my poor little Hervé must have known.' And so the angel of the dawn took pity on him in his gropings, while he slept.

Next day Patrice and Thierry decided to stay on at Jouy-le-Comte to enjoy its peace and solitude, and to make the most of their rather inarticulate conversations, which both soothed and stimulated them. At the end of one of these queer duets Patrice pricked up his ears. 'I probably know more than any one alive to-day,' he thought, 'about the functioning of the liver cells. But this unsophisticated lad of mine has his private stores of knowledge. Perhaps the great mystery of life is basically a very simple affair. And yet we scientists go on dressing things up in algebraic formulae and assembling mountains of statistics.'

On Monday morning Patrice and Thierry went back to Paris, accompanied by Mme Hortense, who had been plunged into gloomy surliness by what had happened, and whose attitude to everything, like that of a disillusioned oracle, was 'I have said so all along.'

For Périot the idea of Paris was inexpressibly repugnant. The prospect of plunging into the crowd again, of seeing once more the faces of his friends and his enemies, and even of his own daughters, could not fail to threaten the very unstable equilibrium, which young Thierry alone had miraculously built up for him. Moreover, he would have to plunge into a mass of papers, feel the ring of the telephone cutting his nerves like a saw, offend importunate callers, and listen to his own mental meanderings in the streets—such were Patrice's thoughts during the short homeward journey.

The house was aired and ready for him. Christine must have left early, but the curtains were drawn back and some of the windows were open to the mild Parisian spring. Thierry went to his room and Patrice Périot retired to his study, where he was not surprised to find Maurice Ribeyrol usurping his own one-armed chair and absorbed in reading the newspapers. The Ribeyrols had a key to the flat, and always made themselves completely at home there.

'I beg your pardon, father.' The young man looked anxious, and his nose twitched. 'Excuse me, one moment.'

'There's no need to apologize, old chap,' said Patrice Périot, throwing a case full of manuscripts and books on the divan.

Maurice Ribeyrol immersed himself avidly in the newspaper spread out on the desk. He was breathing so heavily that Patrice Périot was bound to remark on it.

'Is there anything the matter, Maurice? Are you ill?'

'No, I'm not ill, but I'm furiously angry. It's an absolute scandal.'

Patrice Périot realized at once that he must pull himself together, for something totally unexpected and probably stupid was awaiting him here in his Paris stronghold. His decision to come back had clearly been a sound one, and it was going to be necessary for him to face the situation with a bold front.

'Does this concern me?' he asked tentatively.

'Most certainly it concerns you, father. And us as well. You know that I come here sometimes to read your papers—I may say that I wouldn't be seen dead with them, or support them personally for anything in the world. Well, this is what I was reading when you came in just now.'

Maurice Ribeyrol spread out the newspaper and got up to allow his father-in-law to sit down comfortably. At first glance Patrice Périot saw a portrait—of himself. It was a photograph, taken at the laboratory some years before, showing him holding up a glass flask filled with turbid liquid, which he was examining against the light. Underneath the portrait was the caption: 'The great scientist, well known for his generous views, never despairs of discovering the truth.' Patrice's eye travelled to the head of the page. As is usual all over the world to-day the headlines were in huge type. Patrice read: MYSTERY DEATH DEMANDS ELUCIDATION.

'Read it, father,' said Maurice Ribeyrol impatiently. 'Read it carefully.'

Patrice Périot then read the following:

A scientist who has earned the respect of the entire world, and whose work is a credit to our country and our generation, has recently suffered a severe blow to his heart and to his pride alike. One of his children, one of his two sons to be exact, met his death at the end of last week under circumstances which are so far unexplained and which in our opinion are sensational. Young Hervé Périot was in his early twenties. He lived with his father, his brother, his sister ('Comrade Vera' to us), in a quiet part of Paris 18e. He was apparently devoted to the study of literature and took no interest in politics, which is to be deprecated, but this fact simplifies the problem and makes it easier to view in its proper light.

About the middle of last week, probably on Wednesday if we are to believe our reliable sources of information, young Hervé left his father's house. Apparently he was in the habit of absenting himself for a day or two without telling any one, and none of his family were unduly concerned. Towards the end of the week one of his sisters thought it necessary to inform his father, who was immersed in urgent personal work, that the young student was still away from home. At that very moment terrible news was awaiting the family. The young man's body had just been dragged out of the Seine by fishermen near the Île de Billancourt, to the south-west of Paris, and had been taken immediately to the Medico-Legal Institute.

We consider it our duty to comment freely on any aspects of this mysterious drama that can be elucidated. The suicide hypothesis can be dismissed straight away. It will surprise those who are unfamiliar with the secrets behind officialdom to learn that a burial permit was issued without an inquest. We who are actively seeking and are only concerned with the truth are constrained by all we know to see the work of some criminal agency behind this tragedy.

We have a great respect for Professor Périot. We may not always see eye to eye with him in ideological matters or in the ultimate significance of his researches. But we always regard him with pride as one of our acknowledged leaders, and even as a comrade in the fighting line. We bow before his personal grief. We cannot bring ourselves to believe that the crime, if crime there has been (and all the evidence seems to point to it), will be allowed to go unpunished, for reasons which would be repugnant to our sense of justice.

The article was unsigned. The cold impersonal style was, however, reminiscent of certain talks Patrice Périot had had recently with the person he had described in the heat of the moment at public meetings as 'the distinguished author of *Deep Waves*.' Moreover, it was this morning's issue of Gérin's own paper *Solidarity* which contained the article.

Patrice Périot read and re-read the words two or three times with a sort of pained perplexity. Then

194

he shrugged his shoulders, and once more became aware of the presence of Maurice Ribeyrol, whom he had completely forgotten.

The relations between Patrice and his son-in-law, ever since the latter's marriage to Edwige, could by no stretch of the imagination be described as friendly. The thought that he had given his daughter, his firstborn, to this dry-as-dust, suspicious arithmetician often filled Patrice with uneasiness amounting to resentment. The internal quarrels of the Ribeyrol *ménage* used to bubble up around the paternal hearth, exacerbated, at least as far as Christine was concerned, by political passion, for Maurice Ribeyrol was a monarchist and took every opportunity of announcing the fact. His usual line of talk was of emigration with his wife and children to Bolivia, where there was a shortage of expert engineers, or to South Africa, the land of gold and diamonds, 'The country of the future,' as he called it. He had too much respect for academic qualifications to call in question his father-in-law's scientific ability, but Patrice's political opinion and his general attitude to life irritated him to the point of exasperation.

'I want you to realize, father,' he said, stammering slightly as was his habit when annoyed, 'that we have refrained from cross-examining you during these trying days. We have been forced to assume that Hervé fell into the river and that he could not swim. We had some grounds for thinking that he might have thrown himself in. . . .'

Patrice Périot looked so bent and care-worn that Maurice Ribeyrol came closer to him.

'I hate having to talk to you like this, father, on this very painful subject, but since these disgusting newspapers are interesting themselves in our family tragedy, silence is no longer possible. What are we going to do about it? What are we going to say to the people we meet? Take my own case. From to-day onwards my career is in danger. So what is to be done?'

He elaborated the theme, dwelling on his various grievances, and failing to get any response from Patrice, who was staring out of the window, he made for the door.

'If there is any information to be had I am strongly of the opinion that the members of the family should be the first to have it.'

'There is none,' said Patrice in a grief-stricken voice.

When Maurice Ribeyrol had gone Périot pushed aside the pile of letters on his desk. Undoubtedly there were many expressions of sincere sympathy among them, but what would become of that sympathy when the whole affair, as a result of uninformed publicity, became a matter of public scandal and curiosity? He made an effort to control his emotion, but his wretchedness got the better of him.

He decided to stay in his room, and hung a note on the handle of the front door saying that Professor Périot was unwell and could see no visitors. Then he disconnected the telephone and opened his note-books in a superhuman effort to recapture the thread of his ordinary work. The totemic fly was going round and round the ceiling, as it did in the beginning, and ever would do, world without end. Hervé was no longer there to throw paper pellets at it. . . . Hervé's voice! Patrice Périot had only to close his eyes to hear that voice once more, slightly quavering and so full of unhappiness . . . it should have been impossible to miss that note in Hervé's voice, and he should have foreseen what it portended.

Unexpectedly Patrice succeeded in concentrating on his work for a couple of hours, after which he ate a meal provided for him by Mme Hortense and then forced himself to write a few more pages. Like Charles Nicolle, his friend of former days, Périot was of the opinion that the discoverer of a scientific truth should try to express it, not in esoteric language but in popular terms, as Pasteur and Claude Bernard did, for the future welfare of science. His work brought him some relief, and when he stopped writing it was only to seek fresh fields of thought from which to win mental peace and comfort. Newspaper gossip could have no lasting effect, since it was aimlessly motivated. It would die of inanition and peace would return once more to those that were left.

Nevertheless by the evening he was of a different mind, and taking his hat he crossed the landing and went down the stairs. He rounded the corner of the rue Caulaincourt, where no one knew him and where he could buy the evening papers without the risk of being recognized and asked awkward questions. He slipped the papers into his pocket and hurried home.

They all, whatever their politics, carried some comment on the leader in *Solidarity*, mentioning what they called in popular journalese the 'repercussions' of the Périot mystery. The *Red Torch*, a left-wing evening paper, printed a strange photograph of Patrice Périot in a dressing-gown with his arm upraised, bearing the caption: 'The famous scholar says let there be light.' This Patrice recognized as one of the flashlight pictures taken by the photographers who had snapped him unawares in the corridor of his flat, just as he opened the door to send them away. The same paper carried a short article, printed in heavy type, which began with the words:

We offer our friend and teacher, the great French scientist, our assurance that we will not desert him in his hour of need. The inertia of the public authorities, far from hindering us in the pursuit of our inquiries, will have the opposite effect. From now on we are on the side of justice, and the assassins will eventually be unmasked. . . .

Patrice Périot glanced through the other papers. Curiously enough the right-wing papers did not contradict their natural enemies. All alike referred in the vaguest terms to mystery, crime, and investigations. Patrice re-read the *Red Torch*, and shrugged his shoulders. 'What is the idea behind all this? I ask for nothing from them . . . why won't they leave me alone with my grief?'

He felt an urge to look for an old snapshot of himself and Hervé, taken on a country walk during the war, when Hervé was still in his teens. Although there was no one at home he tiptoed into Hervé's bedroom, as if he were afraid of rousing ghosts.

The room already smelt dusty and stuffy. Since Hervé's death Mme Hortense had closed the shutters and drawn the curtains. The bed was unmade and the bedclothes were neatly folded and piled on the mattress. Hanging on the walls were drawings and paintings of the 'abstract' school, so-called because it attempts to portray the truth beyond reality, which though unnatural was yet capable of being both profoundly disturbing and illuminating.

198

Luckily the photograph Patrice wanted was on the mantelpiece, slipped into the frame of the mirror. He picked it up. Being in no hurry to leave these doleful surroundings he sat down on a chair. In front of him was a desk covered with grey blotting-paper, and beyond the desk was a chest of drawers where the boy used to keep his linen and possibly some of his papers. The thought that there might be papers there and that one day, if the gutter press had their way, strangers would come and ransack them for titbits of news, prodded him into activity.

He moved his chair over to the chest, switched on the light, and began to open the drawers.

The top drawer contained nothing but linen. Mme Hortense must have been keeping her eye on it up to the last, because it was in good order. The second drawer contained text-books and exercise books, suggesting somewhat half-hearted study. In the bottom drawer Patrice Périot found letters, loose leaves, sometimes grouped in folders or pinned together, and note-books full of illegible scribbles, which he decided to take to his study for closer examination. He bundled them all together, and before leaving the room he ferreted into everything, turning out the pockets of the coats on their hangers, finding nothing except oddments such as visiting-cards and metro tickets, evidence one would have said of an ordinary, uneventful life.

He turned off the lights and carried the bundle of papers to the divan in his study. He had always made it a rule to respect the personal lives of his children and not to exercise supervision over them or limit their freedom in any way. He carried off Hervé's last relics with the stealth of one who was lending himself to wrongdoing.

It was soon painfully evident that his fears were groundless, for the dozen or so letters were non-committal and uninteresting, dealing with appointments kept or missed, club meetings, and gambling. The gamblers' jargon was meaningless to an outsider, and Patrice shoved the letters into a cardboard box. The other writings consisted of a jumble of skeleton poems and rough drafts of short stories.

Patrice read one of the stories carefully, which turned out to be about a man who had wronged and then robbed his best friend. The guilty party experienced remorse in proportion to the disapproval of others, and the censure of his personal friends. But he soon began to realize that the disapproval was too mild and the censure almost non-existent. Far from reassuring him this so preyed on his mind, that feeling that he could never be anything more than a petty criminal he put a bullet through his head. . . . It needed patience to decipher this scrawl. It was carelessly written, with numerous spelling mistakes, despite the fact that the boy had several diplomas to his credit. After a moment's reflection Patrice slipped the manuscript into his desk.

Despite the bitterness of the phantasy, if phantasy it was, this short story presupposed a certain moral attitude and some adolescent difficulties in the author. Périot said to himself: 'I knew nothing about all that. I did not know my son. How little we know of our children!'

He made an effort to read the poems, some of which were dated. Those that appeared to be the most recent had no meaning at all for a man of Patrice's generation. By looking at the unequal lines, formed from words in juxtaposition, one could vaguely sense an implied petulance and even ill humour. But after a time the mind, groping in the darkness, could detect, beneath the clash of words and syllables, a music that was harsh and sardonic, and above all grief-stricken and desperate. It was an authentic cry of anger and near-hatred from a generation that had been brought up in an atmosphere of anxiety, humiliation, privation, and resentment. Chaotic and tangled though it was, this poetry had a sense and power of its own.

Patrice turned through the note-books, recently held together by a piece of ordinary string, and the hands of the clock seemed to turn back for him. The earliest poems were unsophisticated and straightforward. Some of them dealt with family history, as for instance when Patrice Périot had taken his son Hervé, then quite a child, for a trip to the country. Patrice could still remember the hotel they stayed at, and he read the following poem, scribbled on a piece of the hotel note-paper:

Il fait froid dès la porte.
Ici les couloirs ressemblent aux galeries des catacombes.
Une lumière funéraire s'endort dans les couloirs.
Les chambres sentent la dent creuse,
Les armoires sentent le mort,
Les tables de nuit sentent le pot.
Les cuvettes sont pleines de poils qu'on n'a pas apportés
    soi-même.
Le voyageur s'assied sur le vieux fauteuil,
Et le désir du néant lui refroidit les jambes.
Une rumeur de jazz en bouteilles monte des profondeurs.
La servante est triste et se plaint d'être seule.
Elle pleure dans l'ombre au fond du corridor. . . .

Patrice closed the folder with a feeling of dismay. His own memories of this pre-war holiday with the youngster were friendly, lively, and happy ones. Now his little companion's private thoughts were revealed to him. 'I should have taken him to Chabot long ago,' he thought; 'Chabot would have taken care of him, might even have cured him. It is really shocking. I can hardly believe that I have failed so signally in my primary duties as a parent.'

He slipped all the manuscripts into a folder, securing them with a band. The newspapers lying on the desk caught his eye and brought him back to the present.

We insist that an inquiry be instituted into the 'person or persons unknown.' We see no reason why the unknown should be regarded as unknowable. We have our own methods and sources of information, and when the Government officials prove themselves to be incapable, it is up to the general public to be vigilant in the maintenance of law and order. . . .

Patrice Périot read this without fully taking it in. Could there be any imaginable connection between this bombast and the poetry of a lost child, the bitter memories of a father in mourning. His reflections were interrupted by a knock at the door, and before he had time to collect himself Clement Romanil came in.

Romanil sank into the arm-chair, as he always did after climbing the four flights of stairs. He waved his hand in friendly greeting but was too busy getting his breath back to utter a word. The two old friends looked at each other in silence, and Patrice Périot raised his eyebrows as if to say: 'I know that you wish me well, but my heart is heavy and I am full of care. . . .'

'I have called for you,' said Clement Romanil.

'Where are you going to take me?' Patrice made a gesture of weariness. 'Everything turns to dust and ashes in my mouth.'

'Quite so,' Romanil replied. 'Being rather depressed myself I thought we should get on well together. So I'm going to dig you out, drag you away from your troubles, and take you out to dinner with me. . . .'

Patrice made a sign of refusal but the old man went on: 'Stop worrying! We're going out to dinner, just the two of us, so stop worrying. We'll go to a little wine-merchant's place I know near the Porte Saint-Ouen, or somewhere else, if you prefer. There'll be no one there, and nothing much to eat, but that's not the point. You're coming out of your lair for an hour or two, and I'm not going to utter a word, not a single word.'

Patrice Périot stood up without answering, and went to tell Mme Hortense that he would be going out. On his return he noticed that Romanil was reading the papers spread out on the desk. Since Romanil made no comment Patrice kept his mouth shut. Hat in hand he pushed Romanil into the hall.

The silence lasted while the two friends were walking down the rue Lamarck. Eventually Patrice broke it with a sigh.

'Of course you know that all this sensational stuff in the press is completely off the mark. Hervé was a sick man, though I didn't realize it myself at the time, to my everlasting regret. Now my son's poor ghost is being exploited for heaven knows what purpose.'

Clement Romanil kept his bargain of silence, and so Patrice continued: 'You are my only friend in court.

You know that I have never asked for anything but justice and peace. . . .'

'Oh yes,' growled Romanil; 'I know all that. You don't expect much, do you? You're not difficult, are you?'

'You're just making fun of me.'

'On the contrary, I admire you. Indeed I admire you and I pity you in the same breath. Look, there's a quiet-looking pub, let's go in. No excuses. Not hungry? Nor am I, but we'll eat all the same, if only to keep the glands secreting, and the old engine ticking over. Right! You were saying just now that all you ask is justice and peace. Some programme! You wanted to plunge into public and political life, and now you profess to be surprised at what it costs you. There is a large element of pride in all philanthropists. . . . But I mustn't carry on like this.'

'Please do go on,' said Patrice Périot, amused by Romanil's heated eloquence and smiling in spite of himself.

'All right, since you wish me to . . . it is sheer pride to imagine that one can meddle in other people's affairs and solve all their problems, or pacify angry and embittered men.'

Patrice Périot took up the challenge. 'Suppose that one does nothing at all, suppose that one is always merely an impassive spectator? That indicates not pride but shame.'

'Thanks, old man, that's one for me.'

'It's not, as you well know.'

'I'll take it to myself, all the same.'

'For you, Romanil, who are one of the pure of heart, I have nothing but praise and gratitude.'

204

'Praise! I know what that's worth. I've had some. Talking about pride, most of the gentlemen who keep the conscience of the world in their pockets are monsters of pride. I know them through and through. They may not preserve their nail-clippings for distribution, like Mahomet, but that's only because they've never thought of it. I shouldn't be surprised if they autograph their toilet-rolls for their admirers.'

'You're disgusting.'

'I'm merely honest according to my lights. I can afford to be. I am a free man.'

'Romanil! You are no more free than I am.'

'Well, I never!'

'You belong to the party of the party-less, and are therefore partisan. Who, I ask you, can escape ties of some sort? Explorers, you may say, climbing Kilimanjaro or Aconcagua, or travelling the Polar regions. But all those people are simply enjoying a truce, so to speak, and they can be recalled at any moment by radio-telegram to declare themselves.'

'You certainly know how to argue. In my opinion the real saint is the man who humbles himself, who keeps out of the limelight, and doesn't even know that he is doing so.'

'An idiot, in fact!'

'If you like to put it so. The genuine saint, the only saint, the only just man, is after all a kind of idiot. Blessed are the poor in spirit! And to think that I am supposed to be taking you out of yourself by talking nonsense!'

'That's precisely what you are doing, old boy.'

Whenever the two old men met they slipped back naturally into their youthful ways of talking, an easy

205

inarticulate style that was more or less unintelligible to other people. They spent the rest of their dinner together in a burlesque exchange of controversial ideas on every subject under the sun, to the surface of which, every now and then, bobbed up their real experience of life. Romanil was satisfied. He had intended to rescue his friend from useless introspection and he had succeeded. On their way out he took Patrice's arm.

'Stick to your guns,' he said. 'The French genius is aggressive and destructive. As a nation we are no respecters of persons, and that applies to you like the rest. We assassinate our great men——'

'Our great men! Come off it!'

'If you don't like the word great, let us say famous. Take the Germans. They know how to build up a national hero. Out of half a Victor Hugo they would have made three Goethes. They have the recipe. . . .'

The two men stopped for a moment outside Patrice's house before separating and Patrice felt his old misery flooding over him.

'If that's fame,' he murmured, 'give me disgrace every time.'

'Don't talk rubbish,' said Romanil. 'You don't know the first thing about disgrace. There's still time for you to learn, however—and for me too.'

On this note they parted and Patrice went up to his fourth-floor flat. Crossing the hall he saw a light in Christine's room. He was about to walk past on tip-toe, but Christine was too quick for him, and she opened the door.

'Will you come in for a moment, daddy?' she asked in her cool, colourless voice.

Patrice went in and sat on the end of the bed.

Seeing that he remained silent, Christine announced enigmatically: 'We know what to hope for. . . .'

'Indeed? With regard to what, exactly?'

'With regard to Hervé's death. The criminals will be run to earth, and in the very near future.'

Patrice was suddenly seized with all his old anxiety. 'Listen, child,' he said, 'I haven't said anything to you for very obvious reasons. You know, or you ought to know, that your poor brother killed himself.'

'That is the official story. But truth will out.'

Patrice got up angrily. 'Don't be absurd,' he growled. 'Surely I am in a better position than any one else to know what I ought to think about my son's death.'

The girl said nothing, her face set in an obstinate expression. Patrice shrugged his shoulders, muttering as he left: 'The inference is that truth is non-existent, and that no one knows, or ever will know, anything about anything.'

CHAPTER XIII

ON Tuesday morning Patrice was thoroughly
upset by the newspapers, which he tried
without much success to wade through systematically. 'My eyes fly from column to column,' he
thought, 'and then from paragraph to paragraph,
and what's the use of it all? Is it not enough that I
have lost my son? Am I not even to be left in peace
to drink my cup of bitterness to its dregs? Romanil
reminds me, in his friendly fashion, that I am now a
public man and that I therefore have only myself to
blame. But I cannot see that I am a public figure in
that sense. All I have done is to proclaim my love
for my fellow countrymen, and declare myself on the
side of the oppressed in the name of justice and peace
. . . and yet my life is as shattered as if I had preached
discord and destruction. What a mad world it is!
The very people who call themselves my friends
exacerbate my grief, and rush to my defence when all
I ask of them is silence. They sing my praises when
all I ask is to be forgotten.'

Having read the morning's delivery of newspapers
Patrice Périot resolved to devote himself to his work.

He cleared his desk of superfluous papers and opened a large folder entitled *Physiology and Philosophy of the Reflexes*. He made an effort to concentrate on his note-books, with the graphs and figures summarizing his experimental findings, but his mind wandered. From his pocket-book he drew an envelope and carefully re-read Hervé's last short letter, more in anger than in sorrow. 'The whole thing is crazy and intolerable. I feel as if I am being thrown to the lions along with the poor little corpse of my own child.'

The morning wore on. Abandoning his resolve Patrice Périot reconnected the telephone and called a number. As soon as he obtained a reply he said in clear and deliberate tones: 'This is Professor Patrice Périot. I want to speak to M. Gérin-Labrit, editor of *Solidarity*.' A girl's voice replied to the effect that she would inform M. Gérin-Labrit, who was now in his office. After a short interval the young tele-phonist spoke again. 'M. Gérin-Labrit much regrets that he cannot come to the telephone, as he is in conference.' That seemed to be quite reasonable, and so Patrice Périot went on: 'Could M. Gérin-Labrit drop in to see me to-day? I am not very well and shall not be going out.' The voice faded into a murmur in the background and then came back again with the words: 'M. Gérin-Labrit is very sorry, but he will not be able to leave his desk all day. If Professor Périot can call here, M. Gérin-Labrit will expect the professor at five p.m., when he will be glad to listen to what the professor has to say.'

'Tell him I will be there at five o'clock this evening,' said Patrice Périot.

'There you are,' he thought, replacing the telephone.

'Only a little while ago, when they wanted something from me, Gérin-Labrit and his friends were coming to see me at all hours of the day. Now the roles are reversed. I am on the asking end, and they have dropped their respectful politeness. What is it exactly that I am asking? The most difficult thing in the world—just that I should be left alone to suffer in my own way. I am asking to be spared an unfounded scandal and that I should not be involved in this undignified wrangle—because unfortunately these offensive statements will not go unchallenged.'

The thought of the coming interview so upset him that he frittered away the best part of the day. He caught a glimpse of Christine, who seemed to exude silence, and he had a short talk with Thierry, who was spending all his time at the university getting ready for his examinations. For some reason Thierry was not as effusive as usual; he seemed to have withdrawn into himself, and would not say anything about what he was really thinking. As he parted from his father, before embracing him, he looked at him long and earnestly in a way that moved Patrice more than any other demonstration could.

At about four o'clock he left home, alone, for the Bourse district, walking by way of the back streets where he would be least likely to meet any one who knew him. These little streets had their own feverish activity, and Patrice fell to dreaming at random. 'The side streets of Carthage, of Memphis, of Athens, or Rome must have been just as crowded and noisy, but our modern technical civilization bids fair to inflame every passion, every ambition, every desire, every folly. I am afraid of falling out of love with this world, although I still hope to interpret its outward behaviour, if not its inner nature, but I am still more afraid of being rejected by its hectic social order. Nevertheless, in my calmer moments I am still happy in my work, and I do not feel unworthy of my honourable task. Why on earth should all these fanatics send their emissaries after me into the very privacy of my hearth and home?'

Gérin-Labrit's offices were on the fifth floor of a large modern block in the Halles district. They were served by an express lift which rushed up and down, creating a terrific draught as it did so. Patrice Périot had never before penetrated this strange sanctuary of modern journalism, and he felt a bit lost as soon as he was across the threshold. He had, moreover, to contend with his feelings of shyness and uneasiness. A young lad, who smoked cigarettes while he worked the lift, conducted him to an office where four stenographers were working in a din that resembled the crackle of musketry.

'Wait here,' he said, 'while I let the editor know that you have come.'

Patrice Périot had to wait for at least ten minutes, looking like a beggar at the gates of some foreign palace. Sweat broke out on his forehead, and he kept twisting his hat in his hands, after the manner of those who seek a favour.

Suddenly the door opened and Gérin-Labrit appeared, carrying a bundle of papers in his left hand.

'I am so sorry that they have kept you waiting here, my dear professor. But what can you expect? Our people, as you know, are not well enough off to run to lounges and waiting-rooms. Come this way, Professor Périot.'

He led the way, keeping up a running conversation with exaggerated protestations of friendship and respect, and showed Patrice into a small office, its walls hung with portraits of famous revolutionaries.

Then, without even giving Patrice Périot time to get his breath he turned his handsome emaciated face towards him and went straight into the offensive, as was his habit. 'My dear professor, I hope you realize that your friends are still your friends, despite temporary differences of opinion, and that they will leave no stone unturned to help you in this tragic affair.'

Patrice Périot was so put out by this exordium that he spent more than a minute in complete silence without finding any possible answer, and he even began to wonder why he had ever been so rash as to let himself in for this interview. 'Gérin is very smart,' he thought, 'a good talker with plenty of courage. He intends to tie me up in knots and disarm me. I should never have come to see him. I should have—I should have . . .'

While his thoughts were thus at the mercy of every stray wind Patrice Périot suddenly summoned a sort of brutality that in his case was akin to courage at critical moments, and said in one breath: 'My dear Gérin-Labrit, I have come in the name of the friendship to which you have just alluded, to ask you to put a stop to the press campaign which you have initiated without my consent, and which is now being taken up by the rest of the newspaper world.'

Gérin-Labrit picked up a paper lying on his desk; apparently he had been reading it before the professor arrived. 'Just a moment!' He ran his eye over the print with an expression of disdain and disgust, holding the paper with the tips of his fingers as if it would soil them. Then he took a red pencil and marked two columns before throwing the offending organ on his desk again.

'Now then,' he went on, 'you have obviously read the excellent article in this morning's issue of our paper by our mutual friend and collaborator Dupré-Mollard, who has been put in charge of this inquiry. We are now in a position to state categorically that your unfortunate son has been foully murdered by the Royalist clique of ex-service men well known to the special police as "Gaëtan 4" group, from the name of their leader, who has been condemned to an ignominious death no less than three times since the liberation. . . . Satisfied? Eh?'

Patrice had risen to his feet in a state of violent agitation. For a moment he stood erect and motionless, and then without uttering a word sank down into his chair and sighed.

'It's all a pack of lies. Utter, nauseating rubbish.'

Gérin-Labrit remained unperturbed. 'Despite our desire for justice and national security we were on the point of abandoning our campaign, because of the pain all the publicity would cause you, and of leaving it to the police to take the necessary steps after our warning. But now our opponents, with indescribable impudence, are spreading the story in their filthy papers that young Hervé Périot was secretly executed by the Communists. Two reasons are given. The first is that following a difference of opinion between Professor Périot and the genuine revolutionaries—these gentlemen seem to be well informed and one cannot but ask who their informant is—the revolutionaries would no longer have any motive of gain in that quarter. These are their own words. The second reason, according to these gentlemen, is that the Communists, in view of Professor Périot's well-known "advanced" opinions, would have an excellent pretext for fixing the crime on their opponents. Such is the theory propounded by the evening paper, just arrived on my desk, that has the temerity to call itself *The Real France*. Take it and read it for yourself. As I told you, professor, our intention up to this very morning was to call off our inquiry and let the veil of silence fall. But this dastardly attack by our common enemy makes it incumbent on us to take the matter further. It is a question of honour, yours and ours.'

Patrice Périot cast a horrified glance on the paper that had just been put in his hand. He could not bring himself to read even two sentences consecutively. Eventually he replaced it on Gérin's desk, breathing deeply in an endeavour to regain his self-control. At last he succeeded in steadying his voice.

'The journalists who write such infamous stuff are despicable.'

Gérin-Labrit nodded his head gently, like a schoolmaster encouraging a pupil to say his lessons. 'Go on, professor, go on.'

'I'm going on all right, don't you worry. These despicable creatures deceive themselves and everybody else. My poor boy was not killed by the Communists.'

'I am glad to hear you say that.'

Patrice Périot ignored the sarcastic tones with which Gérin-Labrit coloured his last remark, and went on calmly, his head on one side as if to think more clearly.

214

'No, my poor boy was not killed by your friends, but neither was he killed by your enemies.'

'Really?' Gérin's manner was judicial. 'You surprise me. And how do you know? Were you by any chance a witness of your son's last moments?'

Patrice Périot looked steadily at his questioner. 'I am certain that my son Hervé was not assassinated, and that it is pointless to search for criminals.'

'I do not know what proofs you have,' replied Gérin-Labrit, 'but I do claim to know something of you. Great as your spirit of appeasement is, I cannot imagine for a moment that you will take a line of least resistance such as the hypothesis that it was an ordinary suicide. Your son was healthy in mind and body.'

Patrice Périot seemed to be rapidly withdrawing within himself, and Gérin-Labrit went on in icy tones: 'You have devoted your life to the service of truth. At least, that's what you claim in your own writings. I cannot believe that you would blind yourself to the truth about the death of your own son, when disinterested parties are prepared to reveal it to you.'

Patrice rose to his feet, frowning. 'If I were in the slightest doubt I should call in the law myself.'

'From now on the dispute no longer concerns you alone, and we can only regret that we are not to have the benefit of your advice.'

'Good-bye,' said Patrice Périot, and left without another word.

He let the lift go, preferring the privacy of the staircase, and hurried down to the street. It was a warm and lovely evening in early June, but Patrice Périot saw nothing of all this and walked the pavement like an escaped criminal, afraid of recognition. With lowered head he dived among the cars at the risk of his life, until he reached his home and shut himself up in his room. He sat in his arm-chair until dark, when he heard the telephone ring. He had omitted to disconnect it after making his appointment with Gérin-Labrit.

As Mme Hortense was out he went into the next room, intending merely to put an end to the insistent ringing. Then it occurred to him that neither Thierry nor Christine were home yet, and he picked up the receiver. 'Hallo, hallo,' said an unknown voice, 'is that Professor Périot?'

'Yes, speaking. What do you want?'

'I am the Baron de Vivier-Salabert. I want an appointment with you to demonstrate an invention of mine for acclimatizing palm-trees as far north as latitude 44 in seaboard countries. It's a marv——'

Patrice Périot replaced the receiver with a sigh. A little later the telephone rang again. He shrugged his shoulders and disconnected without even putting it to his ear.

In the evening, after supper, Patrice Périot was alone in his office, a prey to dark thoughts, when the door opened and Christine came in. She switched on the light, and without saying a word laid a copy of *The Real France* on her father's desk, having red-pencilled the notorious article, just as had been done elsewhere earlier in the day. Périot waited till Christine had gone and threw the paper into the waste-paper basket. 'The world has gone crazy,' he muttered. To complete his humiliation and distress a coarse comic song of his student days came back to haunt him, one that he and his pals used to yell together, a meaningless jingle he had never even thought of for fifty years, rising from the murky depths of the past for no reason at all except perhaps some basic rhythm or association of ideas. 'The world is crazy, and all the people in it. I shall end up as mad as the rest of them.'

Early next morning Maurice Ribeyrol came to see him, and proved to be more communicative than Christine. The young man brought the daily newspapers with him, having picked them up from the concierge and read them on his way up. He threw them on the desk, stammering with rage.

'We have made our reply,' he said, 'and now they are counter-attacking.'

Patrice Périot spoke sharply. 'I hope, Maurice, that you haven't committed the unpardonable blunder of making any sort of reply to these lucubrations.'

Ribeyrol could not conceal his anger. 'No, of course not. When I say "we" I mean those whose opinions I share, and who are now being unjustly vilified. Read this morning's article, father.'

'Well, it is evident that you are all determined not to leave me in ignorance of this devastating nonsense. Christine shows me the articles in *The Real France* and you make me read the diatribes in *Solidarity*. Every avenue of escape is systematically denied me.'

'I should have thought, father, that you ought to be the first to know what is being said about a member of your family. You ought to follow closely both the manœuvres of your enemies and the reactions of your friends.'

'My friends!' cried Patrice Périot furiously. 'I will thank you, my boy, not to talk to me about either friends or enemies. I disown them both, whether of the left or of the right. As far as I am concerned they are a collection of hotheads in the grip of hate. My son is dead and, as I have already told you, he was not murdered and this story of an assassination is just a crazy invention. My son is dead and they are tearing each other to ribbons about a poor little ghost, whose last thoughts, if the word is permissible in this connection, I know. All right. Let them fight it out, since it amuses them! When the sound and fury are spent, calm will be restored.'

Maurice Ribeyrol began to back towards the door with the parting shot: 'You are making very light of a controversy that may well affect all our lives.'

Patrice was on the point of following his cross-grained son-in-law to remonstrate with him for his rudeness and egoism. But he refrained. He felt as if he had reached the end of his courage, while everything around him, even his children and their associates, conspired to expose him to shame. Fortunately there was Thierry, but Thierry seemed to have vanished in the storm clouds. What had become of his beloved Thierry? Was it possible that Thierry was not at his father's side when he was so urgently needed?

Among the letters Patrice received that evening was one typed and left unsigned. In polished legal phrases, devoid of all verbal offensiveness or coarseness, the anonymous correspondent informed Professor Périot that his daughter Christine (in politics Vera Périot) was Gérin-Labrit's mistress. The letter was short, but it contained information of the type referred to as 'chapter and verse,' that is to say it gave the address of the flat where the lovers met and even the actual time of their rendezvous.

Patrice Périot, who had long considered himself to be invulnerable to anonymous attacks, was momentarily so deeply wounded that he could not contain himself. He paced first his study and then his bedroom. He had a wild desire to smash the furniture, tear up his manuscripts, burn his notes, and then set fire to the house. . . . The realization that he had been robbed of all balance and common sense so mortified him that eventually he sat down to think things out. His family life, so important to him, was in effect a total failure. One of his sons had just committed suicide. One of his daughters, the more intelligent one as no one would dispute, had foolishly given herself to a man who . . . He hunted round in his mind for suitably insulting expressions, only to realize the poverty of his vocabulary in this respect.

He refused dinner and remained seated at his desk, in the dark, bemoaning his woes. Late in the evening he heard footsteps outside, and tiptoed to the door. There was a light in the hall and he saw Christine.

'Can you spare me a moment?' he said. 'I want to talk to you.'

The girl came in, put down her hand-bag, coat, and gloves, and went over to her father who had just switched on the little desk-lamp, which served to illuminate the desk without revealing completely his troubled face.

'Sit down a minute,' he said.

It was a long time since the conversations between Patrice and his daughter Christine had contained anything remotely resembling warmth or candour or affectionate confidence. Christine discouraged any such sentiments by her attitude, and Patrice always felt repressed or shy in the presence of his little witch-doctor.

'I should like,' he said, speaking with studied calm, 'to show you a letter I have received this evening. I do so with considerable hesitation, but not to show it to you would be to risk the loss of what little peace of mind I have left under the present stresses. So read this, child.'

With these words he handed Christine the letter. She gave one glance at it and said decisively: 'It is anonymous. What are you doing, daddy, reading anonymous letters?'

'My dear child, I am living in a state of absolute torment, and I am ready to grasp at anything, however disreputable, that will throw light on my situation.'

Christine read the letter without the slightest show of emotion and put it back on the desk.

'It is not true,' she said calmly, and seeing that her father waited for her to go on, with an almost hopeful look in his eyes, she added: 'As a matter of fact I have a lover, since the subject has been raised, but he is not Gérin-Labrit. I admire Gérin-Labrit as a writer and as a speaker and a leader. But I don't like him—how shall I put it?—he revolts me physically.'

There was a long silence. Patrice Périot was reluctant to admit, even to himself, that this confidence, offered so quietly and cynically, shattering though it was, nevertheless brought him immense relief. 'I have not brought you up properly,' he murmured. 'Ever since your mother died you have been neglected. I ought—I ought to have found a husband for you.'

220

'No, daddy, no!' said Christine in her level tones. 'No, I tell you! Your regrets are completely unfounded. I could get married. I could marry my—— Oh, you don't know him, and there's no point in my telling you his name. My reason for not marrying him is that I have no wish to do so. I am twenty-five, and I know what I am doing. I am living my life in the way I intend, as a free agent.'

On a sudden impulse she picked up the letter again, coolly, and scrutinized the typing with an expert eye. 'I wonder if you have ever seen any of Maurice Ribeyrol's business letters, which he types in his office? No? Well, he has a Swiss typewriter of a very distinctive kind, and it's the only machine I know that types "and" as a single letter in that particular style.' When Patrice said nothing Christine went on, in level unemotional tones, with that astonishing self-control which her father sometimes envied her: 'Don't get it into your head that I am going to have a row with Maurice Ribeyrol or to bother my head about him. He is a nonentity. I may bring myself to thank him one of these days, because through him you now know something you have a right to know, something I have been hesitating to tell you myself, since your ideas about life differ so profoundly from mine. We do not speak the same language.'

There was a long silence and then the little witch-doctor got up to go. As she left the room she said: 'These news stories are beginning to take on a sinister aspect. Try and put your mind on them, daddy. They are more interesting and more serious than my personal affairs.'

Actually this conversation disturbed Patrice Périot

so deeply that for the next few days he could not concentrate his attention on the controversy in the papers. He had not the courage to face the fact that Christine's pronouncements, far from upsetting him, brought him considerable relief. Twenty times a day he beat his breast in mortification. Naturally he had not the same views of life as the younger generation. Marry off Christine! It was an old-fashioned idea belonging to a world that had gone, a bourgeois expedient. During his wife's lifetime they had seen their daughter Edwige safely married. This conventional and outwardly normal procedure, though he would not admit it openly, had not given him the slightest satisfaction. He had given his lovely girl to a querulous sarcastic man, a man for whom he had never succeeded in feeling a grain of affection, to Ribeyrol who aroused in him a secret and bitter, almost physical, jealousy, Ribeyrol who did not even know how to make his wife happy. Could he be surprised, then, that Christine should use unexpected methods of her own in pursuit of the wayward myth of happiness? Although she was so different a person from himself he yet admired his enigmatic Christine for her scintillating intelligence, and the thought that she should have fallen for Gérin-Labrit had been unbearable and had caused him hours of bitter suffering. Then the knowledge that the seducer was not Gérin-Labrit had brought him sudden relief. The great thing was that Gérin-Labrit, Gérin of the long nervous hands, the steely glance, the inexorable logic, should inspire in Christine that feeling of repulsion which she had admitted from the outset. As to the other man, whoever he was, some sort of arrangement might still be possible. Time would show. There were many such illicit relationships which appeared in the end to be more honourable than some formal marriages. . . .'

Patrice's thoughts went milling round in this key while he paced the room like a wild animal in a cage. His anger flared up and he cried: 'Oh, that I could get through life without ever needing to see them again! Fortunately my blood-pressure is low—my prostate is another matter. Yes, I know that if I were to die they would be sorry. But pity is no substitute for love and respect.' A thought struck him and he beat his forehead. 'Thierry! Thierry! How unfair and ungrateful I am! Actually I see very little of Thierry nowadays. He comes home late and goes quietly to bed. Of course he's taking his exams, I know. Yet when we meet he gives me a filial kiss— one look from him bowls me over. He always seems to be expecting miracles, whereas I have based my whole life on the distrust of them.'

These contradictory and confused ruminations prevented Patrice Périot from thinking about the other drama which was then exercising Paris opinion, nourished by the gutter press, with himself as the laughing-stock. Several times a day Maurice broke into his solitude and left newspapers, marked in red pencil, on his desk. These occasions were alternated by visits from Christine, who came and threw a different lot of papers in the same place on the same desk. The two adversaries might have been playing some silent and ruthless game of cards. As soon as they were both out of the room Patrice Périot gathered all the newspapers together and crammed them angrily into the waste-paper basket. When he went to the window he

223

could see his grandchildren playing on the balcony across the way. It was a well-built and spacious balcony and the two boys were riding their fairy-cycles round it. Patrice admired their grace and dexterity, and their presence of mind. He let the curtain fall and thought: 'I am afraid they'll get hurt! How idiotic! They're amazingly skilful. Obviously, in the modern world, it pays better to be skilful than cautious.'

On Saturday evening, after having kept to his room for several days, Patrice had a visit from Romanil. The latter's usual good-humoured expression was gone, and he was looking depressed and anxious. 'I have not seen you since the beginning of the week,' he said. 'What are you playing at? You are torturing yourself. However, I am not going to talk about that. Possibly you do not even read the papers—not that I blame you—it's an attitude that's open to question, but it's defensible. But in case your children haven't told you——'

'I am completely fed up with my children—with some of them, at any rate. For the time being I prefer not to listen to anything they say.'

'Very well then, I am going to put you wise. Don't worry, I shall be as concise as possible. The right-wing die-hards and the left-wing extremists are at the moment engaged in a fierce battle over your son's grave, a revolting, mud-slinging contest in which I verily believe you count for nothing, but which in my opinion is thoroughly bad for the moral health of our unhappy country, already unstable enough, heaven knows. I can tell you now, since you neither know nor are willing to find out for yourself, that Gérin-Labrit's paper—I can't bring myself to call him your

224

friend—is organizing a great public demonstration
with a procession which will stretch from the Bastille
to the Place de la Nation. Yesterday the Government
issued a statement to the effect that the police authorities
were not failing and would not fail in their duties, and
that any disorderly behaviour in public would be
sternly repressed. The left-wing papers have replied
this morning that the demonstration will take place
in the name of a truly vigilant and impartial order of
social peace and justice. These are their own words.
The so-called reactionary press are talking of staging
a counter-demonstration, and are claiming police pro-
tection to quell any disorderly elements.'

Clement Romanil spread his hands on his knees and
waited.

'Why are you telling me all this?' asked Patrice
Périot in a low voice.

'So that you shall not remain in ignorance. After
all, there may be some part for you to play in this
morbid comedy.'

Patrice Périot hunched his shoulders and kept them
hunched as if to show his powerlessness to act. The
two friends remained silent for several minutes, and
finally Clement Romanil took his departure.

It must have been past eight in the evening when
Patrice heard Thierry's voice. The young man
bounded into his father's room. He was obviously
excited, despite his look of affectionate concern.

'Now I can be with you again,' he said, 'for I have
done all I had to do. I don't want to worry you, but
I must tell you that the concierge has reached the end
of her tether—she is having to cope with about fifty
reporters a day. You are not aware of this because

P   225

Mme Hortense has been performing prodigies, but she can be very bad-tempered, can Hortense, despite her good qualities. I am going to have dinner with you, even if you don't eat a thing, and I am not going to let you out of my sight from now on.'

'I was thinking,' Patrice Périot ventured nervously, 'of asking you to go instead of me with a letter to Uncle Gustave to-morrow. . . .'

'I understand, dad. I'll go on Monday. I'm going to spend the whole day to-morrow with you, and if you get bored I shall read to you. I'll choose a nice book. You know how well I can read the books I like—at least that's what I'm told. Now come along and eat—and not merely to please old Hortense!'

CHAPTER XIV

SUNDAY began in an atmosphere of unusual calm, the lull before the storm, Patrice thought. At an early hour he heard someone moving, and guessed that Thierry was going out to hear a low mass. The thought that Christine was probably at home did not worry him unduly—he needed time to collect himself before thinking over Christine's problem, and he made several attempts to swallow his scruples and accept the situation.

He drank a cup of tea, and then sat down at his much-neglected desk. Day after day he had sat thus, and he had not been near his laboratory for over a week, contenting himself with telephoning to his assistants to the effect that he was unwell. Who could blame him? He was on the point of bringing a long spell of research to an end by writing the most important work of his life. Would he be allowed to complete this task? And if not, did it mean that all his work would be wasted? None of his pupils was capable of turning out a complete and coherent account of all that had been ceaselessly fermenting in his own brain.

To-day would be clear of newspapers and letters.

What a welcome relief! He found some escape from his own mental insecurity and distress in fantasies of universal upheavals, cosmic disasters, floods, volcanoes, and earthquakes.

It must have been about ten o'clock when Thierry called out from the hall to know whether he might come in. Patrice Périot flung the door open and Thierry came in to give his father a kiss. He had the smooth fresh complexion of adolescence such as men worn out with work and care cannot contemplate without a feeling of wonderment mixed with regret and pity and a contagious access of confidence and hope. He no longer had the look of innocence and smiling delight which in his infancy had made his mother call him her 'angel-face,' but he was as calm and fresh and pure as a morning in June.

'Don't get up, dad,' he said. 'I don't want to disturb you. I'll stay around, or work in my room, whichever you like, but I might as well have a moment of your company.'

'Stay here, son,' said Patrice Périot, in a voice that expressed so much gratitude that it brought a blush to the young man's cheeks.

Thierry sat easily and naturally on a corner of the desk. 'Listen, dad,' he said, 'I have just been reading the various books of yours which you have given me from time to time—I didn't want to tackle them until I thought I could understand them. Now I have read them and I believe I do understand what you're getting at. I hope you'll forgive me for having left them so long—it was not indifference, believe me—rather that I was doubtful of my ability. . . .'

'But I have never held that against you, Thierry.

228

The problems that have occupied me all my life are in the territory which lies between experimental science and philosophy, between a branch of science of which you know very little, and a philosophy from which you, with your religious gifts, would find it very hard to derive any mental satisfaction.'

'That's just where you're wrong, dad. As regards the technical or laboratory side I have nothing to say, and I will take care to say nothing, but I think I understand your philosophy, and I do not believe we are irreconcilably separated.'

'Thank you, my son, but allow me to sound a warning note! Do not let yourself be carried away by love or affection, or by what the politicians call "expansionist zeal." I do not suppose you have any clear recollection of Charles Nicolle. He used to come to Jouy to spend the day with me occasionally. You were very small then—he died in 1936. Later in his life, during a holiday in the mountains, he met a very brilliant Jesuit. Nicolle was a Normandy man, from Rouen, a man of very subtle intelligence, and feeling himself ill and grievously perplexed by the problems of life and death, he asked the Jesuit whether, in order to be reconciled to the religion his mother had taught him, it would suffice to concede that all biological phenomena could not be explained on purely rational grounds. Naturally the Jesuit, himself a man of great understanding, replied that that should suffice. Shortly afterwards Nicolle died, and no sooner was he dead than well-meaning souls began talking of his conversion. When my friend and colleague, Lucien Cuénot, writes that the doctrine of evolution is simple and straightforward, but that it does not explain everything and that cosmic evolution has a meaning—if my memory serves me these are Cuénot's own expressions—and when my friend Cuénot points out that this meaning implies irrational guidance and talks about anti-chance, people immediately label this brilliant and broad-minded man a repentant Christian, a pilgrim on the road to Canossa. That is not very logical.'

While Patrice Périot was speaking he watched his son's attentive and composed expression, and could not help thinking: 'This boy manages me as if I were an elephant. He senses that I am anxious and unhappy, and so he talks about the very things that still interest and excite me, my work and my ideas. He wants to distract me from my suffering, and he succeeds admirably. . . .'

'You need not worry, dad,' said Thierry, speaking with the deliberation, unusual in him, of one who is finding his way, step by step. 'You need not worry. I understand your line of thought. I have too much respect for it, and I find it too interesting, to risk spoiling it by a clumsy interruption. Not so long ago I used to say, foolishly: "You are one of us." I say that no longer.'

'Be more explicit, Thierry.'

'I want to behave reasonably. I'm impatient, and the last thing I want to do is to irritate you or cry wolf in the hope of deflecting you from your path. If one of these days your way crosses mine—I don't say coincides with mine, I should not be such a fool—if your road ever crosses mine I shall make an act of thanksgiving and no one in the world will be happier than me.'

'Dear Thierry!'

Little by little the old man began to feel himself won over. At the beginning of the conversation he had kept listening anxiously, with heart beating fast, for heaven knows what noise or catastrophic news from the outside world. Now young Thierry, with his lisped words and his candid looks and his unselfish enthusiasm, was beginning to lighten his burden and show him the way to peace of mind. And Thierry showed no sign of relaxing his efforts.

'I do not know, dad, whether you are the first of your school of thought to remind us, as you did in your latest book, that we have no positive control over the functioning of our essential organs. That is your theory, isn't it? We feed them, but we can neither stop them, nor speed up, nor retard their action, except by the administration of drugs and poisons. Our only power would be to destroy ourselves—forgive me, but I am trying to get at your meaning. So you see, the ignorant and backward pupil will make no further demands upon you. Furthermore, I am not trying to censor or interpret your thoughts. Put simply, without explanation, they seem to me to be more eloquent and more disturbing than any long philosophic dissertation with notes and appendices.'

'It is extraordinary,' thought Patrice Périot, 'that this boy has discovered the only slant that could break through my misery and make it possible for me to possess my soul in patience. Paradoxically he consoles me in my present misery by talking to me about our eternal misery. He deflects me from contemplating the Périot tragedy by inviting me to explain to him the tragedy of life itself.'

With intermissions the conversational thrust and

parry went on until the end of the morning. The other children had given no sign of interest, or even of their existence, and father and son ate their midday meal quietly together. Thierry, with his affectionate gestures and his naïve yet intensely sincere questionings, kept his father talking continuously.

'I have often talked to you about Charles Nicolle,' said Patrice; 'well, Charles Nicolle used to say that the intelligence of nature has nothing in common with the intelligence of man. And I seem to remember that Daniel Huet, who as Bishop of Avranches was an ecclesiastical authority, made a very similar claim: "God's intelligence is of an entirely different order from man's." I am quoting from memory.'

'But it is in the Bible, father: "For my thoughts are not your thoughts; nor your ways my ways, saith the Lord."'

Patrice Périot nodded assent. 'Yes, everything is to be found in the Bible: hope and fear, peace and conflict.'

After the meal Patrice Périot stretched himself on the divan in his study, and Thierry offered to read out a passage from Pascal entitled: 'Prayer to God for the right attitude in sickness.' In turning through the book Thierry said: 'I haven't read this for two years or more. You realize that it is philosophical rather than devotional reading. Pascal is not a saint, but first and foremost a learned writer.'

He sat on a stool near his father, and began to read slowly and distinctly, pausing after each phrase. '"Lord, who art so good and so gentle in all things, and who art so merciful that not only the successes but the failures of Thy chosen ones are attributable

232

to Thy divine pity, grant me Thy grace to accept the state to which Thy justice has brought me. . . .'"

He read these moving passages until every now and then his father made a signal to him to stop for a moment. Patrice Périot would listen to the distant murmur of the city and then sign to his son to read on. '"But, Lord, what shall I do to invoke the descent of Thy Holy Spirit on this world of sin? Everything that I am is hateful in Thine eyes, and I can find nothing in my heart that could be acceptable to Thee. I see nothing there, Lord, save only my sufferings which bears any resemblance to Thine."'

Patrice Périot turned a look of profound sadness on the young reader, who hid his face behind the book and said: 'It is beautiful, isn't it? And so simple.'

'Go on reading,' the old man begged him.

Thierry read another couple of pages, and he soon noticed that his father's breathing was becoming quiet and even. He lowered his voice and then ceased altogether. He could not tell whether Patrice was asleep or lost in thought. His appearance of perfect calm suggested the approach of death, or at least a renunciation of life. But the old man continued to breathe regularly, and the tie knotted loosely under his chin was moving almost imperceptibly. For two whole hours there was silence, until Patrice emitted a groan. In a low voice Thierry resumed his reading where he had left off. '"Grant, O God, that I may accept every eventuality with equanimity, because we know not for what to pray. . . ."'

Somewhere about six o'clock in the evening Thierry thought he heard a noise in the hall. He put his book down and went out on tiptoe. Patrice Périot rose from the divan, ran his hand through his mop of grey hair, and went to the window, from which he watched the families out for their Sunday evening walks. In a moment or two Thierry came back and shut the door carefully.

'It's Edwige,' he said.

'What did she want?'

'She didn't want anything. She came to give us a bit of news.'

'News?'

At first Thierry made no reply, and Patrice Périot, his hands folded on his breast, walked into his study, and thence to the room crammed with books which they dignified by the name of the library. He picked up the telephone, apparently in extreme exasperation.

'Who are you ringing, dad?'

Patrice Périot replaced the instrument and said, striking one hand against the other: 'I don't know. I haven't the faintest idea.' Then, turning to his son: 'What was the news you were talking about just now? What has happened?'

Thierry went pale. 'Serious news. The demonstration took place, despite police warnings. At the top of the avenue Ledru-Rollin they met a counter-demonstration organized by the society called Guardians of the Real France.'

Thierry hesitated and Patrice Périot said impatiently: 'Yes? Go on, for heaven's sake. What happened? Were there any casualties? Any one killed?'

'According to the radio there were no deaths, but more than a dozen wounded have been taken to the Saint-Antoine Hospital. The police have made about twenty arrests. For the moment it is all over—

Maurice has had a look round and he says that everything seems to be quiet now. They say that there is to be a protest strike to-morrow with a march past the Prefecture of Police and the Palais de Justice.'

Patrice Périot sank into his chair and hid his head in his hands. 'Why?' he cried in a voice of anguish. 'Why? I told them that any agitation would be absurd and criminal, and what is more, absolutely without any justification. If only they would stop fighting over my poor boy's dead body, if only they would leave me in peace, to suffer and to die in my own way!'

He was so prostrated, with his head lying on the desk, so painfully agitated, that Thierry was too frightened to breathe a word. The young man was always rather pale, but gradually his youthful and fine-drawn features hardened, as if under the influence of some inner force. He approached his father gently, and took advantage of one of his moments of exhaustion to say: 'Daddy, give me that letter.'

Patrice Périot raised a haggard face. 'What letter, son?'

'The letter—you know well enough—the letter Hervé left for you.'

The old man looked obstinate. 'I told you, and your sisters, that the letter was of no importance.'

'Exactly. If it is so unimportant there is no reason why you should not let me see it.'

The professor could find no answer to this logic, and after a few ineffective head-shakings he pulled out his wallet, and drew out an envelope which he finally handed to his son. Then he turned on the light and drew the curtain, for the daylight was fading.

Thierry read the letter his father had given him once, then again, then a third time. It was written on a sheet of typing-paper, and the sprawling handwriting covered one side of the paper and half the other side. Frowning, Thierry read and re-read the letter, and appeared to be lost in thought. At last the old man turned round suddenly, stretched out his hands, and said: 'Don't you see, this letter is too simple, too terrifyingly simple. Hervé protests his innocence for no apparent reason. You see that, don't you, Thierry, now you've read the letter. Your brother had contracted a gambling debt—what could be more simple?—what could be more foolish? He owed a hundred thousand francs to people I don't even know or wish to know. You see the position, and how absurd and humiliating it is. Twice he came and asked me to give him a hundred thousand francs. Hervé had not much common sense, as you know, and I didn't take his request very seriously. Incidentally I hadn't got that much money—I am not a rich man, and I have nothing saved up, Thierry. And so I refused him—yes, I refused him point-blank, and probably harshly. I can't remember. I had frequent arguments with him—one more or less, what does it matter?—and then I refused once, and again a second time, to give him those wretched hundred thousand francs. At last he must have suddenly made up his mind to commit suicide. He could have done it for a thousand other reasons; why did he have to go and pin it on that? As you see for yourself, Thierry, the letter is written in such a way as to throw the blame on me. Oh dear, oh dear, oh dear, judging from that letter you'd say that my son is dead because
236

I wouldn't give him a hundred thousand francs I didn't have to give, to pay off a gambling debt to people who weren't even pressing him for the money, because if they had been they would have got in touch directly or indirectly with me.'

Patrice Périot stopped for breath. He was now no longer angry but worn out. He went on in calmer tones: 'I didn't intend to show that letter to any one, not even to Dr. Chabot or my old friend Romanil. It is a particularly unfortunate letter, for it accuses me unjustly. I gave my word of honour to Chabot that Hervé committed suicide, which is true, and that's how the burial permit was arranged. I thought that I could then suffer my grief and humiliation in silence. Apparently not! Apparently the whole world wants to meddle in it! Apparently the whole world knows better than I do how and why my son met his death. And I cannot, I dare not, tell the truth, because I am ashamed to. I don't know what to do, and indeed there is nothing to be done.'

Thierry, his head bent, was gazing vacantly at the desperately unhappy letter, and was on the point of folding it and putting it back in the envelope. Suddenly he threw it on the desk, seized his father by the lapel, and in a voice charged with emotion said: 'Dad, there *is* something to be done. Neither of us knows what yet, but we can and will find out.'

'What do you mean?' said the old man, moved by the burning intensity in the voice.

'Dad, we must ask for help and advice. Don't be ashamed. Kneel down with me and pray.'

Patrice Périot's expression was one of astonishment. 'My dear boy, you must be mad. Pray? Pray to whom? I no longer know how to pray. You can pray, my son, but I—I would not dare. I am not mad—I am very unhappy, but I am not mad.'

'I will teach you, dad, and we will pray together. To pray is simply to ask for help and counsel when we are at the end of our tether. Come on, kneel down with me!'

'My dear boy, I will gladly get on my knees since you ask me, but I tell you that it is an unaccustomed position for me. What do I have to do when I kneel?'

'We will make up a prayer that we can say together. Repeat after me, father: "O Thou whom I know not, but who art my only refuge in this hour of trouble . . ."'

'I will gladly say that,' said Patrice Périot, in broken tones. '"O Thou whom I know not, but who art my only refuge in this hour when I am so miserable . . ."'

'"Grant me Thy counsel and inspiration, help me in my wretchedness to find my light and my way."'

Patrice Périot, childlike, echoed the second phrase.

'Now be silent!' said Thierry.

Silence fell, and Patrice, now completely submissive, watched his son's expression of ecstasy. Thierry was the first to get up, and he took his father by the arm. 'Stand up, stand up!' he said.

Patrice rose to his feet with difficulty. 'I have no idea why I'm doing all this. My knees hurt. What an experience! Please help me back to my seat.'

Thierry led his father back to the arm-chair and knelt beside him. His youthful colour had come back, and he said: 'Now we know what we must do.'

'What, Thierry?'

'You are going to let me copy that letter. I shall make two copies, and you and I will go together to

238

see this gang who are tormenting you and humble ourselves in their presence.'

'How, exactly?'

'By telling the truth.'

Patrice Périot now looked calm, and at the same time completely exhausted. 'Yes, you're right, it's the only possible thing to do. When that is done I hope they'll keep quiet at last, and if they think I'm a bad father it can't be helped. I have been through enough to have expiated my guilt, if guilt it can be called.'

Thierry was sitting at the desk, copying the letter, and from time to time he glanced up. 'I will go and see these madmen myself, and I shall insist on their leaving you alone.' As soon as the copy was ready he went to his father again and whispered: 'There's nothing to be ashamed of, dad; on the contrary, you should be grateful. I'm not asking you to think particularly of Him, or indeed of any one else, for that matter. Look at the sky above you—no one can help doing that—and again I say, be grateful!'

Patrice Périot threw his arms round the boy, as he used to do in the old days, the happy days when he was a young father, and said: 'My first thanks are due to you, my son. Now have it your own way; do what you can; but watch out! Beware of all these people, beware of everything and everybody.'

CHAPTER XV

SURROUNDED on all sides by the exuberant foliage of June, Patrice Périot said to himself: 'Green undoubtedly contains within itself a quality of rest and peace, an effect which is difficult to explain and must originate in the retina or in the visual centres. But for green to have its full effect the human animal must be left to itself, free from the interference of reason. It makes me laugh when people talk glibly about the great peace of nature. Except where man succeeds in establishing by force some sort of order, I see only cruel and horrible confusion. Battle, murder, and sudden death everywhere. Everything is either on the attack or on the defensive, and slavery and oppression are rampant. And we, with our facile talk of justice and equality, behave very much like the insidious bindweed and the ubiquitous wild clematis. I have spent four whole days here in nothing but slaughter—flies, mosquitoes, moths, gnats. We have even had to repel an alarming invasion of ants. There was a time when all that did not bother me, and I was only too ready to defend myself, but latterly I have lost confidence. I am past suffering any more. All the same, I ought to pull myself together. I believe I could be like Thierry and make acts of thanksgiving, except that the necessary grace is denied me. And what is grace except a marvellous blindness, a miraculous folly, a total abdication of all intellectual functions?'

While making his way to the house Patrice Périot mentally reviewed the events of the past week. On Sunday night he had lived through some hours of utter despair. Then, towards midnight, Thierry had come back in a state of high exaltation. He had seen and talked with Gérin-Labrit. He had read him the copy of the letter, and far from begging favours he had spoken up boldly as the protagonist of truth and wisdom. The same evening he had been to see the people of the opposite camp, had heaped reproaches on their heads, and had returned from the interview with the radiant look of a youthful Daniel emerging from the lions' den. And Patrice had honestly thought that, reassuring as Thierry's confidence was, it would all amount to nothing, and that he, Patrice Périot, would have abased himself and beaten his breast in vain; that a mad world would listen to nothing, that everything was foul and corrupt, that the debased passion for publicity would override any probability of a peaceful solution, that the modern age was like that for better or for worse, and that to put up with it any longer would be beyond his powers.

But to his great surprise, either as a result of Thierry's strategy or through the firm intervention of the authorities, peace had come suddenly, as it always does when the press decides to bury a scandal and suppress all further references to it. A few innocuous lines had appeared here and there to the effect that inquiries had been made and that there was no reason to suspect foul play, after which the reading public lost interest, and soon their attention was diverted by other newspaper stunts, and they forgot all about the tasty morsel that had so recently been offered for their delectation.

Thierry was radiant. He was constantly at his father's side, saying: 'What did I tell you! Our prayers have been heard!' Patrice nodded his assent, but he was filled with unutterable weariness. At the first signs of calm, when reporters were no longer bombarding the house, when press photographers were no longer lying in wait for him at the corner of the rue Damremont, and when he could replace the telephone without having his ears split by incessant ringing, he had left Paris and fled to Jouy. Walking behind the wheelbarrow which bore his luggage he thought: 'I don't know what's happened to my physical mechanism, but I have grown twenty years older in a matter of days. I am shuffling along like Pierquin. My heart first stops and then races. Extra systoles, of course. These people have been the death of me, for which I should be thankful. It's only a short step now to my last long rest.'

He had spent four days in these peaceful surroundings, but had found no inner peace. The very waves of silence broke on his melancholy without dispersing it. 'I shall never get over this blow,' he thought, again and again. 'I shall never get over it, chiefly because I haven't the slightest desire to.'

Such were his thoughts as he paced the garden paths, now largely run wild, but his eyes retained the questioning look of the skilled observer. 'Bergson has said that sleep is a loss of interest. Where does that leave us, for death is equally a loss of interest? I long for death, and the solace which it brings, yet I am just as interested in things as ever. But have I earned the right to death's kindly embrace? Here, for example, the gardener has planted convolvulus, at the foot of an old, dead tree-trunk, and he has fixed a string up the trunk. The convolvulus won't twine round the trunk—it prefers the string. Possibly it hasn't the strength to embrace so large a prop. There must be some determining factor operative here, that should be worth studying. And why does the convolvulus twine in this direction? Why right and not left? Again there must be some reason, some law. Some such reason is calling to me, even from the depths of my suffering, and keeps my habitual curiosity alive. This type of reason has nothing to do with hope. In order to survive the pretty convolvulus will stifle everything in its path, everything that is weaker than itself. That is the law of nature. Logically, therefore, the one thing that could bring me consolation and peace of mind, and cause me to fall on my knees, would be to see the graceful creeper sacrifice itself. Is self-sacrifice ever a possibility? For man, sometimes. But then, I am not one of those who regard man as the final achievement of nature!'

A few steps further on Patrice felt other thoughts boiling and bursting from the depths of his mind. Yes. It was very noticeable during the war, when we were short of everything, that the undernourished pregnant woman got thinner whereas the baby, the fruit of her womb, did not suffer at all, however acute the deprivation. Of course this was not within the woman's control. The mother's flesh sacrifices itself to the child. Why? To preserve the species? Is the race a god then, to be able to demand such a sacrifice and obtain it? Is nature a god? What an incomprehensible god to be so indifferent to our wishes!'

Patrice Périot had just encircled the house. He could see the valley of the Oise, and immediately in front of him the gravel drive leading from the house to the front gate. For some time he paused with downcast eyes, and as he was about to go indoors and up to his room he heard a footstep on the gravel. He raised his head to see a human form, soberly clad. 'My sight is beginning to fail,' he thought. 'Who is coming now to torment me in this secluded spot?' The man drew near, fanning himself with his hat, for the heat was oppressive. Patrice Périot felt every fibre of his being grow taut. 'It is Schlemer, of all people!'

The fat man came forward, with the delicate tread that is often characteristic of a man of his build, and without increasing his pace he gave a friendly wave from afar. Patrice Périot waited for him, suddenly filled with anxiety and annoyance. At last the visitor was beside him, offering his hand. Patrice took it reticently, without uttering a word, and Schlemer began at once to talk, somewhat pompously.

'I am fully aware, maestro, that I am violating an agreement. Your son-in-law told me several times —let me remark in passing that that young man is not exactly a model of courtesy—and your daughter, our charming Comrade Vera, herself advised me not to come and disturb you in your retreat. All the same,

I have come, because I feel very sure that, despite minor differences, we are still of the same mind where the fundamentals are concerned.'

Patrice Périot said nothing, but merely nodded his head interrogatively, whereupon the big man resumed the thread of his speech.

'A human life is at stake, a life that is very noble and very precious. Yes, I know that in your eyes every life is precious—you have often told me so and often given proof of it. But I am speaking now of a poet. I am pleading the cause of an Afghan poet, Hemmet Tekrit, who has been in prison for two years and for whose release our papers have been agitating—you read our papers, of course. The great poet, Hemmet Tekrit, has recently been condemned to death, not for his political activities, but for his human, humane, humanitarian views. Weigh well the significance of these three epithets, my dear professor. Hemmet Tekrit is condemned to be hanged, which is disgusting and deliberately humiliating. . . .'

'Just a moment!' said Patrice Périot. 'Come up with me to my room.' He regarded Schlemer's empurpled face, covered with sweat, and added: 'Let me offer you something cool to drink. What would you like? Water? Plain water? Yes, of course, that's best for you, and you shall have it, with a fresh lemon if there happens to be one in the house.'

Five minutes later, when Mme Hortense had brought the drink, Schlemer was seated in an arm-chair continuing his monologue. 'We have lost no time,' he said, 'and we have filed a short and dignified protest. Only twenty lines, as you can see, twenty conciliatory lines, to remind the Afghan Government that we are animated by a sincere desire for friendship. Twenty lines to review Tekrit's career and the international significance of his work, which, as you know, professor, was translated into French last year and published by kind permission of the *Independent Bookshop*. We have already collected some thirty famous names of members of the Institute, professors at the Sorbonne, politicians not only of the militant left wing, as you would expect, but of the centre and right also. We felt that the document would not be complete without your name, and we beg you to do yourself the honour of signing it.'

Patrice Périot's reply was cold and calm. 'I am ashamed to have to admit that I do not know of Hemmet Tekrit. I cannot read everything. I earnestly trust that there is such a person, and that he is in fact a great poet.'

'My dear professor——'

'No, I am not joking. I am in no mood to joke. May I see the text of this appeal?'

Schlemer handed over a sheet of paper and Patrice Périot began to read it to himself. Seeing that he appeared to be thinking over the opening phrases rather than reading on, Schlemer volunteered: 'I quite realize that we may be somewhat rash in asking anything from you so soon after your recent trouble. No one understands that better than I do. Nevertheless, I did not hesitate. I undertook this difficult mission——'

'A mission which Gérin-Labrit would not undertake himself, because he suspects that he has not your persuasive eloquence, Schlemer.'

'I do not follow you, professor. There was no

question of any discussion or choice between our mutual friend Gérin-Labrit and me; we were both perfectly sure of your reaction. As to my reference to your recent troubles——'

'Have no fear, Schlemer, I understood your reference perfectly, and it never crossed my mind that you had come to claim the price of your silence.'

'My dear professor!'

'No, do not be alarmed. Personal feelings do not enter into what I have just said—only my inveterate habit of scientific observation. I am going to sign that paper.' Patrice Périot appended his signature.

Schlemer rose to his feet. 'My dear professor, I really must confess that this is one of the great moments of my life! Such generosity, such nobility of soul! Such a deep understanding of the problems of humanity and charity. . . .'

Patrice Périot was sitting at his desk, watching Schlemer pacing the room. At the word charity he interrupted Schlemer by raising his hand gently. 'Listen to me, Schlemer. I have signed. That's the end of it. I have signed despite all my good resolutions, and independently of any threat of blackmail. I have signed contrary to all expectations. So that's that. Now I want you to listen to me a moment longer —I have not finished yet. You and your confederates, along with the fanatics of the opposite camp, have no longer any hold over a man who has plumbed the depths of suffering. Like your political enemies, without always being aware of it yourselves, you are cunning, wicked, and obstinate. Without realizing it, you, like them, are unworthy to be dignified by the name of man. Schlemer, I tell you that I would sign a similar appeal to-morrow if it was to obtain pardon for your assassin.'

'My assassin!'

'Yes, the man who thought he had the right to judge you and kill you. I would sign out of my horror of the universal cruelty and folly and religious hypocrisy of all parties and sects. I would sign out of pity for the poor unfortunates who allow themselves to be led blindfold, like beasts to the slaughter, and out of pity, too, for the power-maniacs who forge the chains while talking of the freedom of the people and thinking of nothing but their own fanatical ideals. . . .'

There was a long silence before Patrice Périot went on: 'Therefore you will oblige me by not speaking of emotion or gratitude. I am signing first and foremost on my own behalf, and secondarily because this poet, who is unknown to me, is a tool in your busy hands —a pitiable tool, even if he is as great a poet as you claim.'

Schlemer had taken possession of the document and was folding it absent-mindedly before returning it to its envelope. Eventually, seeing that Patrice Périot seemed determined to say no more, he made an effort to smile and said in his well-modulated voice: 'I propose to forget a momentary display of temper that is understandable in a wounded man, to forget your words and simply to say "Thank you." One thing more. Another poet, one whom you do actually know and respect, provides me with an apt ending to our conversation:

> Honte au penseur qui se mutile
> Et s'en va, chanteur inutile,
> Par la porte de la cité!

You will never accept the role of this ineffective philosopher; and that's why you will retain the respect of us all. Please don't disturb yourself, I am going to leave you to get on with your work. A car is waiting for me outside.'

Patrice Périot accompanied his visitor to the court-yard. His expression was now entirely detached and cool. On the way he talked about the shrubs and the flowers, and then about the evening storm rumbling in the distance. He shook Schlemer's moist hand and watched him go off in a car driven by a grizzled man wearing a tartan shirt. Alone at last he returned to his house, and before he had proceeded more than a few steps he determined to think no more about Schlemer and his crowd, and Schlemer's opponents. The remarkable thing was that he met with immediate and complete success in his effort to achieve complete forgetfulness. And so he found himself alone, at last, with his thoughts.

He dined with Thierry in the downstairs room. The young man was once more vivacious and talkative, and ready to expand. While Patrice listened to him talking he indulged his own personal thoughts which he kept entirely to himself. The storm which had been grumbling for a long time in the distance seemed to come closer, heralded by violent gusts of wind which buffeted at the open windows and alarmed the birds nesting in the virginia creeper and in the ivy on the walls. The visit of the great fat clown was completely forgotten. Patrice reverted to the thoughts that had long been troubling him. He analysed them slowly and meticulously, but persistently. 'Christine needs me no longer. She has found a religion, a rule, and way of life of her own. Edwige has her children, her duties, and a husband who is captious enough to make her forget the problems she is naturally inclined to ignore. There is no point in thinking about the dear little grandchildren; they will grow up in a world which we cannot even visualize. And as for Thierry he is safe, safe henceforward whatever may happen because he has been dazzled by a wonderful vision. That leaves me free. Free, free . . .'

After dinner Patrice Périot announced that he was going to his room to work. Young Thierry nodded his assent, but after two or three attempts to speak he gave his father a look which was at once furtive and penetrating. The storm broke, from the south. Suddenly all the lights in the house went out, as happens when lightning strikes a key-point in the circuit. They lit candles and Patrice provided himself with a candlestick. Every now and then a flash of lightning lit up the shadows, revealing through the windows the shrieking poplar-trees in the valley with their leaves blown back like hair standing on end.

Candlestick in hand Patrice began to climb the creaking and groaning steps of the wooden staircase. On the stairs he thought: 'Einstein is alleged to have said that the most difficult thing in the world to understand is that the world is understandable. Einstein is a physicist and that is presumably the reason why he makes such rash statements. He is only taking the temporal and the inanimate into account. He is not speaking as a biologist, and he couldn't possibly be referring to the soul, or rather to the idea of the soul, which is the most difficult reality to grasp.'

On the top step a vivid picture of Schlemer came

into his mind. 'I hope that great lump won't think that he counts for anything at all in my decisions. That would be too preposterous for words.' The thought of Schlemer made him breathe so heavily that he extinguished the candle he was carrying. The picture of Schlemer promptly vanished in the stormy darkness.

Reaching his room, Périot placed the candle on the table and left the window open, so that the flame danced and leaped. He sat at his desk, put a large sheet of white paper on the blotter and dipped his pen in the ink.

Time passed. Patrice brooded, chin in hand. He was in no hurry. The whole night was before him. Suddenly his thoughts became very humble and very clear-cut. 'No,' he said to himself, 'even with an explanation designed to allay foolish suspicions, not a revolver. Too noisy and clumsy and messy. Besides, I might miss my aim. I remember only too clearly the unfortunate Hallop who had an enormous hole in his upper jaw, through which he talked ludicrously. He had no wish to try again, because of the great pain he had suffered—a pitiful picture. No, definitely not a revolver. And not—not drowning, like my poor child. What a conclusion all the fools would draw then! No! And not the top storey. My grand-children would see me from the balcony across the way. So it must be poison, strong poison, carefully selected, certain, and obtained well in advance. Administered intravenously, of course. One hour of sleep. One hour of coma. And then the happy release. . . .'

He pulled open the drawer of his old table and took out two little boxes, evidently knowing exactly where to find them because he picked them up without looking at them and deposited them on the table to his right. One was metal and obviously contained a syringe and needles. As a research worker he no longer had any practical use for such an instrument. The other was unlabelled, and contained ampoules of liquid.

The storm was now passing overhead and could be heard growling in the valley. The tall trees seemed to cry out and every blade of grass sighed with terror in face of the tempest. Sometimes the noise of the thunder followed so close on the heels of the lightning flash that Patrice Périot, detached from life though he was, could not help thinking that the fire from heaven must be falling very close at hand on the village and on the trees. He was not far wrong, for he saw a lurid flash, and one of the tall poplars at the foot of the meadow began to emit pink smoke; the crackle of the branches could be heard from the house. Just then the rain began to fall in torrents, heavy and vertical.

Patrice sat motionless before his blank sheet of paper, thinking in an endless circle. A few minutes later he heard a slight noise, and the door opened behind him. Still he did not move.

Another minute passed. Then he sensed a human presence at his right hand and said in a low tone: 'Is something worrying you, my boy?'

'No, thank you,' replied Thierry in a perfectly calm and easy voice. 'I was in the middle of reading and I suddenly came across a phrase in the book which puzzled me. So as I thought that you were still probably awake I came up to talk to you about it.'

'Is that so?' Patrice Périot did not turn his head or raise his eyes from the blank sheet in front of him. 'And what is it you've found?'

'It is in a book by Louis de Broglie. Broglie says that the progress of physical science may come to an end through lack of words and symbols.'

'Yes . . . indeed. Even in the physical sciences there is a sort of uneasy poetry. For its self-expression this kind of poetry, like others, needs metaphors, flashes of inspiration, striking words which are themselves creative. Ideas create words, and words create ideas.'

'Just so,' said the young man, waving the book he was holding in his hand. 'I was obviously right to come and ask you for help. You have launched me on a study of the sciences, and I find them engrossing and fascinating.'

'Wait a moment, let me think. It is true that I recommended you to read science, especially mathematics and physics, because I couldn't see you, or any of our family, taking to juridical science, for example. But if I ever thought that a clumsy or ill-chosen word from me—I am not of course referring to the excellent book you are just reading—if I ever thought that a perverse remark of mine could have the effect of causing you to lose what you already possess, then I should never forgive myself, to-night or any other night.'

'What I possess?'

'Yes, your faith.'

'There is nothing to fear on that score!'

'My son, you will never know how much comfort those words of yours have brought me.'

'I came to see you to-night, father, in the middle of

a thunderstorm, because I need you so much. I realize it as soon as I approach the vast and frightening world of ideas.'

'You need me! Thierry, I ask you, which of us needs the other most, you or——'

A long and shattering crash of thunder interrupted Patrice. But the storm was now receding, towards the forests of Beaumont. The roar of the rain was like the flood in the Scriptures, a cosmic phenomenon.

'I tell you, Thierry,' the old man continued, 'I and my generation have run aground. We have devoted our lives to a form of reason that is not reason, to a form of thought that gives power but does not bring peace. And we are suffering for it. Perhaps it will be for you, our children, to rediscover the way of hope.'

Thierry's shining eyes were illuminated fitfully by the dancing candlelight. 'I am only an ignorant young man, father. But I believe that there is something great to be done, something that the whole world needs, and that you are the man to do it.'

'I, son? I am too worn out, too disillusioned.'

'You are the man for the very reason that you have suffered. Reason and mystery must be reconciled. I express myself badly, but you understand better than any one else what I am trying to put into words. Pure rationalism! I seem to be able to grasp it, although I utterly distrust it; it leads man to despair, and makes it impossible for him to go on living. We must reconcile intelligence with life and reason with joy, and you are the man to bring that about. I'll help you; in spite of my lack of learning, I'll help you. I'll be your faithful servant and companion.'

'No, Thierry. Perhaps you will take my place.'

'Never. I want only to help you with my love.'

A violent gust of wind blew into the room, laden with such potent sweetness that Thierry leaped to his feet.

'Dad,' he exclaimed, 'what a glorious scent! What can it be?'

'It's honeysuckle, Thierry. It always smells sweetest at night.'

Patrice Périot rose, and went to the window to breathe in long draughts of the freshness of leaves and flowers. 'Yes,' he said, 'it's honeysuckle.'

He sat down at his writing-table again in silence and rested his hands on the sheet of white paper. It was then that he noticed that the two little boxes he had taken out of the drawer and placed within reach had mysteriously disappeared. He turned towards Thierry and looked at him without speaking. Thierry was perfectly calm, sustained by a power which transfigured him.

And so Patrice Périot came to realize that the bliss of nothingness was not to be his, now or for a long time to come, and that he would have to seek consolation meanwhile in this world. He saw clearly that he must continue to travel the road of suffering and affliction until the hour of his destiny with love, and even with hope, in his heart.